"I promised Pa... Aaron pivo... peering at her as though he faced a firing squad "—take care of you."

Hope couldn't move her gaze from his as his words settled over her. For some reason, instead of bringing her comfort, they annoyed her. How could Aaron think that he could take Paul's place? Or that she needed his help?

"Take *care* of me?"

"I—I know this is awkward. It is for me, too, but I...well, it meant something to Paul when I promised to take care of you," Aaron said. "I promised to hold on to Hope." His voice broke. "In Paul's mind, that meant that I'd marry you."

Hope strained to keep her shock from contorting her face, but she was pretty sure that she failed—miserably.

How could he possibly think that she would want a marriage based on obligation? She'd rather be a spinster for the rest of her life....

Books by Pamela Nissen

Love Inspired Historical

Rocky Mountain Match
Rocky Mountain Redemption
Rocky Mountain Proposal

PAMELA NISSEN

loves creating. Whether it's characters, cooking, scrapbooking or other artistic endeavors, she takes pleasure in putting things together for others to enjoy. She started writing her first book in 2000 and since then hasn't looked back. Pamela lives in the woods in Iowa with her husband, daughter, two sons, a Newfoundland dog and cats. She loves watching her children pursue their dreams, and is known to yell on the sidelines at her boys' games and being moved to tears as she watches her daughter perform. She enjoys scrapbooking weekends with her sister, coffee with friends and running in the rain. Having glimpsed the dark and light of life, she is passionate about writing "real" people with "real" issues and "real" responses.

PAMELA NISSEN
Rocky Mountain Proposal

Love Inspired

LOVE INSPIRED BOOKS

ISBN-13: 978-0-373-82869-2

ROCKY MOUNTAIN PROPOSAL

www.LoveInspiredBooks.com

Printed in U.S.A.

Love never ends. As for prophecies, they will pass away; as for tongues, they will cease; as for knowledge, it will pass away.

—1 *Corinthians* 13:8

For Bill, my beloved

Your heart…
Reaching wide as summer's yawning horizon
Glistening pure as winter's white snow
Standing steady as an oak tree come storm time
Burning alive as autumn's vibrant glow

Acknowledgments

Thank you to Steve and Gladys:
your quaint farm and animals reside in the
pages of this book. To my dear friends and family:
thank you for your love and support. To Tina,
Melissa and the Love Inspired family: thank you for
being such a great team with which to work. To my
critique partners, Diane, Jacquie and Roxanne: I am
profoundly blessed by your amazing writing talent
and your loyal friendship. To my wonderful children,
MaryAnna, Noel and Elias: thank you for loving well,
for caring deeply and for filling my life with laughter.
And to my husband, Bill: thank you
for being such a beautiful example of true love.

Chapter One

Boulder, Colorado
1891

Aaron Drake slapped the leather reins, racing his team of horses faster over the dry and dusty road toward the train station. It seemed that all of Boulder was out this evening, moving at a snail's pace through the city streets. His shirt was drenched in dirt and sweat from cutting down trees on this warm May day, but he took little notice as he kept his focus trained on the rutted street.

His good friend, Paul, had sent him to meet the five-forty train, although Aaron had no idea who or what was supposed to be waiting for him.

"Yee-haw! Get on!" he hollered to the team, swerving around a single horse carriage, parked off to the side of the road.

He swiped at beads of perspiration that trickled from beneath his straw hat not from heat but from the anxiety that had wrapped him tight.

Not more than three hours ago, Paul had been pinned beneath a felled tree. Aaron and his brothers, Ben and Zach, had been helping Paul harvest trees in order to build an addition onto his home. They'd been at it from sunup, chopping away at a record pace when the gigantic bur oak suddenly split three ways, barely missing Zach and pinning Paul beneath a section.

Now Paul was struggling to hang on to life, gasping for air even as he'd urged Aaron on to the train station.

Aaron hadn't wanted to leave, but he'd been desperate to do something to help—especially as he recalled how many times Paul had been a lifesaving breath of encouragement in Aaron's bleakest hours over the past months.

Hold on to hope….

Those words had come hard but insistent from Paul as he lay gulping in pain.

Aaron slapped the reins and whistled to the team, praying that Paul would take a turn for the better by the time he returned. Would God hear his plea this time? The past ten months had played out as one senseless tragedy after another, and Aaron had been hard-pressed to find God in the midst of it all. In the grand scheme of things, he had to wonder if there was still hope to be found.

He just didn't know anymore. The day his newborn boy and his wife had died ten months ago had been the day a part of him had died, too.

Tugging his hat tighter over his forehead, Aaron kept his head low, avoiding the stares of several townsfolk. He rarely made an appearance outside work and church. He'd thrown himself into his job building fine pieces of furniture with his brother Joseph, and like so many of the buildings erected here in Boulder, he'd put on a respectable false front, keeping mostly to himself to avoid folks' pitying remarks. Life was just easier that way.

He'd started doubting that the pain of his loss would ever fade. The ache was always with him. Deep down, he blamed himself. And he blamed God. He longed for relief from the crushing weight of it all yet felt helpless to help himself.

Just as he'd been powerless to help Paul.

Pulling on the reins, he slowed the team of horses, drawing them up to the hitching post at the Union Pacific Railroad Depot as he pushed his silent struggle aside. He set the brake and glanced at his pocket watch. He'd made good time but was still twenty minutes late to meet the five-forty. From the ghostly trail of coal smoke lingering in the late afternoon sky, the train had already departed.

Aaron tethered the team and strode up to the platform, glancing around. He wasn't even sure what he was looking for. A package? A delivery of some sort? Maybe some distant relative come for a visit. Paul hadn't been specific, and with the way he'd labored to get out the few words he had, Aaron hadn't wanted to tax him for more information.

He jammed his hands into his pockets as images of the accident flashed through his mind. Clamping his jaw tight against the cavernous feeling of desperation, he dragged in a steadying breath and scanned the platform.

"Goodness gracious, what are you doing here, Aaron Drake?" a voice called with grating familiarity.

It was Mrs. Beatrice Duncan—self-imposed town matron, bearer of any and all information and general busybody. She could irritate a man till he clamored to sit atop the nearest roof, but she could also warm a person's heart with her genuine demonstrations of concern. Right now, though, she was the last person he wanted to see.

He dragged up some good manners, then tipped his hat with a halfhearted nod. "Mrs. Duncan."

She beelined toward him, grabbed his upper arm and tugged him toward a small gathering of folks on the platform. "If this isn't perfect timing, I don't know what is. There's a special someone that I want you to meet."

"I'm kind of in a hurry." Aaron would've dug the heels of his worn boots into the thick wood, but he didn't want to put the woman off balance. "Maybe another time."

"No time like the present. That's what I'm always saying." She waved her hand in clear dismissal. "Say, I don't believe I mentioned it to you last time you were in the mercantile, but I arranged for my niece from up around Longmont to have herself a nice little visit. Thought it'd be nice for the two of you to meet. And wouldn't you know…she just came in on the train." The woman stopped cold in her tracks. The way she peered at him, as though she'd just snared a rabbit for dinner, made his gut clench with dread. "And then here you are, too," she added, her hinting words dropping like bread crumbs down a dark, dreary trail.

He wasn't hungry and didn't feel lost, either.

She perched a hand at her thick waistline and smiled like some well-fed house cat.

He could see what was coming just as clear as the errant wisps of bright orange hair framing Mrs. Duncan's round face. Folks had been trying to nudge him toward remarrying, and Mrs. Duncan had been leading the pack, but it'd take an act of God to get him to love again. He couldn't— not after losing his beloved Ellie. It would feel too much like betrayal.

Ignoring her not-so-subtle manipulation, he did a quick scan of the platform. "I'm afraid I won't be able to meet her right now. There's been an accident out at Paul's place and—"

"I heard *all* about that," Mrs. Duncan put in, as though referring to some trivial tidbit of information. "Poor soul."

Aaron set his back teeth in frustration. On the way into

town he'd stopped and informed Sheriff Goodwin about Paul's accident, and apparently word had already spread. He could only imagine to what degree the story had been distorted by now.

He balled his fists against the trembling that still shook him deep as he recalled the desperate look on Paul's face as he'd pleaded for help. Aaron and his brothers had worked frantically to free him. Finally, with the aid of Paul's workhorses, they were able to lever the log off enough to pull him from beneath the overbearing weight.

Maybe there was a chance—

The grim expression on Ben's face had said more than any words memorized from his medical textbooks.

Once they'd gotten Paul back to the house, Aaron would've done anything if it meant relieving his friend's pain—even a little. Paul had weakly pleaded, "Hold on to hope. Promise me you'll hold on to hope."

Aaron promised, gently squeezing his friend's hand to seal the vow.

"I heard that the sheriff sent for the minister. If you ask me…that does not bear well for Paul." She gave her head a dismal shake. "Not at all. Folks only do that when they're taking their last bow before knocking on death's door."

"Mrs. Duncan, I'm sorry, but—"

"Good thing you and your brothers were there. What was it that happened, anyways?" she prodded, angling her head his way. "Dora Trumm…she heard tell—"

"Really, I can't go into it this minute." Or any other minute. The situation was gruesome, and folks didn't need to hear every last detail of Paul's accident.

"Bea. Come on, we're heading out," Horace Duncan called as he gave Aaron an understanding kind of nod. "Gotta get this girl home before she collapses from her journey."

Mrs. Duncan narrowed her gaze on Aaron. "You'll have to stop over and have dinner with us so that you can meet my niece," she whispered, sliding her proud gaze to the lanky young woman with mouse-brown hair, a long face and even longer teeth. "I figure you're getting ready to start looking for a new wife. It's been what…two years since Ellie passed?"

Aaron swallowed hard, realizing once again that his pain was his alone. No one really understood the way he suffered. "Ten months."

Her squinty eyes sprang open. "Land sakes, that just flew by."

In truth, the time had crept by, scraping nearly every bit of hope from Aaron's soul.

He couldn't go back in time and change what had happened, but conceding to the loss didn't mean he'd peacefully accepted any of it. He'd been struggling to turn over whatever fresh new leaf he could find in the floor of his soul, attempting to find some hope, but so far he'd found pitiful little.

"Bea, are you coming?" Horace called from halfway down the platform.

Mrs. Duncan gave her head a curt shake. "The girl's right as rain, sturdy as an oak, I tell you. But my Horace, he gets himself worked up into an impatient huff."

"You better not keep him waiting, then." Aaron breathed a sigh of relief as she bustled away to catch up to her family.

Shielding his eyes against the sun, Aaron wound around other passengers and those who'd come to greet them, then spotted a woman holding a parasol and an overstuffed satchel. She stood alone on the platform, flanked by five trunks, each big enough to outfit a small army. He glanced around, seeing no other passengers left unaccounted for and no parcels left unattended. Could this be who Paul had sent him to meet?

With a heavy step and an even heavier heart, he approached the woman, who labored to keep hold of her handbag, her parasol and at the same time tuck a fluff of green fabric down into her overstuffed carpetbag. She definitely didn't look as if she was from these parts, especially with the rich-looking, off-white gown she wore. Folks didn't dress like that around here—unless they were getting ready to walk down the aisle, of course. The graceful way she held herself once she got settled, staring off into the distance the way she was, made her appear almost like some fanciful statue, her dark hair gleaming like rich melted chocolate in the late sun.

He came to a stop and swept off his hat. "Excuse me, ma'am?"

She startled then pivoted to face him, nearly dropping her satchel. The brilliant smile lighting her fair face faded to obvious disappointment. "Yes?"

He inched the brim of his hat around in his hands. "Seems that you're waiting for someone. Am I right?"

She swept her gaze over a photograph she held. But when she attempted to tuck it into the side pocket of her bag, her parasol clattered down to the wood planks. "As a matter of fact, yes, I am. I'm sure he'll be here any moment."

"It looks like you have your hands full. Can I help?" He gave her a congenial smile as he bent to retrieve her parasol.

She eyed the frilly fashion contraption. "Thank you, sir. But I'm sure I'll be fine."

Aaron could've walked away right then, but the vulnerable look he glimpsed in her emerald gaze and the almost forlorn way she toiled to keep hold of all of her stuff nailed his feet to the wide-plank platform. "I don't mean to pry, but do you mind me asking who you're waiting for?"

She gave the hem of her fancy off-white bodice a gentle tug as though setting herself right, but as far as Aaron could tell, not one hair or fiber lay out of place—city slicker, no doubt. By the bird-in-a-roomful-of-cats look about her, she'd likely not be around long. Although when his focus drifted to the sea of enormous trunks that surrounded her like servants to some fair maiden, he had to wonder. It'd take a lifetime and then some to wear that many garments.

He glanced around one more time, certain he must've missed a parcel or passenger, because this woman surely couldn't have been who Paul had sent him after.

"I'm waiting for Mr. Thompson." She cleared her throat. "Mr. Paul Thompson. Do you know him?"

Aaron flipped his gaze to the woman. "Yes, I do."

He knew Paul almost as well as his own brothers. As sturdy on the outside as he was on the inside—Paul's faith was unwavering.

Surely, there was something Aaron could've done to prevent the accident. Maybe if he'd been more attentive and noticed that the oak was splitting he could've warned Paul in time.

He pulled in a steadying breath. "Actually, Paul sent me to pick you up."

Confusion crossed her face, and that same faint look of disappointment came once again, making him feel downright awful. "I see. Was Paul detained, then?"

"I'll explain on the way out to his place. Why don't I get your trunks loaded up in the rig?" He glanced at the trunks again as he wondered what relation this woman was to Paul. And more, how he was going to break the news to her about the accident. "My name's Aaron Drake, by the way." He held out his hand to her, but her arms were too full to exchange any kind of handshake. "Here, let me take that for you."

"Thank you so much." The slightest blush colored her cheeks as she handed her bag to him. "It's nice to meet you, Mr. Drake."

"If you don't mind, Aaron is fine." Realizing that the satchel handle had ripped, he tucked it beneath his arm. "We're not much for pretense around here."

She paused. "All right then, Aaron."

"I'm a good friend of Paul's—been friends for years. Are you a relative of his?"

He took in her features, looking for some similarity, but where Paul was hearty and stocky in his build, this woman was delicate and refined. Her fair skin seemed as if to glow where Paul's skin showed the effects of countless hours of sunlight.

The hint of the smile he'd initially seen warmed her face. "I'm his bride-to-be."

"His what?" he choked out.

This woman was as opposite to Paul as a mountain lion was to one of Ben's pampered house cats. She seemed utterly unfit for the West. Was this some joke? Paul hadn't said anything, not *one thing* about some fancy bride-to-be. Surely, he would've shared this small bit of information. He'd often talked of having a wife and family—someday— but he'd never indicated he was already halfway down the aisle.

"Did you say bride-to-be?"

The way her brow inched together just slightly in the minutest look of hurt gave him pause.

"We're to be married today," she answered, her voice soft and vulnerable as she trailed her slender fingers down her elaborate skirt.

"Today?" He swallowed hard.

"Just as soon as the minister is available—at least, that's what Paul had written in his last letter." She took her parasol from him and popped it open. "My name is Hope Gatlin."

He struggled to hold his disbelief in check. It just wasn't like Paul to keep such a monumental secret. "Nice to make your acquaint—"

Hope…

Hope?

Alarm shot down Aaron's spine as Paul's words galloped through his mind with the reckless speed of a wild stallion. *Promise me you'll hold on to Hope. Don't ever let her go.*

Aaron would never give his word on something he didn't intend to fulfill. And he prided himself on wearing loyalty like a favorite shirt, but right now, taking in the gravity of it all… What had he promised?

Chapter Two

"Can you go any faster?" Hope queried yet again, the wagon creaking in protest. She could not remember one time in all of her twenty-two years when she'd begged for a quicker pace, but for the last mile since Aaron had broken the news to her about Paul's accident, Hope had actually made the request three times.

Glancing over at Aaron, she fought to ignore the way her stomach still pitched from the last hairpin curve they'd lurched around. "Please?"

His blue eyes grew wide as he passed a glance from her parasol to her. "Ma'am, I'll say it again. If I go any faster over these rutted roads, I run the risk of breaking the rig." On a sigh, he turned onto a long path leading to a farm. "Besides, we're here. This is Paul's homestead."

She stared ahead at the quaint farm, taking in every rustic nuance: the two-story clapboard house, the barn and chicken coop, the fields, the cows. Paul had described this place to her in his letters. He'd built everything from the ground up and had told her of how the barn had been erected in a day with the help of friends. He'd been slowly adding to the number of cows he had and was looking forward to purchasing more this spring.

Hope had marveled at his love for the land, but having been raised in a family of means in Boston, she didn't know the first thing about farming. She'd told him that she didn't mind hard work and would help out wherever she could, but Paul had insisted that she not dirty her pretty little hands. He'd been set on pampering her.

That sweet memory only added to the lump in her throat and the pain in her heart. She'd never imagined looking for love through the mail-order bride advertisements, but her friend had found love there. Hope had answered an ad strictly to relieve her family's financial burden shortly after her father had lost his small fortune a year ago. With her mother insisting on keeping the house staff and with six girls at home, her father was working himself nearly to his grave, trying to manage, and this seemed the only way Hope could help.

Aaron brought the team to a stop and swung down to the ground. While he strode around to her side, she made a discreet attempt to follow him with her gaze. If the man would crack a smile on his stony face, he might be half-pleasant looking. She took in the scruff of beard on his face and his filthy clothes and couldn't help wondering why his congenial demeanor had changed so abruptly back at the train station. His dirt-smudged face had gone ashen after she'd introduced herself, his already tense expression turning almost angry. For the life of her, Hope couldn't figure out why.

She'd struggled to tamp down her extreme disappointment once she'd realized that Paul hadn't mentioned her arrival to Aaron. Was Paul embarrassed by her, as Jonas had been after her family's financial demise?

She'd been engaged to Jonas Hargrave, a longtime family friend, for two years. She'd loved the idea of marriage to a man who professed undying love. But right after her family had lost their means, she began glimpsing regret in his gaze, and as far as she was concerned, a marriage rooted in obligation would be no marriage at all.

Holding fast to her dignity, she'd eased him off the marriage hook.

He didn't even flinch.

But then she'd met Paul. His letters had been so wonderful—almost too good to be true. He'd shown her the way to God. And her newfound faith had seemed almost too good to be true as well. The ten months she'd corresponded with Paul had been filled with hope and excitement and anticipation. She'd been certain that life would be wonderful.

But now...

Paul had been seriously injured—that's what Aaron had said. If they couldn't get married today, that was perfectly acceptable to Hope. She could wait a day or two. She'd just do what she could to help him get better. Perhaps she'd apply cool cloths to his forehead or fluff his pillows every now and then or prepare some broth to help him keep up his strength.

"Ma'am." The gentle sound of Aaron's voice catapulted her to the present as he stood at her side. "I can't help you get your feet on the ground if you don't pry those hands loose."

Hope looked at where she clutched her parasol and at where she'd curled white-gloved fingers in a death grip over the rough wood seat. She grappled for composure as she released her hold, her hands and arms aching from hanging on so tight. "I guess that perhaps the ride was a bit fast."

He raised his brows over his steel-blue eyes as if to

challenge her *a bit fast* estimation. When he stuck his hand
out to help her down, she glimpsed a tremor of nervous-
ness there. She felt a swell of compassion for the man, no
matter how cold he'd been.

"Do you think Paul will feel up to having visitors?"

He no sooner got her feet on the ground than he released
his hold as though her waist had been beaded with thorns.
"My brother Ben is a doctor." He started toward the house
at a brisk pace. "He's been here with him from the minute
the accident happened, and he's doing everything he can
to make Paul comfortable."

Clutching her reticule and parasol to her chest, she
scrambled to catch up with Aaron, nearly tripping over
the hem of her ivory brocade wedding dress. Wanting to
be prepared for this momentous occasion, she'd changed
out of her emerald-green taffeta dress at the train's last stop
before arriving in Boulder.

"Is he…is Paul in pain?" She almost ran into Aaron
when he came to an abrupt halt at the yawning front porch
that stretched across the front of the house.

His wary gaze passed over her like the dank fog that
often permeated Boston Harbor. "Yes. Ben tried to give
him laudanum earlier, but he wouldn't have it. Said he
wanted to be awake and aware of things until the—well,
for as long as he could."

She considered his words for a moment. Was he bracing her for the worst? Could Paul die—when she'd only
just arrived?

Surely, not.

Imagining her future husband lying in excruciating pain,
she dabbed at tears crowding the corners of her eyes.

"I'm advising you to stay out of the house if you have a
weak stomach," he warned, his admonishing tone border-
ing on degrading. "Paul needs us to be strong."

"Of course. Of course, I will," she assured, but remembering how weak-kneed she'd been when her best friend's little dog, Edward, had howled in pain after being kicked by a horse just last month, she wasn't so sure.

"He's a sturdy man, but a body can only take so much. And believe me…he's endured more than any man I know."

"He is strong, though. Very strong." She remembered the reassuring way Paul had shared his faith with her in the letters. His words had been a lifeline, a fortress in the midst of a very difficult time. Surely, God wouldn't let him die now, just as they were to marry. "I'll do everything I can to help, but I'm sure he'll be just fine."

The door swung open in front of them at that moment, and a darker-haired version of Aaron stepped out onto the porch, his face grim and his eyes red-rimmed.

"He's gone, isn't he?" she heard Aaron ask, his voice low and strained.

The man nodded. Visibly swallowing, he blinked hard.

Hope's knees went weak. Her head spun and her vision narrowed, but she willed herself to stay standing. She could barely take it all in.

Pulling her reticule closer, she strained to hold on to some hope. "Gone?"

Aaron pulled his mouth tight, battling to hold his raw emotion in check.

The slow finality in Ben's nod sent Aaron's heart to his stomach. "He passed away no more than five minutes ago."

"I'm so sorry I wasn't here, Ben," was all he could force out as he peered up at where his brother stood on the porch. Had it not been for Mrs. Duncan waylaying him, maybe

Aaron would've made it back sooner. And then there were the trunks he'd lugged to the wagon; that had taken a fair amount of time.

When he heard a small sniffle next to him, he turned to see Hope's mouth drawn into a line. Her brow crimped. She held her reticule so tight to her chest that whatever she had stashed inside would be crushed.

"I'm sorry." He set a hand on her shoulder to comfort her, feeling anything but natural in doing so.

Ever since she'd given her name, Hope, he'd been silently writhing in sheer panic. He'd tried to be congenial, and he'd worked at being caring when he'd told her about Paul a mile back, but all he could think about was the promise he'd made and what it meant—and how he was loyalty-bound to fulfill his words.

He'd promised to hold on to hope and not let her go.

But he didn't know that hope was *Hope*.

He could pay her passage back to where she came from, though he couldn't exactly make good on his promise to watch out for her from a distance, could he? But the idea of being anywhere near Hope threatened like a gun aimed directly at his vows to Ellie.

It might be easier if Hope was some dowdy spinster lucky to snag a strapping man like Paul. But Hope was nowhere near dowdy. She was beautiful…striking…elegant.

She was also a city slicker.

And that particular attribute was *nothing* like Ellie.

"It's just all so sudden." Her eyes grew moist, sending a trickle of compassion through him.

He braced himself for her to let loose a flood of tears, but instead she drew in a steadying breath, lifted her chin a little higher and ascended the steps.

Ben cleared his throat and motioned them inside. "You must be Hope," he uttered as they preceded him into the house.

"Yes, I am." Her voice shook slightly.

When Aaron spotted a few drops of blood that had splattered on the floor when they'd carried Paul inside, he pulled out his kerchief and hunkered down to rub them away. He wasn't sure how Hope would respond and was intent on getting rid of the remnants before she screeched in fright.

"I'm Ben. Aaron's oldest brother." He closed the door behind them. "Paul just told us about you, Hope. He said you'd be coming."

Paul had told Ben and Zach about her? Aaron angled a glance down the hallway to Paul's room. He could hear the sheriff's voice and Zach's voice, too, and had to wonder what exactly Paul had said after Aaron had left for the station.

She moved into the room and set her bag and parasol at the door. She looked around her as if to get her bearings.

"Where is he now?" she asked, unpinning the matching velvet half of a hat she'd worn and sweeping it off her dark brown hair. Small tendrils wisped down to frame her face. "May I see him?"

Ben sliced a concern-filled look to Aaron.

"I don't think that's a good idea," Aaron finally responded. He and his brothers had done their best to clean Paul up, but all of the care in the world couldn't reconstruct broken bones and reduce overt swelling. "He was in bad shape. I wouldn't want your only view of him to be this way."

She peered up at him with a stubborn tilt to her chin. "I'm sure I'll be just fine. Besides, if this is the only way

I'll see him face-to-face, then that is what I shall do. It's better than not having seen Paul at all."

He caught the shadow of approval that crossed Ben's face and couldn't help but silently applaud her surprising show of strength.

"This way, then." Ben led the way back to the room and motioned Zach and the sheriff out.

Aaron could hear Ben speaking to Hope in the doctorly tone of voice he reserved for grim moments like this. He braced himself for a loud wail or sob from the young woman but heard nothing—not even a sniffle.

And that was almost worse.

Once Ben exited the bedroom and closed the door behind him, Aaron let out a heavy sigh.

"What do we do now?" he whispered as Ben moved over to where Aaron stood with the sheriff and Zach. "I mean, Paul had planned on marrying her as soon as she arrived. We don't know a thing about her."

Ben crossed his arms at his chest and rubbed a hand over the late-afternoon scruff on his chin. "We do know that Paul cared for her deeply, however. Enough that he made arrangements with the sheriff here to have his bank account and land deeded to her name."

"You can't be serious," he ground out.

"As serious as the river's rise come spring, son," the sheriff corrected.

"Was he in his right mind?" Aaron probed, feeling squeezed by the way he'd promised himself between a rock and a hard place.

"Yes, he was in his right mind." The reproving look Ben gave pulled Aaron up short. "In fact, he made a stipulation that if, by summer's end, Hope decides that staying here on the farm is too much, then she can sell. The money would be hers to keep and do with what she wanted."

The sheriff sliced a breath through his sparse teeth. "Don't know what her background is, but one way or t'other, as far as money's concerned, she's settin' pretty now. Just as pretty as the lady is herself," he added with a tactless chuckle.

"Sheriff, do you mind going into town to let folks know?" Ben ushered the man to the door. "That would help a great deal."

Aaron gave a relieved sigh. Goodwin, though well meaning, lacked social grace and would only make things more awkward with his ill-placed attempts at humor.

"Sure will." He tugged at his britches and patted where his gun was strapped to his side in that self-important way of his. "Is there anything else I can get you boys?"

"Not that I can think of. But we'll sure let you know if there is, all right?" Ben slapped him on the back. "But if you happen to know where Jane is—"

"Denver. She's returning tomorrow." The sheriff slid a hand along his belt. "I'll be the one to break the news to her, because knowin' Jane…she might just need a big ole' shoulder to cry on, seein' as how he was her brother and all." Goodwin scuffed out the door, his boots tramping over the porch floor.

Once he was gone, Ben returned to where Zach and Aaron were standing, his expression bleak.

"There's another thing, Aaron." Zach squared his shoulders.

Wary, Aaron braced himself. "What's that?"

Zach and Ben exchanged concerned glances. "Well, after you left for the train station, Paul couldn't stop expressing how grateful he was that you'd made the promise you did."

"That brought him a lot of comfort, Aaron," Zach encouraged. "More than you'll ever know."

"Well, I'm glad for that." He swiped a hand over his forehead. "He was in so much pain I would've done anything."

"I know." Ben clasped Aaron's shoulder. "And you did because that's the kind of friend you are. Loyal. True. Caring."

"Do you remember what that promise was?" Zach prodded.

"I'm not an idiot." Aaron gave his head an exasperated shake, feeling as though he was being crushed by the weight of his promise. "Of course, I remember what I promised. I said that I'd hold on to hope. But I thought he was referring to faith," he uttered, trying to keep his voice low. He raked his fingers through his hair. "I thought he was talking about finding peace and hope again after everything with Ellie and the baby. That's what I thought he meant. He's been saying things like that for months."

After several silent moments, Ben puffed out a long breath. "Well, Paul had other ideas."

Aaron's eyes grew wide. "Believe me, I realized that just as soon as she introduced herself. Paul wanted me to watch out for her. That's what he meant."

"Actually, he meant for you to marry her," Zach said, easing the words out as though he was spoon-feeding a baby.

Desperation constricted Aaron's throat. He forced a swallow past the tightness. He could barely breathe. "Marry her?"

"Yep," Zach answered as if sealing some kind of deal. "Marry Hope and take care of her. Said he couldn't think of another man he'd rather leave his bride to than you."

Aaron's blood ran cold. His entire body shook, yet he

couldn't do a thing to control the vicious trembling. His emotions whipped around in his soul with blizzard force.

The weight of his promise hit him full force. He was a man of his word, loyal to the core. He'd made a promise to a dying friend.

He'd also made a promise to his wife at the altar when they'd married four years ago. How could he possibly honor one vow without dishonoring the other? And how could he possibly enter into something that should be founded on love when he barely knew this woman?

Ben gave his shoulder another squeeze. "I know this is a lot to take in."

"More than a lot to take in," he grunted, feeling as desperate as a cornered and injured animal.

"It wouldn't have been right if we didn't at least tell you what Paul said." Zach clasped his other shoulder.

"No, I'm glad you did. It was the right thing to do." Aaron jammed his hands to his waist and began pacing the floor. He felt helpless to gain some kind of control over the direction his life had suddenly taken. "I'm telling you…I was as sincere as I could be when I made that promise. I just didn't know."

Ben cleared his throat. "It's your decision, Aaron. You have to do what you think is right."

Peering down the hallway, he stared at the bedroom where his friend lay dead, way too soon, just like Ellie and baby Jeremiah. In Aaron's greatest time of need, Paul had been a true friend. He'd been there with quiet strength, not barraging Aaron with empty words meant to lift his spirit. He hadn't ignored Aaron's loss nor had he ruminated over it endlessly. He'd just let Aaron grieve then gently urged his focus to God.

Paul had been a true friend.

Turning to face his brothers, he finally realized that he had no other option. With his fists clenched and head held high, he looked them in the eye. "I made a promise. I'm going to marry Hope."

Chapter Three

On a long, slow breath, Hope endeavored to calm the flurry of emotions blowing through her heart. She reached out and touched Paul's hand, longing for the warmth of life to meet her touch.

He was cold.

She gently pressed her palm against his and entwined her trembling fingers in his, trying to memorize the way his hand, large and callused enough to be strong and protecting, felt in hers. But how could she etch into her remembrance something she'd never truly felt? How could she tuck away the sweet memory of her name on his lips?

She relinquished his hand and closed her eyes, her heart clenching with grief. She should pray, but she didn't know what to pray for. Help? Comfort?

She had no idea a person could feel such tangible fear, desperation and overwhelming sadness at the same time.

Dabbing at her eyes, she stared at where Paul lay covered in a white sheet and simple blue coverlet—so still and so pale. The distinct metallic scent of blood hung in the air, mixing with the musky scent of perspiration that still beaded his forehead.

Hope didn't regret seeing him like this, but it wasn't

easy—growing up, she'd been sheltered from such things. Paul had suffered, of that she had no doubt. She couldn't imagine how he'd survived more than a few minutes, let alone three hours.

But the serene look that lingered on his face had taken her by surprise. Even in the midst of staggering pain, he'd found peace. As strong as Paul's faith was, she was sure he'd been ready to meet his Maker and had probably accepted his impending death.

Hope just didn't know if she accepted it.

For months now, she'd longed for the moment their lives would be joined in marriage. She couldn't understand how God could connect her life with Paul's and then rip him away before she'd ever known the comfort of his embrace.

She'd left all she'd known to join him here in Boulder. With not a single penny to her name, she had no way of returning to Boston. Aaron and his doctor brother were the only souls she knew in this rough-and-tumble land.

And all she could think about right now was the next few minutes and how she would try to hold herself together in front of them.

Standing, she wrapped poise around her like some warm and comforting quilt, hoping that she had what it would take to walk through this alone. She crossed to the heavy oak paneled door and opened it, willing her wobbly legs not to give out on her as she left the room. She resisted the urge to hug her arms to her chest as her mother had always cautioned her, saying that it appeared weak and unladylike.

Well, if ever there was a time where Hope felt weak, it was now. But being alone, she couldn't afford to be weak.

She couldn't afford anything—not even a bowl of soup for her next meal.

The irony of her situation stared her in the face like some fierce predator from the surrounding mountains. She drew her arms to her sides and met the three men's watchful gazes.

"I'm sorry. We did everything we could to keep him alive." Ben's voice was low, tight. "He wanted to hang on long enough to talk with you. But I couldn't—"

"I wouldn't have wanted him to suffer any more than he did." She unfurled her fisted hands, trying to ignore her need for a little consolation. "He must have been in terrible pain."

The studying glance Aaron cast her way left her feeling as if he'd tried to take a peek inside her soul.

She touched her delicate lace-trimmed neckline, suddenly feeling vulnerable.

"I'm sorry about this, ma'am." The other brother offered her his hand, and she shook it. "Name's Zach, by the way."

She struggled to stay collected at his caring demeanor. "Thank you, Zach."

"This has to be a shock," he added.

Nodding, she pulled her mouth tight against the cry that begged for escape. "I'm still trying to make sense of it all. I'm not even sure what I'm supposed to do now."

"We'll take care of funeral arrangements and Paul's body." Aaron swiped a hand over his forehead, glancing over her shoulder to the bedroom. "Don't worry about that, all right?"

She nodded. "I'm grateful."

Ben stepped a little closer, his expression crimped with compassion. "Paul really cared for you, ma'am. He wanted to make sure you were well cared for."

She glanced up at him, confused. Well cared for? Though she didn't, for a moment, doubt Paul's desire to take care of her, he couldn't very well do that from the grave. "I don't understand."

On a loud exhale, Ben pulled a hand over his dirt-smudged face. "When Sheriff Goodwin was out here, Paul made arrangements for you to have this farmstead," he said, gesturing out the windows where fields stretched wide and big fat cows mulled about in the corral. "And also for his bank account in town to be transferred to your name, ma'am."

Hope swallowed hard, turning her wide-eyed gaze from the windows, where the early evening sun poured through the glass panes, to stare at Ben. Had Paul truly thrown her such an enormous lifeline?

"The farm belongs to you," Ben measured out as if realizing her shock. "As well as all of Paul's money."

She glanced at Zach, who gave her a gentle smile and slight nod as if to verify his brother's words. But when she slid her attention to Aaron, she almost startled at the fear that contorted his face.

"Are you feeling all right?" she asked before she could stop herself.

"I'm fine." He dodged her gaze, the muscles at his strong jaw line pulsating.

Ben dipped his head down as if to grab her attention. "I don't know what the amount is in his account, but knowing Paul, I'm fairly certain there's at least enough there for you to live comfortably for many years to come."

She shook her head in disbelief. "I—I don't know what to say."

"You don't need to say a thing," Zach responded.

"But we hadn't even married yet." She fingered the silk brocade fabric of her skirt, feeling uncomfortable and yet next to tears at Paul's extreme generosity. "And what of his sister? I know that he has a sister living in the area, too, doesn't he?"

"Jane lives at the edge of Paul's property in a small home of her own. She's out of town until tomorrow morning—at least that's what the sheriff said. He and Mrs. Duncan pretty much know everybody's business in town," Zach answered, a knowing grin tipping his mouth. "But I'm sure Jane will support Paul's decision. She's nice enough."

"Yeah, I don't think you'll have any problems there," Aaron confirmed, shoving his hands into his pockets.

"Paul was adamant about this, ma'am." Ben motioned for them to move toward the front room where a fire had been lit in the hearth.

She should feel glad for the warmth and comfort of the crackling flames licking around the logs, but for some reason nothing could take the chill from her soul. The farm…the bank account…Paul had known her circumstance and had seen to her future, without him. But could she start a new life alone?

"He said that he wanted to make sure you'd be taken care of. That was all he could think about in those last minutes he was able to talk." With a heavy sigh, Ben eased himself down into the wood rocking chair flanking the fireplace.

Zach plopped unceremoniously down into the damask sofa and hooked one arm over the back of it, staring over his shoulder out the window. "This farm is one of the best around."

"Paul sure loved this land," Aaron added as he motioned for her to sit down in a simply upholstered chair and then finally sat down next to Zach.

"It's lovely. Really it is." She glanced around the spacious home then outside to the fields. She didn't even know what to compare this farm to. Apart from the flowering plants in the greenhouse her family kept, she'd never even been close enough to touch a crop. "But I must admit…I don't know the first thing about farming."

The knowing glances Aaron exchanged with his brothers left Hope wishing she could hear their thoughts.

"Mind you, I'm not completely unfamiliar with how things grow." With a small amount of relief, she recalled how her family had employed both a gardener and a stable hand full time. And the property wasn't even close to this size. "I'm certain the farmhands will be an invaluable help with everything were I to have questions."

Ben cleared his throat. "He's worked the land himself for five years now."

She furrowed her brow, certain that she must've heard him wrong. "Alone? You mean he had no farmhands?"

Aaron shook his head. "Not Paul. He'd work from sunup to sundown. Alone."

"But I—I've never—" She couldn't even begin to imagine herself planting seeds or feeding those big black and brown cows or the squawking chickens she'd spotted.

Once, in a letter, she'd told Paul that she'd gladly work beside him on the farm. She'd meant every word. She wanted to love what he loved. But she'd pictured scattering flower seeds or filling a small basket with carrots she'd picked herself. She hadn't imagined running the place.

"I know this is a lot to think about." Ben braced his hands on his knees. "Paul did say that if by summer's end you aren't happy here that you can sell the place and do with the money what you will."

She gave her head a distraught shake. "I couldn't do that to him."

"Well, Paul seemed to think you might…that you might need some help." Aaron looked about as taut as a tightly strung bow. "I promised him I'd help, and that's what I'm going to do."

With the forced way he'd said those last few words, Hope would've guessed that his mother had been standing behind him, twisting his ear.

She absolutely did not want him helping out of some sense of duty. "I'm sure I can manage."

Aaron gave her an I-don't-believe-you-for-a-second look. Quite honestly, she didn't believe herself either. Why in the world would she make such a claim? She could barely saddle a horse, let alone run a farm.

But when she thought of Paul's tremendous generosity and thoughtfulness, she couldn't bear the thought of not doing her best to honor his efforts with toiling of her own. "I'll do my best to make sure his hard work isn't wasted."

"I'm sure you mean well, but this farm is a lot to take on. And I promised him I'd help," Aaron reiterated as though to convince himself. He stood and crossed to the mantel, his well-worn boots scuffing across the polished wood floor. With his back to Hope, she could see the tension bunching his muscles beneath his ecru shirt as he leaned against the mantel. "I also promised him that I'd take care—" he pivoted slow and steady, peering at her as though he faced a firing squad "—take care of you."

Hope couldn't move her gaze from him as his words settled over her. For some reason, instead of bringing her comfort, they annoyed her. How could Aaron think that he could take Paul's place? Or that she needed his help?

"Take *care* of me?"

He glanced at Ben, who gave him the slightest raise of an eyebrow and inclination of his head. Then Aaron slid his focus to Zach, who held out his hands as if to say, "It's up to you."

With a cough, Aaron turned his complete attention to Hope, and for some reason she wanted to run all the way back to the train station. He'd been avoiding her gaze since the moment she'd introduced herself, and now that his focus was bearing down so totally upon her, she squirmed under the intensity.

But she had nowhere to go. Apparently she had money now, but she also had a farm to run.

"I—I know this is awkward. It is for me, too, but I... well, it meant something to Paul when I promised to take care of you."

"What, exactly, do you mean?" She forced herself to stay seated.

She'd never run from difficult circumstances. Ever. When her family lost their fortune, she'd held her head high and found work at a bakery. And when her fiancé began showing signs of regret, she'd quietly bowed out of the relationship—her family hadn't even known of the real reason the engagement had been called off.

"I promised to hold on to hope." His voice broke. His throat visibly constricted. "In Paul's mind that meant that I'd marry you."

Hope strained to keep her shock from contorting her face, but she was pretty sure that she failed—miserably.

How could he possibly think that she would want a marriage based out of obligation? She'd rather be a spinster for the rest of her life.

Standing, she willed her arms to remain at her sides as she looked him square in the eye. His words pierced her soul, pricking the raw wound that still gaped from Jonas.

She wouldn't marry Aaron now—even if he dropped to his knees and begged. She barely even knew him. Besides, she could list off ten different reasons why this man had likely never married: his emotionless, unfeeling approach to things of great importance, being first and foremost on her list.

"So, I guess that settles it then." He shoved his hands into his pockets. "How soon do you want the wedding?"

"There isn't going to be a wedding."

Her simple, measured answer took Aaron aback. With the fanciful way she'd likely been raised, he thought for sure she'd find relief in the offer and that she'd be glad to have someone take care of her.

"No?" He looked for some kind of hesitation in her gaze.

"No."

Though his pride was a little stung, the way she stared down her nose at him made him immensely glad she'd just declined his offer. They were as different as night and day. And she was nothing like Ellie.

He wasn't exactly sure what Paul had seen in the woman, although it could've been very easy for her to hide her true colors in letters. She was a highfalutin city slicker. The way she held her head high, he guessed that she probably considered herself above those here in the West.

But she didn't seem dull. In fact, she struck him as being intelligent, so why would she travel all the way from the East if she knew what she was getting herself into? Had it truly been for love?

She slid a hand down the buttoned front of her waistcoat and then adjusted it as if it was askew. "If you'll excuse me, gentlemen, I believe I'll go outside for a breath of fresh air."

Her heeled, brown-booted feet tapped in quiet succession from the room and to the front door where she grabbed her parasol on the way outside.

After she'd made it down the steps, Aaron collapsed

onto the sofa next to Zach. He held his head in his hands, willing the incessant pounding that had started suddenly to stop.

"Do you think you could've been any more insulting?" Ben's terse voice reverberated in Aaron's head. "I mean, really, Aaron. *So, I guess that settles it?*"

"How soon do you want the wedding?" Zach mocked.

He glared at them. "What was I supposed to say?"

Ben gave his head a sorry shake. "I don't know, but that definitely *wasn't* it."

"A woman doesn't want to feel like some obligation," Zach scolded, slapping his knee.

Narrowing his gaze, Aaron turned to peer at him. "And how would you know? You're not even married."

"True. But do you think Ellie would've wanted to be proposed to in that manner?"

Aaron pulled a hand over the back of his neck, trying to massage away the pain. He scrambled for some reasonable excuse to support his actions, but no matter what justification he grasped for, it fell apart in his hands. "No. But this is different. It wasn't a proposal—well, not exactly, anyway. It was more like a *business* arrangement."

Zach just stared at him in that way he had that made a man feel small. "Regardless, that sure was a dead-fish way to go about it. Remind me *never* to ask you for romantic advice."

Aaron held his hands up. "Believe me. That area of my life has been sealed and shut for good. There is no way I'll ever love again."

"Don't be so sure," Ben cautioned, raising his brows for a fleeting moment.

Aaron dragged his hand over his scruffy face, thinking for the first time today how disheveled he must look. He hadn't had time to clean up before racing into town to meet the train—before everything had changed, before life had taken another jolting turn.

"I'll watch out for her and help her on the farm," he muttered. "Since she doesn't want to get married, at least I can do that much."

"What about your job at the wood shop? Won't Joseph need you?" Ben queried.

Aaron recalled the orders they had waiting to be filled. "I'll talk with him. See what we can work out. He's been getting along so well on his own."

"That's good to hear. But he'll still need you, won't he?" Ben was protective of Joseph. Since Joseph had lost his sight in a shop accident about a month before Ellie had died, he'd been making great strides, but Ben was always watchful.

"I'm sure he will, but apart from lunch I'll be working my usual hours."

"Well, I'll do what I can to help." Ben clasped his hands between his legs.

"Me, too, but with calving season here, I'll be hard-pressed to get away from the ranch much." Zach stuck his legs out in front of him, draping one foot over the other.

"Speaking of seasons…planting season is breathing down our necks. There won't be time to try and find a hired man." Ben peered into the fire as if looking for some answer there. "Besides, Paul said that any man she'd hire had to first go through you." He pinned Aaron with an intense gaze.

"You can be sure that there'd be men clambering for the job, but I wouldn't hire someone unless I could trust them up one side and down another." When he thought about how delicate Hope was, how vulnerable she'd seemed on the depot platform, the need to protect her rose up like some distant call. "In fact, at least for the first week or so

I'm sleeping out in the barn. That way if she runs into any problems I'll be close by. I'm not taking any chances with her being here all by herself. Not when she's so—"

"Beautiful?" Zach finished for him.

Aaron slanted a challenge-laced glance his brother's way. "If she's so beautiful, I'm surprised you're not stuttering around her."

"So am I." Zach's gaze shuttered as though he was remembering the difficulty he'd had some years ago. At eleven years of age, an embarrassing case of stuttering had set in after he'd been trapped in a cave alone for two days. He hadn't talked about the incident much and had worked hard the past few years to overcome his stutter. But once in a while he'd have a relapse—especially whenever he was around a pretty woman.

"Frankly, I'm not even sure she'll consent to hiring someone. She seemed downright determined to get her hands dirty." Aaron shook his head as he imagined Hope up to her elbows in garden dirt. "I can't picture her dirtying those perfectly manicured fingers of hers, though. Can you? And did you see the way her skin looks like it's never seen the light of day? Or the way she walks all straight and tall like some princess?"

His brothers exchanged a goading look that set Aaron's hackles standing on end.

"Don't give me that," he warned, feeling oddly defensive. But he had nothing to defend. Or did he? "I couldn't help but notice. She stands out like a sore thumb."

"I wouldn't exactly say a sore thumb," Ben corrected.

"Well, she's not who I would've expected Paul to marry, that's for sure." Aaron shoved his gaze to the pine floor, downright irritated by their provoking.

"Why? Because she's such a fine-looking lady?" Zach prodded.

Aaron scowled. "Paul didn't exactly look like the underside of a plow. I guess I thought he'd marry someone a little heartier. Like himself."

"She might be heartier than you think." Ben pointed out the front window. "Look."

Aaron wrenched around in his seat to see Hope standing in the middle of the herd of cattle, her arms stuck straight up in the air as she shimmied through the livestock. When she suddenly dipped down, disappearing into the mass of beasts as they closed in on her, his heart came to a complete stop.

"Oh, for the love of—" He catapulted off the sofa, through the room and out the front door to rescue her. Already.

As he raced out to the corral, he wondered how in the world he'd be able to keep track of her from his home, two miles away. But as she sprang up with a yellow tabby kitten in her hands then bravely edged toward the gate, gentling the cattle in spite of her obvious discomfort, he wondered if the barn or even two miles away would be far enough.

Chapter Four

"I'm coming, Hope. Whatever you do, don't make any quick moves," Aaron warned. He slowed his pace, resisting the urge to throw open the gate since doing so could spook the cattle. His pulse pounded through his veins. The situation could turn disastrous in a mere fraction of a second if she panicked…if he panicked.

She hurled a cursory glance his way and then yanked the hem of her dress, tearing it free from beneath the hoof of a black Hereford bull—a bull, that minutes ago, had been corralled in a solitary confinement of sorts. With an irritated huff, she turned and gave the bull's wet nose a single swat, eyeing the massive creature as though he'd purposely ruined her garment—her wedding dress.

"What in the world!" Ignoring his own trepidation, Aaron wedged himself between this woman and the cattle that had closed in on her like a giant litter of two-thousand-pound, menacing puppies. She either had a death wish or was completely naive to the unpredictability of ranch cattle—especially that of an aggressive bull. Wrapping his arms around Hope, he couldn't miss the way her entire body trembled or her indignant look as he steered her through the small opening to safety.

Once he'd latched the sturdy wood gate and gathered one gigantic steadying breath, he turned and clamped a scolding gaze on her and folded his arms at his chest as he attempted to calm his raging pulse. "What were you doing entering the corral like that? You could've been injured or worse."

"This poor little guy…" Hope nuzzled her cheek against the yellow tabby. Her hands quivered as she pulled the bedraggled kitten close. "He was about to get trampled beneath all of those enormous feet. This sweet little kitten's life could've tragically ended right there."

The kitten gave the smallest, most pitiful meow as it strained to climb higher, right into the crook of Hope's slender neck.

"Shh. It's all right," she whispered, placing a kiss on top of the kitten's head, its long hair fraying every which way.

"So you not only entered the corral, but you opened the bull's pen and went in after the kitten?" he prodded, dreading the thought of having to coax the bull back to his own pen.

If Aaron hadn't been seeing this with his own eyes, he might not have believed she could be so oblivious to the danger she'd put herself in just seconds ago.

"What else was I to do? He wandered in there."

"You could've called for help," he answered, remembering how enormously afraid Ellie had been of cattle—all cattle. He'd always wanted a milking cow and a few beef cattle, but Ellie had been outright terrified, and he refused to put her through the stress it would've caused. "We would've been out here in no time."

"There was not a *second* to waste." Her incensed gaze drifted up to Aaron and then shot over to the cattle as though to wound them straight through. "Badly done, cows. Shame on all of you."

Amazed by her complete naivety, Aaron made no attempt to hide his dismay as he stared, slack-jawed, at Hope.

Her perfectly arched eyebrows furrowed for a brief moment as she took him in. Then she glanced down at her sullied dress and tattered hem. "I can barely believe the nerve of that cow," she whispered, her words obviously meant for the kitten she cradled like some baby. She glared straight into the eyes of the bull at fault, her audacity making Aaron question whether the sturdy gate could withstand a sudden charge.

The angry puff of breath forced through the Hereford's flaring nostrils was a sure sign that Hope was treading on shaky ground. "That's really not a good idea, ma'am."

"To what are you referring?" She narrowed her gaze on the guilty party again.

"Staring at him that way." Sidestepping, Aaron made an effort to block her view of the accused.

"But look at him." She craned her neck to glare at the culprit. "He's being a bully."

"They don't call them bulls for nothing." Incredulous, he gave his head a slow shake as he closed in on her, grasping her arm firmly enough so that she'd know he meant business and tenderly enough to assure her that he meant no harm. He led her away from the corral, stopping only to grab her parasol from where she'd dropped it.

When he recalled the trace of fright on her face as she'd bravely made her way through the herd with the kitten in her hands and then the sweet and tender way she cradled the scrawny tabby—likely a stray who happened to be searching for a scrap of food in the wrong place—he had his answer. She had no idea.

"We best get you back to the house before that bull decides to rally his friends and break through the gate."

She gasped. "He wouldn't dare."

"This isn't the cultured streets of Boston, ma'am."

When a confused and almost fearful look passed over her fair features, he had a hard time getting mad at her. She was a delicate city flower dropped into the West, where only the heartiest took root and grew. And for some reason he felt compelled to make sure she was well protected.

After Aaron had accompanied her to a safe distance from the anxious herd, he brought her to a halt. "Listen, I know you've been in Boulder less than two hours and that your world has been turned on end, but if you're going to stay here then there are some things you should know."

There were plenty of risks she should know about, and if she was going to survive the next twenty-four hours on Paul's farm, and if Aaron was to have peace, he'd have to set her straight. But even then he was sure that serenity would elude him, just like the river bass always dodged his fishhook.

But when he looked into those emerald eyes of hers, he suddenly had a hard time remembering those precautions that had seemed so imperative only seconds ago.

"Yes." Her voice eased him from his silent perusal.

Jamming the toe of a boot into the dusty soil and kicking up a cloud of dirt, he struggled to clear his mind.

"What is it that you wanted to tell me?" She raised her chin a notch then glanced over to the herd of agitated cattle mulling about at the fence line.

Aaron cleared his throat. He gently grasped her chin and turned her head to look her in the eye. "First of all, never, and I mean *never,* stare into the eyes of a bull."

"But I—"

"Never," he interrupted, with more severity than he'd

intended given the way she shuddered. But as the image of Hope getting trampled dashed through his mind, fierce protectiveness for her rose up strong and sure—and completely unbidden. "Do you understand me?"

After a long moment, she gave a single, conceding nod.

He shoved his hands into his pockets, desperate to wipe away the tingling sensation coursing through his fingers from holding her chin. "They take that sort of thing as a challenge. As unfair and rude as you think that fella was being to your little friend there—" he nodded toward the purring kitten "—or stepping on your dress the way—"

"My dress is simply an irritation. Nothing more." She cuddled the kitten in the crook of her slender neck. "It's this helpless one who gave me such a fright."

"Lady, *you* gave *me* a fright," Aaron choked out. He set a hand to his chest. "My heart nearly pounded right out of my rib cage. In fact, it's still pumping like there's no tomorrow," he ground out, the admission carelessly spilling from his mouth without warning. It wasn't as if he was fond of her. But he did feel obligated—no, honor-bound, he corrected himself, remembering Zach's scolding—to watch after her. "If that bull decided to take you on," he added, perusing her slight, feminine form, "all five-foot-two of you wouldn't have a fighting chance."

Just then he glanced over to find Ben and Zach standing at the window, their arms draped in a lazy fashion at their chests and irritatingly innocent grins plastered across their faces. They peered with shameless mirth through the crystal clear window as though watching some theater production. They'd done nothing to help him out here. They appeared to enjoy the fact that he'd pledged himself to this woman's safekeeping.

He had to wonder…did he have a fighting chance?

* * *

The sun's first light bathed the spare bedroom at the back of Paul's home in a soft, rosy glow. At any other time the effect would've been soothing, but Hope didn't feel any more at peace than she had eight hours ago. She'd lain awake all night long, thinking, praying and trying not to be angry.

She was angry at Paul for leaving her so soon.

She was angry at God for taking him.

She was angry at Aaron for being so unkind and severe.

Restless, she pulled in a deep breath, bracing herself to face the unknowns that today would bring—meeting Paul's sister, going to the funeral, tending to duties on the farm…her farm.

Did she belong here?

After the way Aaron had scolded her about the whole cow fiasco, as if she were a small child, she had to wonder. And knowing what a contrast this kind of life was to her privileged upbringing she questioned even more. But she had no choice. Paul had been kind and loving enough to ensure her well-being. Even though he'd given her a way out at summer's end, she couldn't let him down.

Moreover, she couldn't let herself down by giving up.

Reaching for where the kitten slept beside her under the covers, she stroked the tabby's downy-soft fur. Theodore was what she'd named him, although she often called him sweetie. With all of his fluff of orange fur and his perfect little face, she couldn't bear letting him fend for himself when he'd almost died right in front of her eyes. Besides, she'd never had a kitten of her own. It was nice having something to hold when it seemed she was so alone.

Last night after Aaron and his brothers had left her to herself, she'd brought Theodore inside. Hope's mother could never stomach animals, inside or otherwise, but Hope had never understood the reasoning. And Aaron, as nervous as he was acting yesterday, would probably tell her that this innocent little kitten was liable to scratch her eyes out.

Aaron had seemed pretty intent on doling out a list of don'ts—almost as if he didn't trust her to walk five feet without making some kind of grave or dangerous mistake.

She'd make mistakes, of that she was certain. But surely he was being a bit overbearing. Take the cows, for instance. They'd seemed perfectly fine to her. Certainly she wouldn't have ventured into their midst had it not been for Theodore nearly being trampled, but really they'd seemed gentle enough. Even that lonely cow in his own pen had seemed sad when he'd received her scolding swat on the nose. Why, she was almost sure she'd heard him sniffling.

She'd just have to get to know the farm and the animals as quickly as possible so that she didn't feel so out of sorts.

When a long all-encompassing yawn commanded Hope's attention, she realized that she'd not gotten more than an hour of sleep combined. But even so, she had to get up and face the day.

When she felt Theodore nestle in closer against her legs, she lifted the covers and peeked at her kitten. The adoring way he squeezed his eyes shut and purred brought a smile to her face. She wasn't alone. She had this sweet one. And Paul had once written that God was always there in the best and worst of times—that He an ever-present help in times of trouble.

Picturing Paul's broken body, she had to wonder if God had been a help for Paul when he'd been pinned beneath the tree. She'd counted on Paul showing her the way in her newfound faith. Would her miniscule understanding of God be enough to find what had been so real to Paul?

Maybe Paul's sister would be a help. If she was anything like her brother—kind, understanding, tenderhearted— then Hope would have nothing to worry about. She'd be all right. She had to believe that from here on out there would be an endless swath of blue skies.

Jane was *nothing* like Paul.

In fact, Hope would've vowed the woman was some imposter, if not for the way Aaron and his family and the townspeople crowded around her now. They'd all gathered for Paul's funeral beneath one of the large pines anchoring the small cemetery. And now they offered their condolences as the lanky undertaker dropped shovelfuls of reddish dirt, reminiscent of his mat of red hair, over the simple pine box.

Hope struggled to steady her hand as she dabbed at her eyes and grappled for composure. Closing her eyes, she listened to the last bit of musky earth being thrown over Paul's grave and then the shovel's dull clang as the undertaker struck the soil to pack it down—as if to seal Paul's fate.

When she opened her eyes to see the gangly man yield one final clanging blow to the earth, she wished she would wake up from this horrible nightmare…to open her eyes and find herself standing at the church altar, at the very cusp of a brand-new life with Paul.

She grieved the man she knew from his letters. She grieved the life they could have had. But seeing the way each person in attendance was wrought with such deep sorrow, she realized that she grieved never really knowing Paul.

These people…they'd known him. They'd seen how he

walked and how he rode a horse. They'd heard his voice, his laugh. They'd felt his touch.

She was an outsider.

There was no mistaking that Jane was incensed by Hope's presence and clearly thought she was an intruder. From the outset this morning when Jane had arrived home, she'd been cold and frosty whenever she was alone with Hope. She'd made no bones about her displeasure with Paul's deathbed decisions. Jane had seemed equally incensed by Aaron's assurance that he would watch out for Hope. She'd even said as much.

Witnessing the way the woman's shoulders heaved on a loud sob, Hope's heart swelled with compassion. After all, Jane had lost her brother, suddenly and tragically.

When she felt a gentle touch at her elbow, she looked to find Aaron standing at her side.

"I'll see you and Jane home now—that is, if you're ready." His voice was low, and his blue eyes were moist and undeniably sad—a sadness that seemed to be almost permanently etched into his roguish features.

"That'll be fine. Thank you."

When he gestured for her to walk with him down the footpath, she turned and stared at where Paul had been laid to rest beneath the newly turned earth. "Will you give me just one more moment, please?" She glanced back at Aaron.

When he nodded and walked away, she approached the grave and stood there for a long moment. She'd had no problem dreaming of what life would be like with Paul when she was back in Boston, but the harder she tried to generate some kind of image of herself with him now, the further removed she felt. She couldn't seem to see anything other than the glaring fact that she barely knew him.

"He was a real nice feller, wasn't he?" The undertaker

stood beside her, wedging his shovel into the earth and barely missing her foot.

"Yes, he was." She tucked her right foot next to her left one, resisting the urge to turn and see just how far away Aaron had gone. "A fine man."

Pulling one overly large floppy glove off, the long-limbed man reached out to shake her hand. His razorlike Adam's apple bobbed so severely she thought it likely to cut straight through his throat. "Name's Pete. Pete O'Leary."

"Nice to meet you, Mr. O'Leary." She shook his hand, struggling to school her expression against the way his sweaty palm clamped against hers.

"If'n you ever need anything. You jest give me a holler."

She smiled, though not enough so as to encourage the man in any way. "Thank you for your kindness, but I'm sure I'll be just fine."

"I heard that he went and left his farm to you. And that you was to be married. Is that the truth?" he inquired with as much candidness as Hope imagined possible.

Just then a weasellike animal poked its head out from a pack strapped to the man's back. "All right, Conroy. You seen the perty lady. Now you get yerself back in there, ya hear?" Mr. O'Leary reached over his shoulder and gave the animal's head a gentle pat. "Conroy's my ferret. Bought him off'un a travelin' salesman."

"He's a fine-looking ferret," she commented as the adorable animal wiggled his long-whiskered nose at her and then dived into the sturdy denim pack.

"He goes with me most places—cept'n fer church. Though, Lord knows that bein' there'd do his thievin' soul some good." Mr. O'Leary leaned a gangly arm on the shovel handle and sighed as the ferret rebelliously popped up again, perching his front paws on the man's rail-thin shoulder. "The critter can't seem to keep his dishonest paws from takin' that which ain't his."

The earnest show of the man's distress and the delightful look of innocence on the ferret's whiskered face coaxed a smile from Hope. She was grateful for the diversion so that she didn't have to field the man's inquiries. "With a face like that, how could he possibly mean to be ill-behaved?"

"That's what I been tellin' myself, but after a while a body's gotta wonder." He shrugged out of the pack and folded his legs beneath him, then tucked the long, lean ferret back inside.

"This is *not* social hour at the opera house." Jane's terse voice sounded at Hope's ear.

Hope turned just in time to see Jane's cutting glare swing from her to the undertaker then back again, but she refused to cower in response.

"Stop your fraternizing and come along. Can't you see that we're waiting for you?" Pivoting, the woman stalked down the trail toward the wagons, not even bothering to give Mr. O'Leary an appreciative look for his labor and not thinking enough to pass one last look at her brother's grave.

"Thank you for your hard work, Mr. O'Leary." Hope peered up at the man, deciding that although he was a little rough around the edges he seemed harmless enough.

"Glad to do it." He looped his arms into his pack and tugged his shovel out of the dirt. "It's my job."

Turning, Hope made her way down the trail. She caught Aaron's gaze fixed on her as if he'd been watching for a long while. Had he sent Jane up to get her? He'd seemed completely oblivious to the woman's spiteful ways.

When she'd almost reached the cluster of mourners, Aaron came to meet her and guided her toward his wagon.

"My family, as well as a few others, will be coming over in a little while with plenty of fixings for a meal. I hope you don't mind the lot of us barging in on you, but this is how we do it here in Boulder."

"That's perfectly fine." She managed a dim smile as she maneuvered through the tall grass. "As soon as we get there, I'll do what I can to get things prepared."

He shook his head. "You won't be doing anything, Hope. That's what the others will be there for." He came to a stop and stared down at her as if to enforce his point.

"Until the past twenty hours, these people had no idea that I existed. To be counted among family now," she reasoned, thinking about how Jane clearly viewed her as an outsider, "is a bit uncomfortable." And to have Aaron telling her what to do settled over her with equal unpleasantness. Besides, she would rather busy herself than to field the questions she was sure would come her way—just like with Mr. O'Leary.

How did you and Paul meet? How long had you corresponded? When were you to wed? And most inevitably, why had Paul not told us about you?

"Paul obviously didn't view you as an outsider," Aaron argued.

"Please. It's not that I don't appreciate your consideration—" she tugged on the strong thread of gracious manners that had been woven into her from the time she was young "—but I would feel better if I could be helping."

For a long moment, Aaron peered down at her as though taking her full measure. Yesterday she'd refused his apathetic proposal of marriage. Honorable, though it may be, seeing as how this man considered it his job to make decisions for her, declining his hand was a very wise decision—just like breaking off her engagement with Jonas had been.

"Aaron," Ben called, motioning him to the other side of the grassy knoll, "Jane's going to need your help here."

Hope followed in Aaron's wake, lifting the skirts of her cobalt-blue dress as she picked her way around the tender spring flowers that had poked through the soil. She hadn't dreamed she'd need traditional mourning attire upon her arrival, and her lack of it only seemed to irritate Jane further. Paul's sister had scanned her up and down not once but several times today, as though to make some silent barbed statement.

"She says she's feeling pretty weak," Ben commented, his voice low and measured. When he slid a cautious gaze to Hope, she couldn't miss the hint of apology there.

"Oh, I am, Aaron. Very weak. I'm so glad you're here." Jane's breathy whisper filtered to Hope. The woman threw herself into Aaron's arms—almost.

When he sidestepped to gain his balance, Hope stifled a gasp. But she could hardly fault the woman for being given to exceptional outbursts of emotion after suffering such shock.

"You are a great strength to me. I'm sure that Paul would offer his gratitude if he was—" Jane's eyes suddenly pooled with fresh tears. "I don't know what I would do without you, Aaron. Honestly, you are meant for me."

He passed a disconcerted glance to Ben, his throat convulsing as though he'd just swallowed a small horse. He stared down at where Jane had circled her arms around his chest and burrowed her cheek into his dark gray vest. "Well, I, uh…I'm glad to help."

"Thank you," Jane whispered, one side of her thin lips lifting in what looked to Hope like a triumphant grin.

Clearing his throat, Aaron pried her arms loose and took one sizable step away from her. "Don't you think we should probably go since the others will be coming soon?"

"Yes, of course. You're right, as always, Aaron." The way Jane latched onto Aaron and led the way, Hope half wondered if she was making a silent claim. The icy look she sent Hope could've frozen one of the yellow spring blooms dotting the grassy knoll within seconds and furthered her suspicion.

"We'll be right behind you to help with the meal, Hope. Don't you worry about a thing," Ben's wife, Callie, called as she took her husband's hand and climbed into their wagon.

Hope waved and trailed behind Jane and Aaron, watching as Jane nearly sprinted the last few feet to claim a seat at the front of the wagon, not even bothering to wait for assistance.

"You'll have to sit in the back again, Hope. There's just not room up here. You won't mind, will you?" She gave Hope a sickeningly sweet look, her face all pinched in apology as she took great care spreading out her skirts as though decorating an elaborate layered cake.

Hope struggled to prevent her disbelief from making its way to an all-out expression. "Of course, I don't mind."

With a firm but gentle touch, Aaron easily lifted her into the wagon and then took his own seat next to Jane. When Jane clasped a possessive hand over Aaron's muscular arm, Hope determined that Paul's sister was definitely marking her territory. As far as Hope was concerned, Jane could have the man. But being a woman of principle, the fact that Jane was being so nasty about the whole thing just didn't sit right.

Once Aaron had the wagon headed down the road, he glanced at her with a concern-filled look. "Are you sure you don't mind all of us coming to your house for a gather—"

"Paul's house," Jane corrected darting her attention to Aaron then back at Hope. "It's Paul's house."

Hope determined to find some common ground on which to stand with Jane if this day was going to be anything more than horrible. "I'm sure that Paul would've wanted it that way."

Jane twisted in her seat. "Excuse me for saying so, but honestly, how would *you* know what Paul would've wanted?" She narrowed her hazel-eyed gaze and pursed her thin lips, making them nearly disappear. "You never even met him."

"I—I just thought that Paul, being as kind-hearted and giving as he was—"

"Yes he was, wasn't he? So generous that he gave you his estate."

"Jane," Aaron admonished.

"It's all right, Aaron," Hope placated. "She's had a very difficult day."

Jane's shrewd expression suddenly turned sorrowful just like that. "Oh, I'm just so beside myself with grief. My dear, dear brother Paul…dead," she sobbed, hugging her arms to her chest and dabbing at her eyes.

Surely, this woman couldn't be so shallow as to exercise such pettiness—especially at a time like this. Hope would love to give her the benefit of the doubt, but she'd deny her own intelligence in doing so. Instead, Hope reminded herself that she was irrevocably connected to this woman, and although she couldn't help feeling incredulous at Jane's flagrant show of melodramatics, she must be as gracious as humanly possible.

Aaron gave Jane's arm a brief squeeze, bringing a peculiar stop to the lamenting. "Why don't you decide where you think we should have the gathering? How does that sound?"

Jane sniffled. Dabbed at her eyes. Hiccupped. "Thank you. Thank you so much."

After several moments of silence, the woman sniffled once again as if for good measure. She stared up at Aaron, her shapeless loglike eyebrows bunched inward. "I know my brother better than anyone. Why don't we all gather at Paul's home?" she announced, as though the idea was brand new. "I'm sure he would have wanted it that way."

Hope nearly bit clear through her tongue. She couldn't imagine how a woman could be so petty—especially at a time like this. Determined to stay strong, she silently conceded that Paul's sister would be *no* help at all. Hope was in this alone.

Chapter Five

Aaron watched from the front room as Hope made her way to the small spare bedroom to put her shawl away. His throat grew tight as she passed by Paul's bedroom, pausing momentarily and peering inside, her slender hand curled around the etched metal doorknob. She quietly closed the door and entered the room across the hallway.

She'd been stalwart all day long, from the time he'd dragged himself from the hayloft early this morning to take care of the chores until now, when at least two dozen people she didn't even know were set to arrive. And she'd been so patient with Jane.

It'd taken Aaron by surprise, the downright rude way Jane responded to Hope about the gathering on the ride here. Paul had mentioned that Jane could be testy, but Aaron had never seen that side of her.

Ever since his wife and baby's death, Jane had been the picture of neighborly support. She'd shown up at least once a week at the wood shop, a basket laden with baked goods hanging from her arm. She'd even brought a noontime meal by on several occasions. Aaron had been grateful for the offerings, but he'd never seen them as anything more than kindly gestures.

Now he wasn't so sure—especially with the way Jane had taken to clinging to him like mud to a pig.

Hope had held her own with Jane. Oddly enough, that had struck a chord of satisfaction and pride in his heart, but still he felt compelled to watch over the situation. He'd dropped Jane off at her house on the edge of Paul's property, hoping that a little rest before the meal was served would remove the woman's sharp edge. Although Hope had smoothed over Jane's rudeness today with understanding—a surprising trait, given her fancy ways and attire—he hadn't missed the way embarrassment had colored Hope's fair cheeks when Jane had glared at her earlier today as she'd climbed aboard the buckboard in her bright blue dress.

As far as Aaron was concerned, it shouldn't matter a lick what color a person wore to a funeral. And frankly he didn't think God much cared, either. What mattered most in Aaron's book was honoring life. Paul's life had been honored today—that was certain. It was honored by his friends and neighbors who'd recalled his kindness and acts of mercy and also by this woman he'd been set to wed. She'd honored him in the quiet strength she'd shown in the face of a difficult set of circumstances, in the gracious way she'd answered questions from some of the townsfolk earlier and in the patient way she'd endured Jane's near-tantrum this morning when Aaron and Ben had informed Jane of Paul's deathbed decisions.

But life had only just begun for Hope here. There was plenty to be done, and the complete naivety she'd shown around Paul's cattle was proof enough that she didn't have the first idea about farm life. Aaron couldn't imagine her continuing on with such poise and courage when faced with milking the cows or digging her hands into the soil.

He'd help her out and keep an eye on the situation with

Jane because he'd promised and because it was the right thing to do. But he'd do so with as minimal contact with Hope as possible because for some reason he couldn't keep his thoughts from straying straight to her.

Last night when he'd finally nestled into the hayloft to sleep he couldn't seem to stop thinking about the way Hope had saved that barn kitten from sure death, the way she'd kept her calm, the way she'd said, "Excuse me," to the cattle as she made her way through their midst and the way she'd met Aaron's concern with such innocence and determination in her gaze.

"Well, where is she?" Katie, his brother Joseph's wife, asked, intruding on Aaron's thoughts. Thankfully.

"Who?" He hadn't even heard Katie and Joseph enter the house.

"Hope. That's who. I met her at the funeral. She's a dear." Katie peered at him as though he'd spoken some foreign language. "Is she all right?"

Concern for her rose within him just as fast as a rainstorm in the mountains. "What do you—"

"There you are." Katie crossed to meet Hope as she entered the room and set a stack of dishes down on the table. "How are you doing after everything?"

"I'm fine." The faint smile on Hope's face was far from convincing and strummed another unexpected chord of compassion in Aaron's heart. "I was just freshening up." He gave her a quick once-over. She hadn't looked disheveled when they'd arrived home. In fact, she still looked picture perfect.

It was the exact opposite of the windblown, no-fuss, natural way Ellie had always been.

"I thought that perhaps we could use some of the dishes I brought from home for the gathering today," she said as she glanced back at the fine china. "I just unpacked them."

Was Hope putting on airs? Was she intent on impressing the lot of folks here with her obvious trappings of wealth? Folks here weren't so easily awed. Oh, maybe some of the ladies would fawn over the flourish of it all, but most folks put more stock in hard work, endurance and good living.

Katie strode right past surface pleasantries and encircled Hope in a hug. The rigid way Hope had held her shoulders back and head high all day seemed to lessen some, and for that Aaron was thankful. "I think the dishes will be a lovely touch to the gathering, Hope. Thank you for offering them."

As much as he was uncomfortable with this whole situation, he couldn't bear seeing her try so hard to be strong. He was worn out just watching her and was intent on making sure she rested throughout the gathering.

"Hope, I want you to meet my husband, Joseph." Katie glanced over her shoulder at Joseph.

"I'm sorry about your loss, ma'am. Please accept my condolences." He stepped closer and held his hand out to Hope. "Paul was a good man. He'll be missed."

Hope hesitated for a moment then took his hand as though suddenly aware that Joseph was unable to see. "Thank you. It does come as quite a shock."

Joseph had been without his sight for almost a year now. Aaron had encouraged him that he'd done a remarkable job adapting, but Joseph would funnel all of the credit to his wife, who'd initially come to Boulder as his teacher.

"I want to assure you that I'll do without that brother of mine as much as I can so that he can be here with you." Joseph gently draped his arm over his wife's shoulders, the clear look of self-satisfaction pricking Aaron's ire.

Be here with her?

Why would he say that? Sure as shootin', he could've come up with something else to say. Aaron could only hope that Joseph felt the annoyance he was aiming in his direction.

"Oh, it won't be necessary for him to miss work." Hope's brow furrowed slightly. "I'm sure I'll be able to manage. I already informed Aaron as much."

Katie sidled up next to Hope. "Don't look a gifted horse in the mouth, my dear."

"That's a gift horse." Joseph chuckled.

"The horse could be gifted, too, I suppose," Aaron added watching as Joseph pulled his wife close and gave her a hug.

"You two…" Katie melted into her husband's embrace. "You knew what I meant."

Aaron was glad for Joseph's happiness, but whenever he witnessed the love that Joseph and Katie shared, his own loss seemed to grow deeper and stronger, like a stubborn root. Time hadn't healed his heart, as some well-meaning folks had assured him. Instead it had exaggerated the pain. Someday, maybe, he wouldn't be plagued with the familiar ache, but never again would he love.

The idea that he'd almost entered into marriage yesterday made his heart lurch to a grinding halt. What had he been thinking?

He'd been thinking like a Drake, that's what. Honor your word. Let loyalty and right-living be your trademark.

He could be grateful until his dying day that Hope had been good enough to turn him down.

"As I was saying," Katie began again, "Aaron will be a great help. Besides, Joseph has been talking about hiring on another craftsman."

"What kind of gossip am I missing out on?" Zach edged

into the gathering, standing beside Aaron as he slid Katie a playful wink.

"Don't you go winking at my wife, Zach," Joseph warned. "Do you hear?"

Zach waggled his eyebrows at the lot of them. "And how would you know I did that?"

"Because that's what you always do. You're predictable," Joseph added with a grin.

Zach grabbed at his chest, winking at Hope this time. "You wound me, Joseph. Predictable? No man wants to be thought of as predictable."

"We know you up one side and down another." Joseph chuckled. "Face it. You've got the cowboy nod and wink down to a science. You could teach a class on it at Boulder College—that is, if they offered such things."

"Ben, Joseph and Aaron like to accuse Zach of being the quintessential ladies' man," Katie explained to Hope.

She turned an amused expression on Zach and studied him for a long moment. "Perhaps they underestimate you?" The warmth of her smile made the air suddenly seem unbearably stuffy.

Aaron pulled at his collar. If there was one thing he didn't want to do, it was give his brothers any kind of weakness to pounce on. It wasn't that he didn't trust them, but with the way they'd acted yesterday about Hope, he couldn't help but feel like they were pushing for something that could never be—plain and simple.

"Now there's a smart woman," Zach proclaimed, sweeping his Stetson from his head and making a grand bow toward Hope. "I'm barely acquainted with her and already she knows me better than my own flesh and blood."

On a sigh, Aaron gave his head a shake. "My family. I can always count on them to be welcoming to strangers and to make awkward situations more comfortable."

Like now. Hope had to be overwhelmed by everything she'd gone through the past day. He doubted she was eager to have a houseful of strangers, but at least his family would be here to buffer the discomfort of it all.

And there was Jane to consider. She would need support.

Besides, he and his brothers had all agreed that, though they'd like to put it off for another time, they'd have to talk with Hope at some point today about the farm—how she wanted to handle things, what kind of chore schedule they could work out and if she was considering hiring a farmhand.

If that was the case then no man would work for her unless he passed to Aaron's satisfaction. Even then he would insist on closely guarding the situation. A woman like Hope—beautiful, helpless and alone—would be a dark-minded man's dream.

"I just figure if I keep my contact with the ladies to a harmless wink here or there then I don't have to worry about stuttering." Zach jammed his hat back on his head. "Although, thank the good Lord I hardly ever have a problem with it anymore."

"Are we missing out on something?" Ben asked as he closed the door behind his family, Callie—his wife of six months—and her seven-year-old daughter, Libby.

"Uncle Aaron, Uncle Aaron," Libby squealed as she ran the short distance and jumped into Aaron's arms.

"Well, hello there, Libby-Loo." He gave her a big hug.

Callie had shown up on Ben's doorstep last October, wanting a job. Little did they all know that this stranger was their brother Max's widow. Having endured seven years of abuse and suffering at Max's hands, Callie had sought Ben out, per Max's dying words, as a last resort. Aaron gulped past the lump that always formed in his throat whenever he thought of the situation and how she'd been reunited with her daughter from Max after he'd used the child, a newborn at the time, to pay off a gambling debt. He'd lied to Callie, saying that the baby had died just as Callie had passed out with the final birthing push. God had definitely redeemed many a heartache.

"I been missing you, Uncle Aaron." Libby wrapped him up in a gigantic hug then pulled away and held his face between her small hands. "You have to come see the new kitty Papa brought home. She's real pretty."

"Really? A new kitty, huh?" Aaron glanced at Hope, thinking about the helpless yellow tabby she'd rescued.

With the way Hope was gazing at him, her eyes full and bright and laden with enchantment, he couldn't seem to look away. He didn't know what was getting into him. Why did he seem so captivated by her?

"Uncle Aaron, did you hear me?" Libby tugged his head to square his focus with hers. "I said the kitty is all white. Like a bride. Like Mama was when she married Papa."

"Oh, how sweet," Hope whispered.

Libby twisted in Aaron's arms and peered at Hope, as if noticing her for the first time. She wiggled out of his hold and went to stand in front of Hope. "You're a pretty lady."

Hope's cheeks suddenly flushed to pink as she clasped her slender hands together in front of her. "Why, thank you. Might I say that you are a very pretty girl."

A sweet smile spread across Libby's face as she studied Hope. "I like your blue dress. Mama said that Miss Jane thought your dress was too blue, but I—"

"Libby." Bending over, Callie whispered something in the girl's ear.

Libby tucked her chin a notch. "Well, I think it's very pretty. Don't you, Uncle Aaron?" She peered up at him.

Heat instantly infused his cheeks. He brushed his hand down his arm, dusting imaginary dirt from his sleeve.

"Uncle Aaron, you're not listening to me." Libby furrowed her brow in that adorable way of hers that always tugged at Aaron's heartstrings.

"Yes, the dress is very nice. Beautiful." He set his gaze just over Hope's shoulder, but even out of the corner of his vision he caught a whisper of vulnerability cross her face.

If he looked at her now, straight in the eyes, she might be able to see the way his soul had suddenly begun churning with the smallest bit of tenderness, attraction.

He was being ridiculous. He was as silly as a smitten schoolboy. He'd been widowed for ten months. He'd not spared any woman a single glance. So why would he now? Aaron struggled to pull himself together as he wondered what had gotten into him.

"You have a lovely dress, too. Pink is such a charming color—just like you." Hope nodded at Libby with a fair amount of fancy manners. Which probably went far with Libby seeing as how the girl considered herself an expert in ladylike ways.

The way Libby perched her hands in front of her in the same manner as Hope provoked a few light chuckles from his family.

"My name's Libby." She reached out and fingered Hope's satin dress. "What's your name?"

She knelt and met Libby, eye to eye. "Hope."

Hope. Aaron's promise once again unfurled in his mind like a heralding banner. He'd like to just roll it up and stuff it away, but try as he might, he couldn't seem to catch the thing and bring it back.

"I like your name. Hope. Mama and Papa say that we should always have hope." She turned and looked at Ben and Callie, her earnest expression melting Aaron's heart. "Don't you?"

"Yes, we do," Ben answered on a wink. He pulled a hand over his mouth as though to wipe off a grin. "We're all for hope."

Aaron couldn't feel any more cornered than he did right now. Ben, Zach, Joseph, Callie and Katie....

At least sweet little Libby hadn't forsaken him.

Just then Libby peered back at Hope, reached out and took her hand. "So I guess that means you're gonna be part of our family."

Hope yawned as long and wide as she imagined humanly possible. Five o'clock in the morning was far earlier than she was accustomed to rising, but after Aaron and his brothers had set her down yesterday and noted the numerous chores and details of the farm for her, she was quite certain that this ghastly hour wouldn't be nearly early enough.

All night long she'd been deliberating the enormous changes in her life and had just nodded off when a loud cackling call from outside her window had pierced her slumber. Once again, she peered out the bedroom window, watching as the large chestnut-colored rooster strutted as pretty as you please, right underneath her opened window. With one eye aimed her way, he stared up at her as if to get a glimpse of the newcomer.

She tugged her long white opera gloves on as far as they would go, adjusted her pale green silk dress, then drew her shawl around her shoulders and walked out to the barn. Her warm breath fanned out in a ghostlike cloud into early morning, the hint of purple, pink and orange hanging on the horizon, heralding the day. When she opened the barn door, an earthy, not exactly unpleasant, scent met her square in the face. Holding a lantern before her, she stepped inside, the dim light lapping up the darkness in warm, gentle waves.

The crude dwelling closed her in but not so that she felt unsafe. Holding the lantern high, she looked the barn over, noticing the sturdiness and how solid and thick the beams were that endured the weight.

Just then a shifting sound came from somewhere up ahead. Then it came again followed by a low groan.

She froze on the spot and slid her gaze to the left where the noise originated. When another low groan met her, she nearly dropped the lantern.

Her heart pounded hard and fast inside her chest as she scanned the dwelling. She held her breath, images of a mountain lion leaping from the shadows and pouncing on her flashing through her mind. The hair on her neck stood on end. With needlelike claws, fear pierced deep, delving into her peace, her mind, her composure.

The noise came again followed by a distinctive mooing sound.

Squeezing her eyes shut, Hope sighed in the most unladylike way she'd ever permitted herself. "It's only a cow."

She was being silly. Aaron had cautioned her on many issues, but milking the cow had not been counted among them. There was nothing to fear. Right?

In truth, she could find trepidation in nearly every place she looked. But if she let fear guide her thoughts, she might not have the fortitude to manage on her own. Growing up in a wealthy Boston family, she'd never been exposed to farm animals except for the horses that had pulled their carriages to and fro. She'd often begged for a cat or a dog to love, but her mother had refused, noting that animals belonged in the country.

Willing one foot in front of the other, she followed a generously large, dirt-packed corridor to a stall where a fat brown cow stood, its tail swishing from side to side as it chewed on something. It peered over at her, its big brown eyes looking no more malicious than its thin, long tail looked like a weapon.

"Now, then, aren't you a fine-looking cow?" She willed her pulse to even out.

Nonplussed by her greeting, the creature continued chewing in a slow and lazy way.

She opened the latch to the wood-plank half door and squeezed inside, quickly closing it behind her. Although this four-legged being seemed docile enough, Hope couldn't be sure that, given the opportunity, it might not escape. And she definitely didn't fancy the idea of chasing it about the farm yard.

"You must be the cow I'm going to milk this morning."

The beast sighed, its warm breath hanging like a peaceful mist in the crude stable. Aaron had cautioned her never to stare into the eyes of a bull, but he'd obviously never met this cow.

"Well, I can assure you that I shall honor your modesty in every way possible." She hung the lantern on a hook by the entrance then draped her shawl over the door. "And I shall be as quick and as thorough as possible—though you'll forgive me," she added, peering behind her at where the cow stood as amiably as a child on his first day of school. "With this being my first time tending to such a chore, it may not go quite as well as what you are accustomed to."

While she secured her long gloves once more, she tried to remember what Aaron had said last night about this chore. He'd mentioned something about a stool.

"Would you be so kind as to point me in the direction of the stool?" she asked, addressing the gigantic beast to calm herself as much as it—in case it got aggravated by her presence.

Spotting a rough-hewn stool hanging in the corner, she hiked up her skirts and picked her way over two overly large piles of dung. When she had the stool in hand, she set it next to the cow, then stroked her hand down the cow's side where the soft and warm feel of his fur met her touch.

The gentle beast turned a bored look on her as if to say, "Enough with the pleasantries. I'm ready to be milked."

She smiled at that as she stood back and assessed the situation. "Aaron had insisted on coming over and doing all of the chores this morning, but I thought I'd beat him to it." She moved up to the cow's head and gave the beast a scratch behind the ear. "Just between you and me, I'm fairly certain that he doesn't believe I possess the strength and perseverance to keep up with everything."

When the cow turned its head, nearly knocking Hope off balance, she dragged the stool back an inch or two, a little unsettled at the thought of sitting so close to such a powerful animal.

"Well, Mr. Aaron Drake has a bit of a surprise in store for him, doesn't he?"

The cow swished its tail from one side to the other as though offering some kind of agreeable response.

"Being alone and new to Boulder, I have nothing better to do than to take care of the farm, right? After all, how hard can this really be? At least once I am well-acquainted with every little nuance. I'll show him that his precon-ceived idea of Hope Gatlin as a useless city bauble is not even *close* to being true."

Just as quickly as her ire raised thinking about Aaron

and his judgmental bossy nature, it diminished to barely a trace as she recalled the compliment he'd given her yesterday regarding her dress—and the way it seemed to have cost him dearly. She also recalled how loving, how very gentle he'd been with his niece. Hope's heart had fairly melted in that moment, seeing the sweet way Aaron had interacted with Libby and the way Libby adored him.

Hope knew little of Aaron—only that he loved his family. That had been evident in the way he'd related with them. She'd also noticed that something weighed heavy on the man. The telltale marks of sadness in his gaze had pierced her heart on several occasions.

She would never forget his tortured gaze as he'd watched Joseph and Katie, the tender, loving way they acted with each other. The image of Aaron stealing admiring glimpses at them stirred Hope's compassion, her sympathy and a deeply buried vulnerability.

And that she most certainly couldn't afford. She must stay strong.

Although, she had been very grateful for his patience and kindness yesterday. She certainly hadn't expected to be treated like a fragile flower, but she was appreciative of his understanding and his seemingly genuine consideration for her well-being—even if his duty was misplaced.

If not for the way he rubbed her wrong, with his general doubt regarding her fortitude and his obligatory offer of marriage, she might consider him a saint—at least in the way he treated Jane.

Hope trailed her hand down the cow's back to where a long tail ended in a wiry tuft of hair. Jane's image instantly came to mind, her frizzed, unkempt hair poking out from where she'd pulled it back in a haphazard fashion. When the woman had arrived at the gathering yesterday, the amiable conversation with Aaron's family had come to a screeching halt. In a matter of moments, Jane had swung from public displays of near-sobbing to private, vindictive barbs directed at Hope. And whenever Aaron was anywhere near Hope, Jane would descend on him like a vulture, with talons so sharp Hope was almost certain she'd witnessed Aaron wincing once.

The cow's low mooing sound jolted Hope from her thoughts.

"I'm sorry. I almost forgot about you." She chuckled at the very idea that she was about to milk a cow. "All right then, if you're ready to begin, why don't we get started?"

Grasping a handful of her skirt with one hand, she straddled the stool and sat down. She retrieved the two teacups she'd brought with her from the crude drawstring bag she'd found in Paul's pantry and wrapped around her wrist.

She gave the cow's belly a whisper of a pat, marveling at just how close she was to it. "I was told that when all is said and done I might get two full containers, if I'm lucky. So, here they are." She held up the two china cups for the cow to see. "Aaron informed me of that. You might know him. He frowns often, but, in fact, he's very handsome, rather roguish in his features, really. But I daresay, he would *never* make a good husband."

Chapter Six

Aaron fastened one of the buttons on his shirt, swallowing hard as he stood at the stall door, his gaze riveted to Hope, her fancy dress and long white gloves as uncommon in a cow's stall as a miner's coal dusted garments in some upscale opera house. His hearing totally occupied by her words…that he was *very handsome…would never make a good husband…and frowned often.*

He had plenty to frown about, but he didn't exactly like the idea that this was the first thing she could find to say about him—and to a bovine, no less. And he'd like to think that he'd made a good husband for Ellie. He hadn't been standing there for more than a minute, but it'd been long enough.

As ridiculous as this was, he couldn't stop the smile from stretching across his face. Threading his arms through his suspenders he realized that Paul's mail-order bride didn't know the backside of a horse from a train caboose when it came to western ways and country living.

She was something, Hope. Here she was perched on a stool in her fancy clothes, ready to milk the cow at the crack of dawn.

Did she even own a work dress? So far, the garments

he'd seen draping her feminine form had been more elegant than most women in Boulder dreamed of owning.

But just seeing her sitting there all elegant and refined looking, he realized that he'd definitely underestimated her. He'd figured that she'd drag herself out of bed sometime around eight o'clock and still consider that early. Well, he was a big enough man to recognize when he was just plain wrong.

"Now, you just let me know if I'm hurting you. All right?" She held the china cups under the cow's teats and waited…and waited, and it was all Aaron could do to remain perfectly silent. "Hmm…maybe if I try this." She slowly maneuvered a long white-gloved hand to the cow's teats. The dainty teacup perilously cradled in her other hand would barely catch enough milk to feed a fat and sassy cat.

Her naive tenacity…now *that* was strangely and undeniably refreshing. It awakened a tender part of his heart he thought had died right along with Ellie.

From this vantage point, he could tell that she was barely touching the cow as she began squeezing—pinching, really. He listened for the ping of milk hitting the vessel, knowing full well that it'd be difficult. She tried again and again, then bent at the waist and peered beneath the cow as though looking for written instructions.

He'd been awakened by the soothing sound of her voice filtering through the barn to where he'd been sleeping in the hayloft. For two nights now, he'd slept up there, and though it wasn't home, it eased his mind knowing that he was within earshot—even if she didn't know it yet. Tucking in his shirttails, he had to bite his lip to keep from grinning at her as she worked so diligently to milk the cow.

When the cow mooed and shifted, Hope startled. She stood suddenly, stumbled.

Aaron sprang into action, bolting through the stall door and catching her under her arms just as she was about to hit the ground.

She let out a muffled scream, and then gasped as her upside-down gaze met his. Swallowing hard she stared, up at him.

He cleared his throat, unable to keep a grin from curling his lips. "Do you need some help?"

Her stunned expression infused her features with a feminine, rosy glow. "Why do you ask?"

He couldn't begin to wipe the smile from his face, especially when she was trying so hard to appear nonchalant as she smoothed a hand down her skirt.

"Oh, I don't know. Just a hunch, I guess." He gave his head an exasperated—albeit amused—shake, perplexed by her stubbornness, stirred by her determination. "I'd be glad to give you some pointers, if you'd like."

He maintained his hold on Hope as she tried to get her footing, but her flourish of skirts caught her up. She scrambled to right herself and stumbled against Aaron, falling backward once again and bringing him down beneath her.

"Oh, my, I apologize," she gasped as she lay there, seemingly helpless as a bug on its back. "How positively clumsy of me."

"Are you all right?" He angled his gaze at her, trying not to notice how her slender form molded to his or how he could almost feel her body sigh with relief, as though she was grateful to have someone catch her when she fell. "You're not hurt, are you?"

He also struggled to ignore the way his heart seemed to exalt—rebelliously so—in the opportunity to hold someone again. He'd cherished his wife, Ellie—with his words, his touch and his deeds. He'd loved her deeply—and he'd been loved deeply. It was as if his arms had ached, these ten long months, for the chance to protect, offer support and to care.

Hope sputtered. She took a deep breath as she rolled off of him and stood. "I'm fine. I'm just so sorry for the awkwardness of this situation. The cow startled me, and when I took a step back I tripped and—"

"No apologies are necessary." He pushed himself up in one solid movement, unable to ignore the way her astute gaze took in his every move. "As long as you're all right, that's the main thing."

"Really, all is well. I'm as good as new," she added, picking bits of straw from her dress and her snow-white gloves.

Aaron righted the stool, determined to hide his unwelcome attraction to her. "Come here. I'll show you."

Hope fingered the hair at the nape of her creamy white neck and kept her distance, but he couldn't miss the way her gaze flitted to him. "He's been just fine. Very agreeable, actually. I'm certain I'll be able to manage just fine from here on out." She retrieved the china cups from the straw.

"Maybe," he half lied. "But just in case—" hunkering down next to the cow, he braced a hand against the bovine's side and grinned up at Hope "—first of all, let's get something straight. *He's* a *she*."

"Who?" Her brow furrowed.

"Your friend here," he answered patting the cow. "Females are the ones who bear babies, and that's why they have these." He pointed to the cow's teats. "She's a cow, not a bull."

She sank her hands on her hips and gave him an I-am-well-aware-of-that look. "So what is a bull then? I was under the impression that cows were cows."

"Hmm...not exactly." He crossed to the small window and motioned her over. Resting his hand on her shoulder, he pointed out at the big bull. "*That's* a bull. See the difference?"

She studied the animal for a moment, her cheeks growing pink as understanding dawned.

"Just clarifying," he added on a brief chuckle, enjoying her obvious discomfort as he hunkered down next to the cow again. "Anyway, this is where calves get their milk." He gently touched the cow's udder, grateful the cow was so even tempered and happy to be chewing her cud to pass the time. "How's that for an agricultural lesson?"

Hope adjusted the hem of her satin bodice. "You are a veritable wealth of information, Aaron. Thank you. I will gladly keep those things in mind," she responded, evenly— too evenly.

He would've been willing to wager his next breath that she'd just pricked him with a barb, however cloaked in politeness it may have been. And for some reason, he was proud of her for doing so.

Patting the stool for her to join him, he studied her for a long moment. "I'm curious as to what exactly is going through that head of yours right about now." She seemed skilled at schooling her expression, an art she must have learned in her upbringing. But the way she held herself... that had a way of slipping secrets to those who were attentive enough to notice. Like now.

"Nothing that would interest you, I'm sure." She clearly avoided his gaze.

With the courage of a brave little songbird facing off a stalking cat, Hope perched on the edge of the stool, her shoulders held back and her hands threaded into a tight ball.

That gave him pause. She was trying—hard. She was

trying harder than most women would when faced with the same situation.

Angling his gaze to her gloves, he tried for an indifferent tone. "Are you planning on wearing those milking?"

She threaded her fingers together as though Aaron was likely to rip her gloves right off. "I had planned on it, yes. Is there something wrong?"

Sure, there was something wrong with wearing long, fancy gloves to milk, but how would she know that?

"Well, not exactly. But I'll give you a little hint." He cupped a hand on one side of his mouth and leaned toward her.

"And what would that be?" She hesitated then leaned closer, the subtle hint of rose petals wafting to his senses.

"It'll be a whole lot easier if you use your bare hands. Like this." Grasping two of the cow's teats, he squeezed and tugged in a well-trained rhythm he'd learned through the years.

When two streams of milk shot down into the straw, she started, but the soft awe-filled gasp Hope gave next coaxed another grin from Aaron's lips.

She held out the teacups. "Here you are." The complete sincerity in her expression was the only thing keeping him from all-out chuckling at the woman—at her innocence, at her earnestness, at her determination.

Aaron settled a bridled expression on Hope. "Sorry, darlin', but those wouldn't hold enough to feed that orange tabby you saved the other day. What was his name...Theodore?"

"Yes." She peered at him. "I'm surprised you remember his name."

"I'm not sure whether to take that as a compliment or an insult." In truth, he remembered her kitten's name and a whole lot more about this woman that he'd just as soon forget.

Her gaze softened some, and that touched him way down deep. "A compliment, to be sure." When she reached up and plucked a piece of straw from his hair, his breath caught. "It seems that you have been sleeping on the job," she teased.

He swallowed hard. "Well, actually, yes. I've been sleeping up in the hayloft since you arrived—just to make sure you're all right."

Her mouth fell open for a brief moment. "There is no need for you to inconvenience yourself."

"Those containers will do the trick," he said, waylaying her protest. He nodded to the corner of the room where a couple of four-quart pails hung from hooks.

She gave a short harrumph. "Did you hear me?"

"I heard you." He'd had a feeling she'd react this way, which is why he'd not informed her sooner. "Like I said, those containers over there will work just fine."

On a semi-defeated sigh, she followed his gaze to the pails then slid her wide-eyed focus back to him. "But I thought you said a single milking would necessitate only two containers."

"I did." He felt the cow's udder, heavy and warm with milk. "But I meant those."

She eyed the pails. "I can hardly drink all of that in one day."

He clenched his jaw to keep from smiling. "That would be a sight to see…you sitting at the table, determined to down that much milk, just to be polite."

The way her eyebrows crowded in ever so slightly doused his amusement some.

"Ahh…don't worry. You won't have to drink it all yourself," he amended.

On a weighted sigh, she lifted the pails from their hooks.

"You can give the rest away to neighbors, if you like, use it for some of the other animals on the farm or churn it into butter. Cheese. Whatever suits your fancy."

Hope handed him the pails, relief evident in the way her shoulders had relaxed some.

"All right now, sit on the stool and place your hands like this on the cow's teats." He demonstrated, his skin tingling as his arm brushed hers.

When she raised her gloved hands to do the same, he cleared his throat. "Are you sure about the gloves?"

"Oh, dear. I forgot." When she rolled the long, silky things down, stripping them from her arms and hands, he suddenly wished she'd left them on. Her arms, fair and delicately beautiful, made his pulse pound a little harder.

Why was he being affected in this way? He was getting all pulse-poundy and grinny and tingly. She was nothing more to him than a…than a woman in need of help. That's all. He could honor his promise and not lose his head over her. It shouldn't be that hard. With her high-class ways, fancy dress and superior attitude, she was nowhere near his type.

But as images of Hope marching through the throng of crowding cattle—and all for the sake of a stray kitten—darted through his mind, he had a hard time holding her to those not-so-complimentary ideals.

Even Ellie would've thought long and hard about going into a corral of unpredictable beasts for a scrawny kitten. Sure, she'd have cared about the kitten's welfare, but she would've been more inclined to scream for help than to take the bull by the horns, so to speak.

He silently admitted that there was something markedly

foreign and vulnerable about Hope that made him want to protect her. He'd seen it on her face two days ago when she'd realized that Paul hadn't come to meet her at the train station and when she was informed that this spread was now hers. He saw it yet again when he'd listed off the duties of the farm for her yesterday.

He'd nearly wrapped her up in a comforting hug at that moment. The way she remained outwardly stoic was in direct conflict to the angst that flashed through her gaze.

"Aaron? Like this?" Her pleasant voice seeped into his awareness. "Is this the correct way?"

He directed his attention to her hands, trying to shake off his wayward thoughts. "Not bad, not bad. Here." He moved a little closer and grasped her hands to make the slightest adjustment.

He froze, completely unprepared for the jolt that traveled all the way up his arms to his heart. It was all he could do not to jerk away, as though he'd just been burned.

But *something* had happened, *was* happening as he held her hands in his. It was as if the seemingly impenetrable vows he'd made to Ellie four years ago had been penetrated. He fought wildly to patch the hole, reminding himself of the loyalty and love and dedication he had for Ellie, for her memory.

This was a harmless, helpful gesture. Right? Assisting Hope in this way? He'd done it for others in the past.

"Am I doing it correctly now?" Hope peered over at him, her eyes all open and honest.

Nodding, he slid his hands from hers. He swallowed past the thick lump that had lodged in his throat as Ellie's smiling image, always there in his mind's eye, seemed to fade some. Aaron braced his forearms on his thighs, realizing that no matter how innocent the action, no matter how much he could chalk this simple gesture up to helpfulness, a carefully guarded part of his heart had been awakened. And he was scared to death that nothing could be done to bed it down again.

Chapter Seven

"It is just wonderful having another sweet breath of eastern air out here in the West, Hope," Julia Cranston twittered as she scooted farther into the church pew to make room for others to get by.

Julia had beelined for Hope just as soon as the service had ended, with a certain air of grandeur that seemed more fitting for royalty. But the moment the young woman had begun talking less than ten minutes ago, Hope couldn't help but like her. She was eastern. She was familiar. And in spite of all of her fanfare, Hope could tell that she was genuine.

She was a lovely contrast to Jane, who'd cast derisive looks her way as they'd ridden with Aaron to church this morning. The ride had been silent, except when Jane would turn and whisper some bit of information to Aaron—even as she did now with some of the young women who'd crowded around her like a protective barrier at the back of the church.

Hope tried not to care what had transpired between Jane and Aaron on the way here, but she couldn't deny that her heart had swelled slightly when he'd return Jane's words with a dismissive nod or an indifferent shrug.

Jealous, Hope was not—certainly not.

After all, she'd lost her husband-to-be three days ago.

But for her entire life, she'd maintained a definite aversion to pettiness and had always taken great pains to champion the misunderstood or wronged, which is one very acute reason why she'd been so hurt when her former fiancé, Jonas Hargrave, had turned a cold shoulder her direction after her family's financial misfortune. She'd tried to convince herself that his indifference was temporary, that he really did love her. But the barest chance that his love was so shallow had undermined any sense of security she'd ever had in his commitment.

She'd called off the engagement and had subsequently born the often-gossiped-about reproach of *wounding* his poor heart. Not knowing the real reason behind the disengagement, her mother had ridiculed Hope for her pettiness, saying that Jonas was a fine man of means who could offer her so much. Hope had refused to buckle under the weight of pressure and had remained true to her decision. True to herself.

"Believe me, it was all I could do not to run straight back to the comforts of Boston in those first few months after Father relocated us to Boulder." Julia patted Hope's arm as though burping a young babe, then peered at her with an expression akin to sympathy. "If ever you need a shoulder to cry on, I shall be here for you."

Hope gave Julia an appreciative smile but remained resolute in her goal to be strong. Running back to Boston was not a possibility for her now—or ever. "Thank you, Julia. Your kindness means so much."

"So, you and Julia have met?" Katie smiled, stepping up and looping an arm through Hope's.

Hope nodded, noticing the way Aaron passed furtive

glances at her from across the room where he was talking with Zach. Ever since he'd walked in on her in the barn yesterday morning, attempting to milk the cow, she'd been particularly aware of his attention. She'd been beyond embarrassed when she'd tripped and had fallen back on him. Her arms and legs had rebelliously refused to move—even an inch.

But when he'd grasped her hands to show her how to milk correctly, she would've been all but dead not to notice the odd way he'd reacted. His breathing had grown short and shallow. His hands, large, work worn and yet so very gentle, had trembled. The pupils of his eyes had grown deeper, wider and more intense as he'd stared at her for a long moment.

Just looking at him then had enticed a distinct quiver at the base of her stomach. She'd never felt that before.

She pulled herself out of the unsettling memory and turned to Katie. "Yes. Julia was good enough to introduce herself to me after the service."

With a self-satisfied smile tipping her lips, Julia slid her gaze from Hope's head to her toes as though she was making some kind of historic, newsworthy discovery. "I knew she had to come from the East, Katie. From the moment I saw her this morning, I was convinced."

"It seems as though we're acquainted with some of the same people back home." Hope adjusted her gloves.

"Really?" Katie slid her wide-eyed gaze from Julia to Hope. "As big as Boston must be, that's remarkable."

"As I've already stated, this is a breath of fresh air. Like having a small bit of home right here with me." Julia inhaled and set her gaze Heavenward, only furthering Hope's embarrassment.

But Hope could hardly fault the woman. Boston was a

far cry from Boulder in so many ways. Even with the amenities Paul had added to his farm—running water inside, a new stove, an indoor privy and bathing room—it wasn't what Hope was accustomed to.

Yet it was warm, comfortable. It was a house she could call home.

"Do tell, how did you meet Paul? God rest his soul." Julia set a hand to her heart.

Out of the corner of her eye, Hope could see Aaron approaching in that steady, western way of his that made her abundantly aware of her eastern blood. Did he still think she was unable to manage the farm after the whole milking fiasco?

Why wouldn't he? She'd given him no reason not to conclude otherwise. He'd essentially done most all of the chores yesterday because she'd been so inept.

So she'd been unaware that her white gloves were better left inside or that a bull was not considered a *cow* or that a chicken could lay more than one egg. Even her attire seemed to fluster him. When she'd embarked on this journey, she hadn't imagined needing actual work dresses. When she'd worked at the bakery back home, she'd worn her everyday finery covered by a lovely little lace apron. Her job had been to take orders and make change.

"Hope, dear? How did you meet?" Julia prodded.

She turned and peered at Julia, guessing that her new friend would likely think the reality gauche. "A mail-order bride ad."

She took Julia's measure but didn't really care what she found there. There'd be no freedom in pretending she was someone or something other than herself.

"A mail-order bride. Oh, the *spice* of it all," Julia breathed in a dramatic flourish. She primped the puffed sleeves of Hope's violet brocade waistcoat. "How daring of you. How brave. And how *very* adventurous."

"Adventure born of necessity," Hope corrected as she set a hand on Julia's arm. She didn't have to emit every single detail, but she would not allow Julia to believe anything other than the truth.

She relayed a shortened version of the misfortune that fell upon her family a year ago and then the hard times following, along with the way she'd let Jonas off the marriage hook.

"That is positively the saddest story I've ever heard. How your fiancé can sleep at night knowing how he must've hurt you, I will never know." Julia closed her eyes and tilted her face Heavenward, as though interceding for the man's shadowy soul.

Hope shared a smile with Katie, guessing that Julia probably hadn't even gotten as far as *Dear Lord*. She was just dramatic. Her unabridged self was comforting and was a wonderful taste of home.

"I consider myself fortunate, really," Hope amended, just in case Julia tended toward tears. "To marry out of obligation is no marriage at all. Besides, through it all, I met Paul."

Julia's eyes grew wide, disbelieving. "But he—"

"He opened up a whole new world for me," Hope finished for her, struggling to grasp the good even when it seemed her life had taken a jolting turn for the worse. When she noticed Aaron standing beside her, his intense, questioning gaze connected to hers, she added, "For that I am ever so grateful."

"That certainly sounds like the right way to look at things." Katie gave Hope's arm a tender squeeze and then peered around Hope at where Aaron stood. "Right, Aaron?"

He nodded, his mouth pulled tight.

"How will you do it—out there on your own?" Julia clasped her white-gloved hands in a prayerful pose. "I've heard from a very reliable source that you plan on running the farm by yourself—not that I was fishing for information, mind you."

Hope grinned at how skillfully Julia had danced around hearsay. "I'll do the best that I can. I learn quickly and am not at all opposed to doing what I must in order to keep the farm running."

"It is a bit of fortune that Aaron Drake will be there to help you with everything, is it not?" Julia nodded to Aaron with an aristocratic air that brought a smile to Hope's face. "He's certainly one you can depend upon."

"I'll second that," Katie added.

"Just doing what any decent man would do." Aaron groaned as he jammed his Stetson on his head. "Now, can we change the subject?"

"You go far beyond a decent man's actions." Katie shot Aaron a scolding look, reached around Hope and gently nudged him. "Joseph has so much respect for you, Aaron. He's often said that he'd have been hard-pressed to make things work in the shop if not for you."

"Did I hear my name mentioned?" Joseph asked, feeling his way around the pews.

Katie reached out and pulled him into their circle. "We were just talking about how dependable Aaron is. And how much help he'll be for Hope."

"Dependable, among many other attributes." Joseph grinned. "Would you like me to list them off for you, Hope?"

"Joseph." Aaron's voice was low and laden with caution.

"He'd risk life and limb if it meant saving those he

loves." In the most casual and comfortable way, Joseph draped an arm around his wife's waist. "By the way, did you all hear that Sam is coming back?"

"Really? That's great." Aaron crossed his arms at his chest, looking immensely glad to have dodged the attention.

"Sam was one of Joseph's best friends growing up." Katie directed her words to Hope. "Beside his brothers, of course."

"He'll be a welcome sight, that's for sure," Joseph said. "I'll never forget how he helped me see things more clearly." When Joseph placed the most tender, cherishing kiss on Katie's head, Hope had to look away.

It was not because she was embarrassed by the show of love—or offended—but because the sweet display, so pure and wholesome, spurred the longing in her heart for the same.

Hope had met all three of Aaron's brothers and was powerless to unearth one unkind thing to say about them. Katie and Callie were fortunate to be loved by such honorable men. And Hope had no doubt that Zach would find his own beloved someday. He was just too personable and kindhearted to go through life unmarried.

But Aaron…she had a hard time imagining him with a bride. If his sometimes glowering nature was a consistent mark of this man, she didn't know a woman who'd welcome that—except for Jane, maybe.

But remembering the sweet way Aaron had caught her just before falling into the straw, or the patient way he'd instructed her in the art of milking, brought her unkind judgment up short—painfully so. Perhaps he really was as good-natured as his brothers. Perhaps he'd been through his own set of circumstances that had colored his view of life. If so, then Hope vowed right then and there to pray for him, to pray that he'd find God's goodness. In several of the letters Paul had sent to her, he'd said the same. She'd been so touched by Paul's faith in God, his faith in her.

"From what I understand, Sam's going to be setting up a law office somewhere in the area." Joseph threaded his fingers through his chestnut waves.

"Actually," Julia began, clearing her throat, "he'll be setting up his practice right here." Her voice trembled ever so slightly, her fair complexion suddenly turning a faint shade of pink. "In Boulder."

When Hope exchanged glances with her new friend, she had the distinct suspicion that Julia was even more aware of Sam's plans than she was letting on.

"Aaron…" Jane's bleating voice called from the vestibule. She straightened her black satin bow in her hair, a frivolous extra the woman had apparently never worn before, given the numerous comments Hope had overheard. Jane strode this way, dabbing at her eyes as though on the verge of tears. "You wouldn't mind taking me home now, would you?" All white-knuckled, she clutched the back of a pew, as though to remain upright. "With all of the activity today, I'm not feeling myself."

"Sure." He turned and looked at Hope in that sideways, roguish way of his that was endearing, really. "Are you ready, Hope?"

Katie grasped Hope's hand. "Why don't you come home with us for dinner, Hope?"

"Oh, yes," Jane agreed almost before Katie had finished her sentence. She fluffed the straggle of curls hanging down her neck—another small change that had surprised Hope since the woman usually only fastened an unkempt knot at the back of her head. "Then you don't have to worry about little ole me. Aaron can see me home just fine." Jane's face grew brighter as she hugged her arms to her waist, the snug black garment she wore bulging at the seams. "Can't you, Aaron?"

"Absolutely." Every bit a gentleman, he nodded Jane's way.

Hope tallied several marks in the kindness column for Aaron.

"You can join us after you get Jane home, Aaron. All right?" A broad smile brightened Katie's face.

Jane's posture suddenly snapped straight, as though someone had shot a rod up her spine. "But I—"

"You do look peaked, Jane." Concern infused Julia's words, but the measured, perceptive gaze she slid to Hope communicated something completely on the contrary.

"It's a good thing you'll be able to rest for the remainder of the day." Katie rubbed her hands down Jane's arms. "You don't want to overdo yourself. Right, Ben?" she called, motioning Ben over from where he'd be conversing with the minister.

"What?" Ben approached with Libby in his arms.

"I was remarking about how we don't want Jane to tax herself with too much activity," Katie reiterated.

"My sentiments, exactly." Ben shifted Libby, who smiled and waved at Hope, to his other arm as he pulled Callie to his side. "After everything you've been through, you're far better off giving yourself ample time to rest."

Jane tangled a thick finger in her lean cluster of curls. "But I—"

"I'll make sure Aaron and Hope bring a meal home for you this evening." Katie wrapped her arms around Jane. "And I'll be over to check in on you first thing tomorrow."

Stiff with obvious anger, Jane hugged Katie back with

one arm, but the sheer look of hatred she shot straight through Hope could've sent a child hiding behind her mother's skirts.

"Just look at all of these chickens. They're quite the lively bunch this morning." Hope knelt and held out a handful of grain to one of the dozen chickens strutting about in front of her. "They're simply delightful, aren't they?"

"They're just stupid chickens," Jane grumbled as she shifted Paul's books to her other arm. Even though Hope had informed Jane that she could take anything of Paul's that she wished to keep, Jane had stalked up into the yard this morning, ready for a fight.

The willing consent and word of sympathy Hope had offered had seemed to ruffle Jane all the more.

"But look at how pleased they are with their grain. They certainly are whimsical birds." She grinned, watching them peck at the ground with such meticulous care.

Ever since Aaron had shown her how to feed them a week ago, she'd been trying to come up with names for each one and had finally decided that as colorful and as full of personality as they each were they deserved the names of famous artists.

Jane grabbed a handful of feed from Hope's bucket and threw it to the ground, hitting one of the birds square in the face. "Get back, you ugly bird." With a thrust of her foot, she shoved the chestnut brown colored hen nestling close to her black dress, aside, making the bird squawk then flutter away a few feet. "When you have what they want—*feed*—then of course they're going to act all eager when it's time to eat."

Hope would've liked to have given Jane a kick for being so thoughtless. Instead, she decided to ambush Jane's irritation with an endearing tidbit about one of the birds. "Look, that's the one who serenades me early every morning." She pointed to the rooster. "If you don't mind me saying so, you have a lovely voice, Michelangelo. The lady birds love to hear you sing, I'm sure."

"Oh, for goodness' sake. That is what roosters do. They crow at the crack of dawn. I can hear that ugly bird from all the way over at my place." In a very unceremonious way, Jane grabbed the bucket from Hope and dumped the rest of the grain on the ground. "No wonder you take so long to do things. You dally about talking to brainless chickens."

Hope's cheeks heated with instant anger as Jane threw the bucket aside, nearly hitting the rooster in the process. "Please, be careful," she cautioned. "You could hurt them."

Pursing her lips, Jane tugged at the thin strand of curls hanging at her neck. "It'd take a cannon blast to kill off these annoying creatures. All they're good for is eggs and a good hot chicken bake."

With a disbelieving scowl, Hope wondered how Paul could've seemed so kind and gentle in his letters when his sister was so spiteful. Swallowing any word of outrage that might surface, she headed toward the henhouse. "I'm going to gather the eggs."

A few of the chickens followed her into the small, narrow building as though looking to her for protection. "It's all right. She never stays long," she soothed as she reached into one of the nests and carefully lifted two large brown eggs. "Good job, Van Gogh," she praised, as the hen picked a path beside her. "Two eggs today. What a fine chicken you are."

She worked her way down the line of eight nests, gingerly plucking through the straw and dusting each egg off before placing it in the basket. She was almost done when she heard Jane talking outside.

"Yes, I just stopped by to see if she'd mind if I borrowed these books—since they help remind me of Paul." Jane's animated tone of voice left no question as to who had arrived.

"I'm sure that helps," Aaron answered. "To have bits and pieces from Paul's life."

Hope continued to the last nest, biting her lip as she took her time searching through the straw for the warm brown eggs.

"Anyway, it seemed that she was running ragged trying to manage everything, like she *always* is, so I thought I'd give her a hand feeding the chickens." Jane's emphatic statement pricked Hope's pride.

She wasn't *always* running ragged, was she?

Aaron cleared his throat. "That was neighborly of you."

"I try when I can." Jane gave a weighty sigh, pausing for a long enough moment that Hope braced herself for what was coming next. "Of course, you know that I want to see her make it here, but honestly, Aaron, I wonder. Did you know that she doesn't even own a work dress?"

"I didn't. But I'm sure that if that's the case, she's already well aware," Aaron responded, his tone curt.

Hope swallowed hard, trying to subdue her anger so that she wouldn't crush the next egg she retrieved. She didn't own the kind of work dress she really needed out here. She'd been horribly naive, horribly unprepared for the unexpected turn her life had taken.

"How can a woman do what she's supposed to on a farm, dressed like she's going to some fancy ball? It's just ridiculous, if you ask me."

Hope didn't have to see Jane to know that the woman had pursed her thin lips to nonexistence.

"I'm sure that she never thought she'd have to work like this," Aaron defended.

Exactly, Aaron.

"Exactly." Jane's terse response whipped across Hope's composure. "Which is why I question whether or not she has the fortitude needed to make it here. On Paul's farm. She could get hurt, and of course, *that* is my main concern."

Hope couldn't know Jane's heart, but the woman had certainly never said or done one thing to show her concern.

"Don't worry. I'm keeping a close eye on things."

The impatience in Aaron's voice was the smallest bit gratifying, but the idea that he had to *keep a close eye on things,* as though she was some child, was more like a slap on the wrist. She struggled to be appreciative as she quietly picked several handfuls of straw from a loose bail and added them to each nest.

"You're a saint. I can hardly believe how much time you've sacrificed away from your job as a carpenter, to help her."

Hope had marveled at the same. She'd also been plagued with guilt over the situation, too.

"I worry about you exhausting yourself," Jane measured out, her voice low and layered with fluffed-up concern. Hope could almost see her now...fingering that lean clutch of curls she'd suddenly begun wearing. "In fact, with all you're doing for that woman, I'm going to have to bring by more of my home-baked goods to help keep your energy up."

Resisting the urge to roll her eyes at Jane's syrup-laced comment, Hope cradled her basketful of eggs. "Good job, ladies," she whispered to the two hens that'd refused to leave her side.

"That's not necessary. I'm fine. Actually, I'm more en-ergized the past ten days than I have been for a long time," Aaron said, his convincing tone making Hope's heart swell with pride. "It must be all of the fresh air."

"And then there's the—"

"Listen, Jane, I need to get busy with chores, but I want you to know that your concerns are valid enough. I've even had some similar thoughts. But we can't go jumping to conclusions about Hope. She's new to all of this. She may surprise us all and really take to things."

"Do you really think she will? Honestly, Aaron?" Jane's tone pricked Hope like rusty barbs.

He gave a big sigh, and she could almost imagine him jamming his fists at his waist the way he did when he was frustrated. "As far as I'm concerned, the jury's still out."

As far as Hope was concerned, she'd do more than just take to things; she'd excel at farming or die trying.

Chapter Eight

"No, no. Naughty goat," Hope scolded sweetly.

Aaron watched in amazement from where he tied his mare to a post as Hope scurried behind the goat, trying in vain to snag her undergarment from the accused.

"Please, you must let go of my skirts," she pleaded.

Just then a second goat snapped another one of her pristine white undergarments from the clothesline and began munching away. Content as she could be, the goat stared up at the line as if to decide what she might have as her next serving.

As Hope hiked up her dress and ran across the yard after the perpetrator, Aaron couldn't even begin to stop a smile from shattering his emotionless face.

She was a willful one, Hope. At first glance, a person could easily think she wouldn't be caught dead being so close to the farm animals, let alone running after a goat. He'd thought the same thing—at one time. But riding into the yard this morning, he was proven wrong—again.

Aaron ate up the distance with his long strides. If he didn't come to her aid, she'd be chasing after the stubborn creatures all day. But when Hope hunkered down, eye-to-eye with the animal, and began speaking in kindly rational tones as one might with a child, he came to an abrupt halt and laughed.

Laughed for the first time in a very, very long time.

She shot her focus over to him as he covered his mouth in a feeble attempt to hide his mirth. Wide-eyed, she gave her head a shake and stared at him as though he'd just lost his senses.

"You're laughing?" Her own smile begged at her full lips. "At a time like this, you're laughing?"

He nodded, feeling his laughter coming from way down deep, as though escaping from some prison. "I'm sorry," he sputtered as he approached her. "It's just too funny."

Out of the corner of his eye, he noticed an orange kitten—the same one Hope had saved the day she'd arrived in Boulder—bounding, head over heels, this way. The little guy looked significantly more filled out, as though Hope had been letting him glean the richest creamiest milk.

"Don't come too close, sweetie," she said, stopping Aaron dead in his tracks.

He stared at her, dumbfounded.

"Not you, Aaron. The kitten." She gave a determined harrumph and then turned to the goat and grabbed a corner of her garment. "Now, if you'll please give me back my camisole, I will escort you over to your pen and feed you a proper meal."

When the animal continued chewing, perfectly content with his fibrous serving, she sighed. She wrapped the corner of the garment around her fingers once, then glanced at where the kitten had gotten waylaid by a crisp brown leaf. Turning her attention to the goat again, she continued. "I do believe that you will be far more satisfied with your hay and grain than this old thing, anyway. So, if you will be so kind as to—"

When the clothesline snapped, she whipped around to

see that the other culprit had removed another one of her whispery white undergarments. Standing, Hope stalked toward that goat. But the guilty party managed to stay one hoof ahead of her.

Aaron was sure she'd give up, but then she lunged forward. She caught the black and white goat around the neck, fell to her knees in the dirt and held on for dear life.

"All right, enough of this play," she scolded in the most patient, kindly way Aaron had ever heard. "Be a good goat, and give me back my garment. Now," she added, with a smidge less tolerance.

Amazed by her sheer grit, Aaron wrestled the camisole from the nearest goat and approached the one Hope had nearly hog-tied. "Here, let me try."

"No. I will get it." She shot him a stay-right-where-you-are look.

He backed off and watched her pry her clothing from the goat's mouth, seemingly unfazed by the garment's slobbered and slimy condition.

"Finally." Collapsing to the dusty earth, she closed her eyes.

"They're stubborn," he muttered as her eyelashes fluttered open. "But not as stubborn as a certain young lady I know."

"I retrieved my garments, did I not?" She levered herself up to sitting, smiling triumphantly.

"Yes, you did. And you look the part of a goat wrangler, too." A fair amount of her silky hair had escaped from where she'd fastened it at the back of her head. The green-and-white striped dress she wore was clouded with dust and grass stains. And her lily-white complexion, dotted with smudges of dirt, had flushed to a hearty rose color, making her appear like some waif—and almost irresistible.

When Aaron held his hand out to help her up, she arched

her eyebrows over her eyes. "You're a bit late on your show of chivalry, Mr. Drake."

"I—I'm sorry for laughing," he muttered, dropping his gaze to the delicate camisole in his other hand. *Bad idea.* He shot his attention to where the two goats were grazing on wiry sprigs of grass. "Really, I am."

Hope smiled then—in the most beautiful, natural way that seemed void of her strict adherence to propriety. And for some reason, he couldn't keep from staring. She'd just chased after then wrestled a goat to the ground and yet she still smiled.

When he pulled her up to his side, he tried to ignore the way his fingers tingled at her touch.

"You fared pretty well, I'd say." He winked at her, before he even realized what he'd done. "One thing you've got to learn about goats, though, is that they'll eat most anything."

"So I see." She brushed her hands down her sleeves then headed toward the escapees. "Come along, Patience. Penelope. You two need to return to your pen."

Aaron caught up to her. "You named them?"

She peered at him as though he was daft then leaned over and fluffed and fluttered her hands to get the goats moving. "Of course, I did. They seem quite happy with their names, as you can see." She fluffed her hands again. "That's the way. Keep going," she encouraged, amazingly enough, herding the animals toward the pen.

"I named the cows as well. And honestly, Aaron—" she threw his direction "—they're really something if you take the time to get to know them."

"I'll have to keep that in mind." He grinned, picturing Hope calling the cattle by name. "Speaking of the cattle—" he glanced over at where they lingered along the fence line, watching intently "—I remember Paul saying that some of his girls—I mean female cows—were going to be calving soon, and I'm guessing that from the way some of their bellies have been looking so plump—"

"Shh. They'll hear you."

"I doubt they'll mind," he dismissed, grinning. "But just to please you, I'll never refer to them as plump again."

"Good, because you never," she grunted, giving the black and white goat a gentle push, "*ever* discuss a lady's age or weight."

"Never again." He held up his hand.

"That reminds me, did you know that that big bull, Caesar, doesn't like being all by himself?" She looked at him only for a moment then shifted her attention to the goats again. "He'd much rather be with the rest of the cows."

Aaron chuckled. "I'm *sure* he would."

"I was thinking that I could probably take over feeding them now," she commented, as though mentioning that she'd just tried out a new recipe. "This way, Penelope. Into the gate." She gave the white goat a gentle pat on the rump.

Amazed and worried by her adventurous spirit, he sighed, positioning himself on the other side of her charges in case they dodged the gate. "As willing as you are, I just can't have you feeding them by yourself. I'd never forgive myself if something happened to you." Aaron tried to understand how he'd grown so fond of this woman—especially when he had his vows to Ellie.

Was he being disloyal to Ellie? Was his honor so weak as to stumble over the first pretty face he clapped eyes on?

Those questions had swirled through his mind with relentless force. He longed to find peace with Ellie and the baby's death, with himself and with God.

He'd thought that he was getting close and then he'd made that promise to Paul. The result of his words had only seemed to rip at his still gaping wound. But maybe that's exactly what he needed in order to heal.

"I'll let you help me, but I don't want you going in there by yourself," he finally said. "Promise me?"

She gave a conciliatory nod.

"Thank you." He sighed with relief as she continued that cute hand-fluffing of hers. When the goats trotted inside the pen, Aaron could barely keep his mouth from gaping open. "Good job there, goat lady."

"I'm determined to do this."

"So, I see." Leaning against the fence, he hooked one foot over the other as Hope secured the latch. "How'd they get out, anyway?"

"I have no idea." She set her hands at her hips and stared at the thick metal closure. "The gate was closed last night after I fed them."

"Are you sure?"

"Absolutely." She nodded emphatically. "Early this morning, I'd hung my wash on the clothesline and didn't notice anything wrong, but when I came out to feed the goats a little bit ago, they were eating my garments."

Aaron wanted to believe that Hope had been attentive in the animals' care, but he had to admit that with the extreme change of lifestyle for her, he had his doubts.

Morning's light peeked through the dirt-clouded windowpanes as Aaron tugged on his boots and downed another gulp of coffee. He'd risen before the sun to get home and do his chores before he returned to do Hope's chores.

Ever since Ellie and his baby had passed away, he'd done everything he could to steer clear of his home, and the cluttered, unkempt condition stretched before him like a bitter, old drunk. Sometimes he wondered if his home's befuddled state was a reflection of his life—piled with so much grief and pain that he didn't have to look beneath the mess and face the bittersweet memories he and Ellie had made under this roof.

Until recently he'd been focused on his loss—not necessarily wallowing in it but coming to grips with the sudden shock and then trying to keep moving forward despite the gaping hole left in his heart.

That is, he did until Hope landed in his life.

Hope.

She'd taken him by complete surprise. And try as he might, he'd been hard-pressed to find reasons not to like the woman—especially after overhearing her interchange with Julia and Katie at church last week. Aaron's heart had been pierced, first by the hardship she'd recounted about her family's misfortune and her broken engagement and then by her determination to focus on the bright side of things.

There was more to this woman than what he'd been willing to notice. On outward appearances alone, Hope was beautiful…stunning, really. Paul would've been pleased. Although Aaron had judged her as a snippety easterner, he realized now that he'd been too quick to shape an opinion.

Standing, he swallowed the last bit of coffee in his cup, recalling that he'd never heard one peep of distress uttered by Hope, although she certainly had every reason to buckle under her circumstance. Instead, she'd been firm, steady and unyielding in her determination to rise to her new tasks.

Raking a hand through his hair, he located the only uncluttered corner on the counter to set his mug when a knock sounded at his door. He scuffed across the room to the door, glancing at the mantel clock to see that it was almost six-thirty.

Opening the door, he found himself peering down at Hope. When she gave him one of her tentative smiles, the kind that seemed to seep straight into his heart like the sun warming the ground after a harsh winter, his dull mood brightened a little.

"Good morning, Aaron." Smoothing wayward wisps of dark hair from her face, she stared up at him.

"Good morning to you." He dipped his head her way.

"I'm terribly sorry to bother you so early." She tugged at her fitted bodice, the lavender color of her dress reminding him of the larkspur dotting the meadows and mountainsides this time of year.

"It's no bother. I was just getting ready to finish my morning chores and head back to your place."

"How—how are you doing?"

"I'm just fine. And you?" he asked, amused by her uncharacteristically shy, odd behavior.

She was something…Hope. She was regal, stubborn, naive and outright charming all in one. Apart from the dirt smudged on the very tip of her cute little nose, she looked ready to attend some elegant affair.

He breathed in the invigorating spring air, trying to clear his head. "So what brings you by so early?" When she hesitated, threading her fingers together, alarm pulsed through his veins. "Is something wrong?"

Opening the door wider, he gestured her in before he thought better of it. His house was a mess with dishes, mementos, clothes—even the handmade cradle where Jeremiah's body had rested in until Aaron had built him a coffin.

The vivid, heartbreaking memories of that day haunted

him day and night, clouding over any solid bit of peace he'd managed to find. Joseph had been there with support and care. In fact, even though he'd just found out that his blindness was permanent, he'd helped Aaron build the coffin. It'd been a painstaking process not because of some elaborate design but because it'd been for Aaron's son—his only child…stillborn.

"I'm sorry if I'm interrupting something." Her tender voice gently tugged him from his silent solitary grief.

"No, don't worry. What seems to be the problem?"

The minutest lines of distress etched in her face. "Well, I'm sure that everything is fine, but just in case, I wanted to check with you."

"What is it?" Pulling a chair out from the table, he dusted it off for her to sit.

He doubted the chair had been used since Ellie had last sat there. It'd been her spot. On several occasions, Katie had offered to come over and clean his house for him, but he'd barricaded his home, just like his heart.

"It's one of the cows—Isabel," she measured out, plastering her hands to her lap. "She seems to be overly restless. She's groaning and mooing and doesn't seem to want to be with the other cows this morning."

"Are you sure?" He pulled out his chair and sat down to her right. He had to resist the sudden urge to reach out and remove the dirt smudge from her nose.

"They're always so kind to each other, licking each other and standing together the way they do but not today. Not with this one, at any rate." If Hope noticed his home's state of disarray as her attentive gaze flitted around for a second or two, she did a remarkable job hiding her shock. "Do you suppose she's sick?"

"I'm not sure, but as soon as I get my last chore done we'll head over there and I'll check her out."

"What do you suppose is wrong with her?" Her shoulders slumped slightly.

"She could be one of the soon-to-be mamas I was checking on last night." He pulled a hand over his jaw. "Was she standing?"

She nodded, her brow furrowed in concern.

"Grazing?"

"No."

Seeing her distress and knowing how hard she worked to keep her composure, he gave her arm a comforting, albeit brief, squeeze, setting his pulse to thumping a little faster. "It's all right, Hope. Don't worry. I'll take care of things."

She pulled in a deep breath, resting her hand where his had just been. "I tried to calm her when I gave the cows grain this morning, but it didn't seem to help. And she didn't even seem to want to eat."

His heart screeched to a halt. "You *fed* them?"

When she gave no response but instead fixed her gaze on the cluttered table, Aaron set his hand beneath her chin and nudged her unwilling gaze to his. "Hope, listen to me. I've been feeding the cattle every morning and night. I told you I'd do that."

"I know you did." She nibbled her lower lip for a fleeting second. "But I have to learn how to do this myself, Aaron. I can't count on you forever."

That struck him dead in the heart. And for some reason he was overcome by an undeniable longing for her to *count on him,* to trust him. In spite of her desire for independence, he wanted her to need him.

"In fact, it is completely unnecessary that you sleep in the barn anymore. I'm fine by myself."

"I don't know."

"Truly, I am," she said.

He pushed up from the table and scuffed over to where Ellie's picture sat, crowded among other things that had been hers, on the fireplace mantel. Folding his arms at his chest he told himself that the admission—that he wanted Hope to need him—was outright wrong. Wasn't it? Every bit as wrong as cutting down the biggest oldest tree in the forest, right?

He'd stretched the vows he'd made to Ellie across his heart like some thick, solid board, barring those who would think to knock and maybe even barring any rogue emotions he might have, from escaping. He'd been certain there'd never be room in his heart for another woman and had thought that Ellie's sweet memory would always stake out the forefront of his mind and heart—forever. Until this past week.

Picking up the small, framed image, he stared at Ellie—nineteen years old, beautiful in her simple ivory wedding gown, young and full of vigor and standing at the beginning of a new life. He was desperate to infuse her image into his mind because she was fading, just like the sepia-toned picture caught behind the tarnished silver frame's glass.

When Hope's chair scraped away from the table, he yanked himself from his thoughts. He scrambled to recall what they'd just been talking about as he set the frame down.

"You stayed clear of the cattle, didn't you?" he choked out, remembering the way the cattle had crowded around her that very first day. "I don't want you getting hurt." His gut knotted at the horrible thought. "Did you stay away?"

"For the most part." She hiked her chin up a notch and pulled her shoulders back in that telling way of hers that promised a fancy-laced boot-to-cowboy boot confrontation, if warranted. "But not entirely. I couldn't stand to hear Isabel sounding so upset, so I went in the corral to comfort her."

He set his back teeth and crossed his arms at his chest, struggling to wrangle in his frustration and fear. She didn't deserve to be treated like a child—she was too much a woman for that. But, compassion or not, he couldn't have her acting without taking into account the dangers she faced.

"Hope."

"Aaron," she taunted in the same exasperated tone. "I fed the cows in the exact way you feed them every morning, and they were just fine. In fact, I believe that all of the animals are getting very well acquainted with me."

Speechless, he shook his head.

She edged closer, enough that he caught that sweet scent of roses that seemed to be Hope. "Do you think Isabel will be all right?"

"It's pretty safe to guess that she's laboring, which means you'll have your very first calf of the season soon." When her eyes grew wide with surprise, he added, "You'll really enjoy that. They're as cute as can be the way they frolic around the pasture."

On a gasp, she grabbed his arm. "We should get Ben. He should be there for the birth."

Aaron covered her hand. He didn't move an inch, mostly because of what her touch was doing to him. The simple connection beckoned some hidden part of him, a deep desire to protect, care for and know a woman. He'd avoided her as much as he could over the past days but couldn't seem to get her out of his mind or his heart.

And by the way her touch sent quivering sensations coursing headlong through his veins, he was pretty sure he'd have a hard time getting that out of his mind, too.

He jammed his hands into his pockets, battling to keep his wits about him. "The cow seemed to be fine last night, but if we run into trouble we can get Ben or go for Zach—he's got lots of experience, being foreman at the Harris ranch," he assured, leaning against the mantle again. "Most of the time, though, these things work out just fine."

Most of the time…

As uncertain and sometimes disastrous as the process could be, Aaron didn't want to scare Hope.

He ran a hand over his freshly shaved jawline. "Unless the calf is breech, we let nature take its course. But just to be on the safe side, I'll stick around at your place this morning to make sure everything goes well. All right?"

"What about Joseph?" she asked. "Will he need you?"

"He knows that if I'm not there that something important came up." His gaze drifted to the picture of Ellie again. When Hope's gaze followed his, he could almost hear her unspoken question. "That's Ellie. She was my wife of four years." He swallowed hard as he forced the next two words out. "She died."

Her mouth opened in silent shock. Understanding dawned in her eyes. "I'm so sorry, Aaron," she whispered. "Did she pass away recently?"

He peered at the picture again. "Last summer. She gave birth to our baby boy, Jeremiah, who was stillborn, and then died a day later." When he felt Hope's hand rest on his arm, he turned and looked at her, wondering if sympathy always felt like this…heart-wrenching and gut-clenching.

Soothing.

He'd tried to be strong. He had deflected sympathy and pity from others because he just didn't want to feel. But maybe he had to feel in order to find healing. "I buried them within two days of each other."

"Oh, Aaron. I'm so very sorry. I had no idea." Her words and her voice were like a comforting embrace. She drew her slender hands to her mouth in a prayerful pose. "Paul had asked me to pray for a friend of his who'd lost…" She peered up at him, her eyes glistening with unshed tears. "I want you to know that I did pray for you even as new as I am to the faith."

He dragged in a long, steadying breath, struggling to hold back the depth of emotion. For some reason, some tangible, weighty reason, just knowing that Hope had prayed for him, a nameless stranger two thousand miles away, settled into the deepest, darkest part of his heart like a healing balm.

"I had no idea it was you, Aaron," she whispered. She ran a single fingertip over the tarnished silver frame. "May I look?"

He held out the frame and watched as she cradled it, with gentleness, caution and great care.

"You know, over the months most folks have seemed to avoid talking about Ellie."

Her eyelashes fluttered down over her eyes for a brief second. "That must hurt terribly. To feel like they've forgotten."

Aaron peered around the room, a flood of memories meeting his gaze in every single place he looked. "I suppose they think that if they talk about her it will make me remember." He pulled a hand down over his face. "As if I've ever forgotten."

"Of course, you haven't forgotten." She inched her concentrated gaze over Ellie's picture.

"That was the day of our wedding." That had been the best day of his life. Crossing to a small table beside Ellie's rocker, he retrieved another picture. "See, this is us after the wedding."

Hope held both frames and was so attentive while she took in every detail. "She's lovely, Aaron. Beautiful." Peering up at him, she smiled in a way that made him feel like maybe she understood his joy and pain. A little. "You both looked so happy."

He swallowed hard and pulled his mouth tight. "We were. Very happy."

When she lightly brushed her fingers over his arm, he felt some much-needed solace. "I can't imagine how hard it must've been losing her—and your only child, too." She gently held the frames to her chest in a cherishing kind of way that made his eyes sting with unshed tears.

He'd done the same countless times, lying in bed at night or sitting alone by a warm fire on a winter's evening, hoping that by holding Ellie's image close he would somehow find comfort. But a picture couldn't give an embrace in return. A picture couldn't talk. A picture couldn't heal his pain. So usually his loneliness only worsened.

He'd decided it was easier not to feel.

Jamming his hands into his pockets, he dragged in a breath. "Losing them was the hardest thing I've ever had to face."

But when he looked at Hope and saw the way compassion had stolen over her fair and delicate features, the way soft vulnerability had masked that stoic composure of hers, he had to wonder if he would face an equally difficult task if he actually allowed himself to feel again.

Chapter Nine

Hope's heart nearly twisted in two seeing the grief that stole over Aaron's features—especially when he'd shared his cherished pictures of Ellie. She'd had no idea he'd endured so much suffering. Knowing that now answered many questions as to his sometimes abrupt and confusing behavior—or his emotionless offer of marriage.

He was brokenhearted. He was sick at heart for having lost the love of his life—and newborn baby, too.

Although Hope's faith was perilously new, she silently vowed, right then and there, to pray for Aaron every day. She had a feeling that Aaron found it difficult to pray for himself. She didn't necessarily know what God would do with all of her prayers, but Paul had once written that if she took the time to talk with God, He'd listen. He wanted to be close to her, to help and to love her through her perils and triumphs.

Aaron sighed and headed to the door. "I'm going out to finish up the last of my chores and hitch up the wagon. Do you mind waiting in here since it'll be a few minutes?" He passed a weary gaze around his home as he clutched the door handle.

She returned Ellie's photograph to the mantel. "That will be fine."

He opened the door and paused at the threshold. "There's a little coffee left if you'd like to warm it up for yourself."

"Thank you," she managed as he walked out and closed the door.

Hope swung her tear-stung gaze around Aaron's house, seeing the clutter and the way things appeared as though they hadn't been moved for months. Likely, they hadn't. Maybe Aaron didn't want to deal with things or wasn't adept at cleaning. Or maybe he would rather avoid this place, altogether—that certainly would explain why he seemed unfazed by the discomfort of sleeping in the barn. Whatever the reason, she wanted to help.

Surely, in the amount of time he was gone she could tidy the place a little. She could do the dishes, at least. After all, he'd worked so hard to help her over the past ten days.

Rolling up the sleeves of her taffeta dress, she found an apron and a kettle nearly full of water, apparently left over from breakfast, on the small stove. While it was heating, she swept the place then cleared the counter to lay dishes to dry. With every dish she scrubbed, she sent up a prayer that Aaron would find peace and comfort and hope for the future.

A satisfied smile spread over her face, feeling the way she did at this moment, so useful and so needed. She was fairly certain that her life, until this very instant, had been rather empty. Yes, this was the least she could do for him. It'd put her prayers into action, and as far as Hope was concerned, that had to be every bit as meaningful as articulating them to God.

After she'd washed and dried the dishes, she made quick work of tidying up the place, collecting Aaron's shirts he'd strewn about the place and fluffing the two pieces of up-holstered furniture. She also stacked all of the stray items she found in a pile so that he would have a clear table on which to eat at again.

She wasn't even close to being done, but she was a far cry from where she'd begun twenty-five minutes ago. Perching her hands at her hips, she stood back and took in the results of her labors.

"What are you doing?" Aaron's voice, tight and forced, broke her silent reverie.

She whipped around to find him standing there, his large muscle-bound frame filling the doorway, blocking out the light. The look of shock, and maybe even anger, that flickered over his face sent a tiny trickle of fear snaking up her spine.

"I—I was just cleaning," she measured out, trying to steady the small quiver in her voice. "And tidying things up for you."

She untied her apron and hung it up exactly where she'd found it, unable to miss the way his intense gaze focused on her every move. Or the almost mechanical way he turned his head and looked at the place.

"I didn't think you'd mind," she added, trying desperately to interpret the mixed reaction etched into his features. "I don't know what got into me, barging into your personal life like this." She slid back a step and braced her hands on the chair behind her. "I'm sorry. Very sorry."

He removed his hat and stepped inside, closing the door with a nearly silent click. "No one has done something like this. At least not since Ellie. Katie tried to get me to let her clean, at first, anyway, but I didn't want her touching things. And, honestly, I'm not sure how I feel about you messing with things now."

* * *

"Uncle Aaron," Libby squealed, throwing open the wood shop door and running toward him. She leaped into his arms. "Oh, say you will, say you will, say you will," she pleaded, her words coming faster than a herd of wild horses.

"What about me? Don't I get a hug?" Joseph grinned as he moved around the workbench where he'd been doing the final sanding on a chest of drawers.

"I gotta ask Uncle Aaron something first. Then I'll give you a hug, Uncle Joseph."

Aaron smiled at Libby's exuberance. She was a constant reminder as to how far he had to go to find simple trust in God again. "Say I will what?" he asked when she hugged him tighter as if trying to squeeze an answer from him.

He couldn't help thinking about the appreciative hug Hope had given him yesterday after he'd watched over Isabel as she delivered her calf. She'd made the whole process alive with awe and delight.

She pulled back and peered at him. "Help Mama and Papa with a fun-raiser."

"A fun-raiser, huh?" he echoed with a chuckle. "Do you mean a fundraiser?"

"Yes." Nodding, she clamped her little hands on both sides of his face to ensure his full attention. "Just say you will. Promise, pleeeze."

"Of course, I will. I'll be glad to help." He'd donate whatever Ben and Callie needed to get the Seeds of Faith boarding house, a home for women in need of a fresh start, off the ground. "Anything for you, Libby-Loo."

He winked at Ben and Callie as they entered the wood shop.

"So, what's the verdict, Lib?" Ben sauntered over

and brushed a lock of dark auburn hair from her round cherub face.

"She's got him wrapped around her fingers and toes. That's the verdict." Joseph grinned in Ben and Callie's direction.

"You're one to speak, *Uncle Joseph*," Ben teased. "So, what'd he say, Libby?"

"He said yes." She scrunched her shoulders almost up to her ears, her expression laden with self-satisfaction. "Didn't you, Uncle Aaron."

"I sure did." He touched his nose to hers.

"That's *very* big of you," Callie remarked, eyeing him as though he'd just consented to the railroad detouring straight through his property.

But when Ben gave him a no-backing-out-now, raised brow look, Aaron set Libby down. He folded his arms at his chest as she scampered to the other side of the work bench to launch into Joseph's waiting arms. "Um…what, exactly, did I just promise to do? Construction of some sort, right?"

Callie exchanged a cautious look with Ben then shoved a wad of papers into Aaron's hand. Her growing smile was too sweet and way too triumphant for reassurance. "You've just agreed to play a part in our fundraiser theater production we're putting on for the Seeds of Faith boarding house."

"Uh…I don't think—"

"Sure you can." Ben clapped a hand on Aaron's shoulder, shoving the rest of Aaron's words back down his throat. "Libby prayed you'd say yes. Didn't you, Lib?"

"Yes, I did. Last night I said, God," she began in earnest, closing her eyes and clasping her hands beneath her chin as Joseph held her, "please help my Uncle Aaron be in the play with me." She popped one eye open and met his stinging gaze. "Did you know that I prayed for my friend, Elsa Lockhart, too?"

He tamped down his frustration and focused on Libby. "You did? Tell me about that."

She opened the other eye then, her sweet face growing serious with concern. "I prayed her daddy would let her be in the play. She can even stand beside me, and I'll hold her hand if she gets scared."

"That's good of you, Libby," Aaron encouraged. "You're a good friend for Elsa."

His heart surged with compassion as he thought of Libby's new friend. Maclean Lockhart and his daughter, Elsa, had moved to the Boulder area just last month to be near his two brothers and his sister after his wife had died. They'd attended church with his sister one time, but the man was very protective of his daughter, and honestly, Aaron couldn't blame him. There'd been whisperings that Maclean's wife had been sick with melancholy and had taken her own life.

Why couldn't folks just keep their tongues from wagging? No matter what had happened, death was death, plain and simple. Although Aaron had only spoken with Maclean a couple of times, he was sure the man was grieving. His daughter was, too, because from what Aaron had heard, the girl had grown mute right after the death.

"You can do it, Aaron," Ben encouraged, bracing Aaron's arm in a sturdy grip. "You've always loved to be the center of attention."

"Yes, but—"

"Yep. I know you can do it," Joseph added, setting Libby down and stepping around the workbench to join them.

Aaron sighed when Libby smothered his hand with kisses, then scurried off to the scrap box where small odds and ends of lumber were stashed.

"How?" he asked, raking a hand through his hair.

"How what?" Callie brushed a hand down her peach-colored dress as if she were covered in dust.

On a long exhale, he raised a hand to his neck and massaged the stiffness there. "How is it that I end up making these promises?"

Ben looked him square in the face in that big brother way of his that always seemed to set things right. "Because you're just that kind of a man. True, honest, loyal..."

Aaron shook his head. "Ah...don't make me out to be a saint. You sent your little girl to do your—"

"And maybe a *little* gullible," Ben added, pricking Aaron's ire.

He narrowed his gaze on Ben, realizing now that he'd been purposely duped. Before Ellie had passed on, he would've gladly jumped at the opportunity to be in the play, but not now. He didn't want to be the center of attention. Folks were more liable to ask him questions or try to tell him he'd be all right or try to set him up with their long-lost nieces, and he'd just as soon avoid that nonsense.

"I'll do it," he finally confirmed, knowing he would never let himself back down from a promise. He slid his gaze over to where Libby was busy building with the blocks. "But *only* because I promised that adorable niece of mine."

How hard could it be to connect the plow to the draft horse?

Hope swiped her sleeve across her perspiration-beaded brow. She adjusted her wide-brimmed hat as she knelt down at the edge of the field to inspect the equipment. Dirt marred her dress, and she'd only just begun. She'd picked the most workaday garment she owned, a light blue cotton floral print, embellished with delicate white lace and elegant ruching, but still she'd be overdressed and way too warm given the way she was already heated. But it couldn't be helped. There was work to be done.

Squinting against the late morning sun blazing overhead, she studied the attachment parts, trying to remember what Aaron and Zach had said yesterday when they'd been over preparing the implement for planting season. She'd asked a long list of questions about the process and had figured that plowing couldn't be that hard. It was just a horse pulling a blade through the dirt in a straight line, right? Wouldn't Aaron be surprised and greatly pleased when he got there to find the field done, or at least well on its way?

Until she'd arrived in Boulder, she'd possessed a mere shadow of understanding as to what hard work really entailed. Now, she was eager to tackle each new task, the enormous sense of gratification she felt at her accomplishments, her sole motivation.

Although she'd be remiss not to admit that the way Aaron had recently begun encouraging her had been lifegiving. She'd developed a hunger for his heartening words of support, his sweet sentiments bearing his genuine pleasure in her efforts.

But even more than hearing his encouragement was the desire to hear him laugh again. The hearty, almost desperate sound she'd heard a few days ago when she'd lost two of her undergarments to Penelope and Patience, undermined her sense of composure more than any naughty goat could. And his smile…the boyish twinkle in his blue eyes and his handsome easy grin had made her knees weak and the base of her stomach all aflutter.

But she couldn't help remembering the sting she'd felt at his response after she'd tidied up his home. Her hurt had been short-lived when she reminded herself just how closed off this part of his life had been.

"Good morning," Jane called from behind Hope.

The woman's, aren't-you-aware-that-I'm-here kind of tone, jarred Hope's senses. It set her nerves on end—instantly.

She dipped deep into her well of manners and stood, straightening her dress. Turning, she waved as Jane strode up the lane, her rigid gate adding to Hope's wariness. She wore the same faded black dress, at least a size too small and an ankle too short. Paul's sister had stopped by several times since the funeral two weeks ago, and although her sneak glares and sideways cuts had all but disappeared, Hope didn't feel the least bit inclined to let her guard down.

"Good morning, Jane." She brushed off her white-gloved hands, noticing the way the gloves were wearing thin. "What brings you over this morning?"

"I thought I'd stop by and check in on you." Jane slowed to a stop, her small-eyed gaze inspecting Hope's attire as though she was some fashion authority. "I see you're not dressed appropriately *again*."

Hope forced a smile to her face, choosing to ignore the caustic barb. "Would you like to gather some more of Paul's things? Or maybe you'd like to join me for a cup of tea?" she proposed, prepared to lay out her finest for the woman.

"I thought I told you already that I don't drink tea." A scorn-filled look creased Jane's high brow. Her thin lips curled.

"I'm sorry." Hope bit her lip trying not to react. "I didn't remember."

Jane waved her hand in clear dismissal. "I actually came

by because I wanted to talk with you about something very important."

"Certainly." When the horse gave an eager snort, Hope had to tamp down the impatience she felt at Jane's surprise visit. "What about, might I ask?"

Hugging her arms to her thick waist, Jane began. "I wanted to let you know how worried I am. About you."

"Worried?"

Jane ambled up to Hope. "Yes. Why, yesterday when I happened to be here when Aaron and Zach were over working on the plow," she began as Hope seriously questioned the *happened to* part of that sentence. Paul's sister seemed to show up, more often than not, when Aaron was here. "Well, you looked so *tired,* Hope. I thought you were going to fall asleep standing up."

Hope's mother would have a fit with the way Jane bunched her shoulders up in that utterly unfeminine way of hers and hugged her arms to her waist as though she was ready to wilt away to nothing, when it was obvious she had more than enough *extra* to carry her through the harshest of times. "I was feeling just fine, as I recall."

Furrowing her shapeless eyebrows, Jane scrutinized Hope. "I think you're trying to do too much." She pursed her thin lips, making them nonexistent. Then she paused for a strategic, baited moment, but Hope didn't feel the slightest bit inclined to bite. "It may be none of my business, but I do worry that this farm is too much for you. After all, Paul had worked every bit as hard as his workhorse." She pointed to the enormous animal, scowling as though the horse had contracted leprosy.

Hope couldn't resist pulling off her gloves and running a hand down the horse's sleek, muscled side. "Chester, isn't that his name?"

"How would I know?" Jane scoffed, taking a cautious

step away, as though the grazing horse was liable to trample her beneath his enormous feet.

"Honestly, it has been a challenge trying to learn how to do everything, but I'm feeling just fine. Truly." She smoothed her hands down her dress. "I never realized just how meaningful it is to work hard."

Jane's crumpled gaze softened some as she turned and peered at the thick timberline flanking Paul's property. "My dear brother worked so very hard, but then I'm sure you've learned that by now. Aaron said that the day Paul died, he'd been cutting down trees to build an addition onto his house." Her attention slithered over to Hope again. "Probably to please you."

Jane may as well have slapped Hope across the face for the impact of her words. Hope had asked nothing of Paul. In fact, she'd felt bad when he'd had to pay her train fare out here. She'd only wanted his love, and he'd offered her much more.

She dearly wanted to defend herself but wouldn't give Jane the satisfaction. Besides, she had to keep reminding herself, she didn't really know what it was like to lose someone so close. Jane was grieving, and sometimes grief could change a person. Death had always been a distant, unobtrusive entity in Hope's life—until she'd come to Boulder.

But even then, her grief didn't seem as deep as what others experienced. She had to wonder just how one-dimensional her relationship with Paul had been; her parents had cautioned her of exactly that. Words, ideals, pledged love…it'd all been her sustenance back in Boston. But had she only loved the idea of a good man? Had she loved the comfort and guidance he'd given in his letters? She had no doubt that, had Paul not died, they would've discovered true love—in time.

"Oh, that probably sounded horrible. I mean, the look on your face." Jane sliced a breath through her teeth. "All I meant to say was that, knowing Paul, he would've done anything for you. I'm sure of it." She hugged her arms tighter to her waist, her slumped-shoulder posture suddenly turning all rigid. "And poor Aaron. It's not as if he doesn't have his own job. But then he has to come over here and help so that Paul's *years* of hard work don't waste away under your care."

Rubbing a newly callused patch on her palm, Hope sighed with discouragement. As harsh as Jane's words were, they were also true. Guilt's burdening weight had been getting heavier with each passing day and with each hour Aaron took off from his job to help her on the farm.

She'd interviewed several farmhand candidates, but for each one Aaron had given an adamant *no.*

She knelt down next to the plow, its blades gleaming and ready to cut through the spring-thawed ground. "Believe me, I'm doing all I can to relieve him of some of the tasks, but he's determined to help."

"Aaron's just too noble to let a woman flounder."

Flounder? She wasn't floundering, was she?

Feeling her poise slip some, she grasped for control, reminding herself that even Aaron had noted how well she'd been doing. His stellar attributes flashed through her mind. He was noble, good, kind and ever so patient. The growing list of his fine character traits would easily fill a page.

She hadn't been able to ignore the way her stomach had fluttered the last few times he'd been here. It was the gentle way he'd spoken, his heart-stopping smile. Even though he'd worked hard just to honor some promise he'd made to Paul, he hadn't once made her feel beholden to him.

But it was his lingering gaze—its warmth penetrating

deep, as though he was peering into the furthest reaches of her soul—that made her feel so utterly undone.

Jane came to stand right beside Hope, jerking her from the stirring emotions. "Do you need some help with the plow?"

Hope bit back a surprised gasp. "That would be wonderful."

"I used to give Paul a hand with this all the time. In fact, he used to say I was as accomplished as any man he'd seen."

Inferiority pricked Hope, but she refused to let it get to her.

"All you need to do is line that flat-looking thing up…" she began with a measure of forced patience as she pointed to the front end of the plow. "With that other—that other *thing*."

"Do you mean this?" Hope crawled over to where the other tonguelike contraption rested on the soil next to where the horse nickered softly.

"Yes, that." Jane rested her fists at her nonexistent waist, producing a patronizing mmm-hmm, every now and then as Hope heaved the plow forward by herself and hooked it up. "Oh, well, aren't you doing a fine job? See how easy that is?"

Hope bit her lip and stood up straight. "All right. Now what?"

"Look at you. It's as if you know just what to do." With a condescending smile, Jane gave a small round of applause, irritating Hope all the more. "Now, all you have to do is just hold on to the reins and plow handles and let the horse do the work. It's *very* easy."

Hope slid her white gloves on and took her place behind the plow. "Like this?"

"Exactly." Jane rewarded her with an enthusiastic smile. "It should be very easy. Why, even a child could do it."

"Thank you so much, Jane." Hope made a mental note to cook something special for her just as soon as she was done plowing the field.

"Oh, please, what are neighbors for?" Jane turned and started walking back down the lane, only pausing long enough to call out, "Happy plowing."

Chapter Ten

Hope fought to pull on the reins, struggling to bring the horse to a halt, but she could barely keep a hold of the plow handles let alone manage the reins. And the horse, he seemed to have a mind of his own and kept plodding over the ground.

She'd probably only been at it for an hour, but already exhaustion had nearly consumed her entire being. She'd long since thrown her useless gloves to the side after holes had formed in short order. Now her hands were blistered raw and her dress was drenched with sweat, the hem ripped in several places, only adding to her frustration when she'd trip on the torn edges.

Just then she stumbled on a dirt clod. She grappled for the plow handles and tripped on her torn hem, landing face-first on the ground as the horse, mercifully, came to a stop.

Tears stung her eyes as she let out a pathetic whimper, loathing the sound but helpless to keep it locked up any longer. Her hands burned fire-red as she pressed her palms into the musty smelling soil to push herself up. She paused for a moment, relishing the way the cool and damp, freshly

turned earth brought a needed bit of relief to her pain and
to the work-induced heat that consumed her body.

When she lifted her head and glimpsed the three rows
she'd labored so hard to plow, her heart sank. There was
nothing straight or even about them. They wandered across
the field like a meandering creek bed with long stretches
where she'd either barely skimmed the surface or had gone
way too deep.

Maybe Jane was right. Maybe she'd taken on too much.

She was floundering like a fish out of water, and her
attempts to breathe and live in this new land did not come
easy. Here she'd wanted to have the field plowed for Aaron,
and she'd barely gotten a start.

To add to her already-long list of chores, she'd promised Callie she'd participate in the fundraiser. She'd been
thrilled when Callie had thought enough of her to ask her
to participate in the play. When Hope was a girl, she and
her sisters used to put on plays with their dolls. But right
now she could barely even hold up her head enough to
finish this one task let alone make it to play rehearsal tonight.

Dropping her forehead to the soil, doubt and despair
pummeled her like thick chunks of hail falling mercilessly
from the sky. She'd been giving her grandest effort over
the past two weeks, but it just didn't seem to be enough.

What else could she do? Aaron had rejected every candidate she interviewed. And she refused to skitter away
like some spoiled child, tired of playing house. She had a
responsibility to Paul, to the land and to the animals she'd
grown to love—and to herself.

Emotion clogged her throat as she searched for some
kind of answer. She was so frustrated, tired and upset that,
if she'd allow herself, she could've watered the freshly
turned earth with her tears—flooded the field, maybe.

But tears wouldn't get the field planted. They'd only prove to be a painfully short relief from her current and growing dilemma.

She rose to her elbows to see the cows—*her cows*—grazing contentedly in the pasture next to the field. She heard the chickens' whimsical bawk-bawking sound. She felt the steady June breeze dance over her sweat-dampened dress and skin, and her spirits were bolstered.

Pushing her weary body up to standing again, she got her bearings about her then grabbed the reins, the worn and smooth leather cutting into her blisters with relentless force. A surge of nausea rose fast. She pulled in a steadying breath. Then she pulled in another as she prepared to set her hands on the rough wood handles once again.

"Hope! Stop!" Aaron's command cut through a chorus of birds chirping in the nearby trees.

She shaded her eyes against the blazing sun to see him racing his horse over the field. Even from almost a hundred yards away, she could see distress etched in his brow.

"What in the world are you doing?" He brought the horse to an abrupt halt and dismounted in one smooth movement. "I warned you not to try this yourself."

Hope's entire body ached. Every muscle screamed in pain.

Her pride hurt just as much.

"Look at you. You're about ready to collapse." He lifted her wilted European-made hat from her head and threw it to the side. He cupped a hand under her chin and looked at her, the concern depicted in his scrunched features, almost her undoing.

Sheer panic coursed through her veins, thinking that he might see just how desperate she felt at this moment, that he might somehow read the words *I quit* in her gaze.

Her knees nearly buckled. Tears threatened at the corners of her eyes as she willed her limbs to stay strong.

"Hope, darlin'. What were you thinking?" Gentle as could be, he brushed at a bead of sweat—or was that an errant tear—trailing down her cheek with the pad of his thumb.

In spite of her pain, she felt a shiver of awareness at his tender touch. "I was only trying to help."

He gently grasped her shoulders. "Can't you see that it's too much for you?"

Thick shame enveloped her as she remembered Jane's words, that plowing was easy enough for a child and that Paul had considered Jane as useful as any man.

Hope couldn't admit that she'd failed miserably to Aaron. The small bit of regard for her that he likely had left would diminish, altogether.

"I'm sorry," was all she could seem to manage.

He slid his grasp down her arms and gently took her hands in his, peering at her palms. "Aww...Hope. Your hands."

She pulled them away and clasped them behind her back, wincing at the way searing pain bolted through the open wounds. "They're fine."

"No, Hope. Your hands are not fine." His fingers trembled as he drew her hands in front of her again, his gaze crimped with compassion. "They're blistered raw. They're going to get infected if we don't tend to them."

"Aaron, please do not worry so. They'll be as good as new tomorrow." She'd heaped as much conviction as she could into her words, given the fact that her hands were torn to shreds and that she was light-headed and nauseous. "I promise."

With the back of her hand, she brushed the hair from her face and tried for an unconcerned expression.

He shot her a worried gaze. "This is no time for you to be trying to outdo yourself—or anyone else—for that matter. Your hands are a serious matter." Aaron reached out and tucked the remainder of her hair behind her ear, as if he knew just how much it hurt to use her hands.

"I just fell, that's all," she breathed, his compassionate gesture nearly overwhelming. "I'm sure that the dirt makes them look far worse than what they truly are."

Whipping his leather gloves out of his back pocket, he held them up to her. "*I* even wear these things when I work."

"But I had my gloves on," she argued, glancing over at where she'd tossed them at the edge of the field.

"Those things?" He pointed to her gloves. "Fancy party gloves were never meant for farmwork. They're useless."

When a swell of dizziness assaulted her, it was all she could do to maintain her balance. "I'm well aware of that now, Aaron. That's why I threw them over there. With the holes in them it was just as easy for me to use my bare hands."

He grasped her elbow as if he could tell that she was unsteady on her feet. "There was a good reason why I told you not to try plowing. Do you see now?"

"It hasn't been all that bad. Really," she argued, trying to convince herself as much as him.

"Well, compared to plowing the rugged mountainside," he retorted, jerking his head to the west, where the mountains stretched Heavenward in unforgiving yet marvelously beautiful lines, "I'm sure it's been surprisingly easy."

Feeling all but defeated, she sidled up next to Chester and smoothed the back of her hand over his thick, muscled neck. She brushed her cheek over his downy-soft nose, loving the scent and feel of the horse.

Aaron gave his head a slow, measured shake. "You are stubborn and determined. I'll give you that."

Both perturbed and flattered by his graceless estimation of her, she stepped over several clods of dirt, toward where he bent over the plow and unhitched the implement.

"Why are you doing that?" She wobbled then caught her balance, willing her blistered feet to stay standing as he loosely draped the long reins over the yoke. "I wasn't done plowing."

When he clicked his tongue, Chester and his horse turned to follow him like obedient dogs. "Oh, yes you are."

Her pulse swished and churned in her head. She blinked hard. "But I—"

"Come on, boys," Aaron said as he scooped Hope up in his arms. "Hope, this is no place for you."

The feel of his strong arms cradling her stopped her protest somewhere between her mind and her mouth. She barely had the strength to loop her elbow around his neck as he set off up the sloping ground. She wanted to be angry at his implication—that she didn't belong here—but for the life of her, she couldn't seem to think beyond the feel of his muscle-bound arms carrying her past the barn toward the house.

"Are you trying to prove something?" His breath fanned over her hot face as he glanced at her lips. "Because if you are, you might as well save yourself the pain. You've proven plenty already."

She indulged herself in the way his blue eyes sparkled in the blazing sun and the way he'd set his perfectly squared jaw in that dashing, signature look of frustration, the way his lightly bronzed skin glistened with perspiration and the way a delightful colic kicked his light brown hair off to the side of his forehead.

The sound of the horses plodding, slow and steady, behind them, was like the graceful lull of some grand hall clock. Her eyes hung heavy, weighted with exhaustion.

"Do you know what, Aaron Drake?" she murmured, feeling heady with utter and undeniable fatigue.

He sighed. Then he pulled her closer, his manly woodsy scent lapping at her poise, undermining her good sense. "What?"

"You're awfully handsome when you're upset," she whispered, closing her eyes and relaxing completely into his powerful arms.

When he grew rigid all of a sudden, her words swung back around and hit her square in the face. She flipped her eyelids open and stared at the brilliant blue sky, praying for a brief moment that God would take her right here, right now.

How could she be so reckless?

So bold?

So unabashedly truthful?

She gulped and braved a glance at Aaron.

From the unsettled look blanketing his face, he was just as shocked. He swallowed hard, his throat visibly convulsing. He stared into her eyes, his face mere inches from hers as he came to a slow stop a good ten feet from the house. "You're right I'm upset."

The way his expression swerved between tenderness and anger and fear in the space of a few seconds struck Hope dead in the heart, jerked her to her senses.

He was grieving, for goodness' sake. She was grieving, too. So how could there be such an undeniable draw between them?

"I'm sorry. I didn't mean to say—"

"Don't," he ground out, his mouth clenched tight.

"Just answer my question. Are you trying to prove something?"

Her throat grew tight. Tears burned her eyes. "No."

On a sigh, he angled his gaze down at her in that quiet subtle way of his.

"Well, perhaps," she finally admitted.

He gave a quiet sigh, his breath fanning over her like a mesmerizing summer breeze.

"I just feel so very guilty."

"Guilty?" Confusion etched his face. "Why?"

The hair at the nape of his neck brushed against her wrist, sending chills up her arm and straight to her heart. "Because I wanted to relieve you of some of the burden you've carried here, and I don't want you doing one single thing out of obligation." *Never obligation.* She hardly felt worthy of his hard work, let alone his sense of duty.

He paused for a moment. "I don't feel obligated."

"Aaron, you've gone way above and beyond what any good friend would in carrying this burden."

"Not in my book." He drew his mouth into a grim line.

"You've even gone so far as to carry me." She splayed her hands, instantly regretting the action when pain shot through the open wounds.

"I had my doubts whether you'd make it back to the house on your own. And, for the record," he added, raising his eyebrows, "this hasn't been a burden. *You* haven't been a burden."

After a long moment, he slowly set her feet on the ground again. She was grateful for his steadying hands at her waist because the blisters on her feet burned anew, sending a wave of nausea tumbling over her. She breathed deep to ward it off.

"I've enjoyed every single minute of my time here," he finally said, his voice decidedly tight.

Jane's words, that Aaron had to be exhausted from having to do so much for Hope, flailed about in her mind. "Surely, you can't mean that."

His eyebrows raised in challenge. "I can. And I do."

"You can't maintain your work here, the chores at your own place and your carpentry job forever, Aaron." She drew in a sharp breath, helpless to ward off the fiery pain that burned her hands and feet. "It will eventually take its toll on you."

He braced a hand at her back, his brow etched with concern. "How 'bout if you let me be the one to make that decision?"

"I've interviewed six men, now. And each time you give an emphatic no," she argued, feeling way too close to tears for comfort.

"That's because I don't trust them. Not one bit." He scooped her up in his arms again and carried her the last twenty feet to the house. "Did you see the last one you interviewed? The way he was gawking at you? It wouldn't be safe for you, Hope." His vulnerable gaze was nearly her undoing. "I'll say it again…it hasn't been a burden being here helping you."

He climbed up the three steps to stand on the sprawling front porch. "And I'll tell you another thing, Miss Gatlin, I never say anything that I don't mean."

Aaron trembled from way down deep as he wound the bandage around the last bit of Hope's blistered hands. Ever since he'd found her out there in the field plowing less than an hour ago, he'd been shaken to his core.

She'd been drenched in sweat, red-faced and barely able to stand. He'd been sure she would faint, and the thought of her falling into the plow blades or hitting her head on some rock protruding from the soil nearly stopped his heart cold.

His heart did stop when he'd carried her back to the house. The way it felt to care for and protect a woman like that—to care for *Hope* like that—had settled in the furthest reaches of his soul, stirring an innate age-old rhythm.

"I'll need to put some salve on the blisters and change your bandages again tomorrow." He swiveled in his chair to place the medicinal supplies back into the wood box.

"I'm sure that I can manage," she dismissed, her voice edged with pain.

"Knowing you, I'm sure you'd try, but I'd feel a whole lot better if you'd let me make sure they're all right." Turning to face her, he folded his arms at his chest as he noticed how her face still flamed red. "In fact, I think I'll bring Ben out to see you later."

She sat a little straighter in her chair. "That is completely unnecessary."

"Maybe," he responded, catching her resolute gaze in his, "but I'm going to bring him by anyway."

When she wiped her brow with her sleeve, he pulled out his handkerchief and gave the fabric a small snap to unfold it. "It's clean."

Before she had time to reach for it, he gently patted her brow and face while she followed his every move with her vulnerable gaze.

"Thank you." She sighed, her breath whispering against his hand and sending a quiver shooting straight through him. "Actually, I'll be seeing Ben and Callie a little later. I can see if he has time to look at my hands then."

"I'm sure he'll make time," he ground out, forcing his rogue emotions to line up.

When she rose from the table and limped toward the sink, he followed behind. "Your feet, too?" He angled a glance down at her brown-booted, dirt-scuffed feet poking from beneath her tattered hem.

Gentle as he could, Aaron grasped her shoulders and guided her back to the chair. "Have a seat."

"I was just sitting down," she weakly protested, collapsing into the chair on a heavy sigh. "I have far too much to do."

"Hope, you won't be doing anything for days if you don't take care of yourself." He hunkered down and reached to unlace one of her boots. "Do you mind if I take a look?"

When she gave her head a defeated shake, his heart squeezed inside his chest. "Aww, Hope. You've got to be in a considerable amount of pain to forgo a protest. I promise I'll be as gentle as I can."

"Of that, I have no doubt." Hope stiffly leaned back against the chair, furrowing her brow as he removed one boot.

"You're an honorable man, Aaron Drake. Honorable and good."

"I'm glad you think so." He was, too, because for some reason, knowing that she had a favorable view of him meant more than he was willing to admit.

Chapter Eleven

Clenching his jaw, Aaron stalked across the town hall stage where the first play rehearsal had just finished. He'd maintained his calm for the past two hours, but his frustration was in full swing now as he moved in on Ben, determined to let him know exactly how he felt about this setup.

"What in the world were you and Callie thinking, Ben?" Aaron jammed his fists to his waist and stared at where he'd cornered his brother near the rear of the town hall stage. "You heartlessly roped me into this like I was some lame calf."

"What are you talking about?" The scrunch of concern carved into Ben's face was as shallow as a puddle and far from convincing.

Aaron edged closer, grabbing his hat from his head. "Don't think I'd be gullible enough to fall for your innocent act."

With a sly grin, Ben winked at Callie as she approached. "Aaron, here, thinks he's gullible."

"No…*you* said I was gullible just the other day," he argued, pointing at his brother. "*I* said—"

"That's what is so adorable about you, Aaron." Callie

stood on tip toes and reached up to adjust his shirt collar. "You're so willing to help—and for such a good cause, too."

"Oh, for land's sake. Now I'm adorable, too?" Rolling his eyes to the vaulted timbered ceiling, he raked a hand through his hair. He then ran it down his neck to massage the knots that had formed over the past hours from plowing, and from fighting so hard to be unmoved by Hope's presence. "Please. Have a little respect for my manhood, would you?"

The minute he'd returned to Hope's place around lunchtime, she'd been out in the field again, trying to rig up the plow. He couldn't believe his eyes. Why would she choose to go back out there?

But the almost desperate, unwavering way she'd sidestepped his anger and concern had pulled him up short—way short. He couldn't help but wonder *why* concern for her well-being affected him to such a degree.

"Where's your sense of humor?" Ben jabbed him in the arm.

"Sorry, but calling me gullible and adorable rub me the wrong way. I draw a line at my masculinity." He lowered his voice a notch in case the cast members mulling about were in hearing range. "What I'm talking about is casting Hope opposite me—and in a play that ends in a happily-ever-after?"

"Coincidence, Aaron." Ben held his hand out. "Strictly coincidence."

"Oh, come on. How old do you think I am?" Aaron flexed his hands, overwhelmed by the instant need to shove his fist into…into something.

"Twenty—" Ben began.

"Five," Callie finished. "Twenty-five."

"Why? Did you forget?" Ben absently glanced at the script in his hand.

"No, of course I didn't forget. But I didn't just drag myself out of the birthing straw." He shrugged off the way his own hands and arms ached from plowing, and he was twice the size and strength of Hope. "I'm not stupid enough to believe that the way you cast the play is coincidental."

Ben turned and peered to the back of the hall, giving a thumbs-up to Luke, his young shadow and the son of one of the women Callie and Ben had been helping to get on her feet again. The boy's erect posture and all-business look on his face as he stood beside his mama, making sure everyone had their scripts as they left the building, brought a smile to Aaron's heart.

"By the way—" Ben tapped his disorganized script into some semblance of alignment "—did I tell you that this play is written by our very own, albeit anonymous, romantic advice columnist here in Boulder? Maybe you should ask for advice for whatever it is—or whomever it is—that's gotten under your skin."

Aaron sighed. "I don't know what you're talking about."

"That would be wonderful," Callie commented, nodding up at Ben with a bit too much eagerness. "I'm sure the woman could help you, Aaron."

"She has enough success stories to create quite a legacy, that's for sure." Ben brushed a lock of hair from Callie's face.

Folding his arms at his chest, Aaron stared at them. "It's a good thing you two are in charge of the production instead of playing a role. You're terrible actors."

"Aw, Aaron, you wound me." Ben held a hand to his heart, his face scrunched in mock pain.

Aaron jammed his hat on his head. "I had my suspicions before—that you all were trying to manufacture a connection between me and Hope. But now…"

"I do believe that *you're* the one who proposed marriage to the woman." Callie angled a glance up at Ben, her overly earnest expression rankling Aaron further. "Isn't that right, dear?" she asked, glancing briefly at Ben.

"You know…if I hadn't grown so attached to you, Callie, I might just detest you right now." Aaron folded his arms at his chest.

"All bark," Ben commented. "And, yes, I witnessed the proposal myself."

"You *know* why I proposed." Aaron shook his head at their lame act. "And it sure as Sunday wasn't because I fell in love at first sight."

The challenge-infused way Ben arched one eyebrow made Aaron want to haul back and hit him square in the jaw. He made a halfhearted grab at good sense, struggled to temper his surly mood and wondered why he was feeling so defensive.

He *hadn't* fallen in love at first sight, had he?

He'd been so fraught with worry over Paul and then confused as to what he'd been sent to the train station for that he'd barely even noticed what Hope had looked like, right?

But he had noticed. And since then he'd dedicated himself to trying to forget.

He'd failed.

The image of Hope standing on the train station platform over two weeks ago, surfaced with brilliant and undeniable clarity—again. It made him almost wish that, in that moment, he'd been as blind as Joseph. Had he not been so intrigued by her, he might not have been so curious about how she would react to her situation. But then he'd been permanently charmed by her determination and her naive innocence. And like some curious and hungry animal following his heart instead of his instinct, Aaron had wandered right into a sunlit valley.

Danger lurked down the trail where his thoughts were headed. If he knew what was best, he'd turn around and head back to where he came from—back to the vows he'd made to Ellie.

He shoved his focus to his brother. "First, you use my cute little niece to get me to volunteer, which, I might add—" he edged a little closer "—was a very low-down, sneaky thing to do to your own flesh and blood."

"If you remember right, she did pray." Callie scanned the room, her face brightening the moment she spotted Libby.

Aaron sighed. "I'm fighting a losing battle with you two."

"Maybe you're fighting against God," Ben measured out, his low voice void of all joking. "Have you given that any kind of serious thought?"

The idea had swung through his mind a time or two. But Aaron had dismissed it just as quickly as it appeared—like now.

He flipped his gaze toward the back of the hall where he spotted Hope standing and talking with Maclean Lockhart, her script in her bandaged hands. Aaron wasn't sure how she'd managed to clean up with all of her bandages and the way she had to hurt. She looked beautiful, in a rose colored dress that matched the hint of color dotting her fair cheeks. In fact, as far as he was concerned, she'd looked perfect this morning, too, all dirt-smudged and tattered and bedraggled.

"If it's really that hard for you, well, then we can try to rearrange the roles." Ben peered down at his script as Callie looked on with him. "Maybe put Jane opposite

Aaron and then have Hope take Jane's part. What do you think?"

"That would be a good alternative," Callie agreed, her index finger resting against her lips. "As fast as Hope memorized all of her lines, I doubt she'd have any trouble with Jane's few lines."

Aaron narrowed his focus on Ben then shot it back to Hope and Maclean. And out of nowhere, a wave of uneasiness, as if some kind of claim on her was being threatened, stole his balance. "Just keep things the way they are."

"Are you sure?" The corners of Ben's mouth tipped upward the smallest bit.

When Hope smiled in that relaxed way of hers as she talked with Maclean, he jammed his hands into his pockets and set his jaw. "Forget I ever said anything."

"All right, then. Forgotten," Ben agreed as Aaron turned to leave.

"Oh, and by the way—" he pivoted to face his brother "—did Hope ask you to check on her hands?"

"She didn't. But seeing the bandages, I did, anyway."

"What do you think?" Concern for her well-being overrode jealousy's tightening chords for the moment.

"I think that you better make sure you're out there as much as possible—" Ben raised his brows and pulled his wife close "—so that she doesn't try something like that again."

"Done," he answered. He'd already decided that much. "Anything else?"

"Just keep your heart open," Ben answered.

Aaron turned and stalked across the stage and down the steps, trying to shrug off the taunting irritation and jealousy nipping at his heels. He grabbed his script from the front row and wound it into a tight roll.

He didn't know Maclean well, but he'd known most of

the other Lockhart clan and had been good friends with Maclean's brother, Brodie, a U.S. marshal. In fact, Brodie had played an integral part in finding Callie's daughter, Libby, last fall.

There wasn't one thing about Maclean that would point to Hope being in danger or at any risk—not one thing.

But there was plenty of danger when it came to Aaron. If his heart continued the way it was heading, she would be in danger of being hurt—by him. Because he'd never be able to love another woman like he'd loved Ellie.

He just had to figure out how he could be with Hope on a daily basis and remain unaffected by her charm and wit and unflappable determination.

"Uncle Aaron, don't leave yet." Seven-year-old Libby raced down the aisle to meet him, stopping briefly to backtrack a few feet and grab the hand of her little friend.

"You did great tonight, Libby-Loo." He tweaked the big pink bow in her auburn hair.

"Thank you. This is my friend, Elsa. Her papa—" Libby pointed at where Maclean and Hope stood "—said she could be in the play with me."

"Good to hear you're joining us, Elsa." He smiled down at the girl, and the sadness that was so evident in her gaze sent his glowering mood packing. He could only imagine the kind of sorrow that could steal the enthusiastic flow of words from a little girl.

"We have to go talk to Mama and Papa cuz Lukey told us we had to have our scripts." Libby looped her arm through her friend's. "And Elsa doesn't have one yet."

"Then you'd better get going." Grinning, he gave Libby a pat on the back as she scampered off with Elsa in tow.

Glancing up, he met Maclean's watchful gaze as the man came this way with Hope.

Aaron nodded to Hope and then held out a hand to Maclean. "Good to see you again, Maclean."

"You as well." The man took Aaron's hand. "Libby tells me she's going to watch out for my young one, then."

"I'm sure she will. Callie and Ben, too," he assured.

"They've said as much. I'm appreciating the kindness shown to her. It's not been easy for her, with all of the changes." He inclined his head to where his little girl stood next to Libby and Luke on stage. "She's pleased to be having a friend such as Libby."

"Libby is delightful," Hope added, her gaze flitting as light as a butterfly from Maclean to Aaron.

"I imagine it's been hard moving and starting over." And losing a wife and mother. Aaron nodded to the unspoken sentiment, knowing from the somber way Maclean met his gaze that the man understood exactly.

"Aye." Deep sadness weighted Maclean's gaze. "I'm grateful to be near my kin again. They've been a help with my little girl. With the ranch, too."

"Brodie said you'd brought a few head of cattle with you in the move."

"That, I did." He nodded, shoving his large work-worn hands into his pockets as he glanced over at Hope. "I brought the best I had but sold the others off else I'd have too many on my hands for the journey."

"Are they adjusting to your new place?" Hope's sweet innocence and concern stirred Aaron's heart. She'd barely even been around cattle and yet treated them as though they were house pets.

Maclean nodded as he set his Stetson on his thick head of dark hair. "The land is good. Better than where we came from, seventy miles east of here. And I've got a large enough plot to add many more head when I'm ready."

"You sure do." The Lockhart land stretched to several

hundred acres, total. With the eldest brother and renowned horse trainer Callen Lockhart's horse ranch and now Maclean's cattle, they needed every bit of the grazing land. "If you ever need a hand repairing fences or outbuildings, you be sure to let me know."

"Thank you." When Elsa walked up and eased into Maclean's side, he reached down and settled his big hand on her shoulder.

Aaron couldn't miss the way Hope regarded the interchange, her eyes shimmering and her hands clasped beneath her chin as Maclean hunkered down and spoke in low soothing tones to the girl.

If Aaron was inclined at all to follow the way his heart had been heading, he better stay focused because, like it or not, he was going to have to come face-to-face with his own pain and sorrow or else risk losing Hope—if he ever even had her at all.

Chapter Twelve

"How did you escape?" Aaron looped a rope around the prized stallion's massive neck, gleaming with sweat. He set his back teeth, irritated that Paul's costly horse had gotten loose. "I'm afraid your fun is over, buddy. I'm going to have to take you back home."

Aaron's mare had come into heat just a few days ago, and he'd been diligent about keeping her confined.

But from the triumphant satisfied look in the black stallion's eye, and the tamed docile stance of his mare as they grazed side by side, not diligent enough.

He led the horse through the gate when a movement from the meadow caught his attention. Turning, he spotted Hope running through the ankle-high grass, waving frantically. Even from a good forty yards away he could see the way worry had etched her brow. He could also see the way her hair had tumbled down in soft chocolate waves around her porcelain face, dotted pink from exertion—the way her feminine form strained against the bodice of her dress with every single breath.

His pulse kicked up a notch—or two. The core of his stomach grew tight as she neared. Sweat beaded his brow.

"Oh, thank goodness, you found Edmund." She slowed

to a jog as she approached the corral. "I was looking all over—"

"I found him, all right." Aaron ran a hand over the stallion's massive shoulder, feeling the horse's power bunch beneath his touch. Knowing how this could mess up his mare's bloodlines. "And believe me, he couldn't be happier than he is right now."

Bending at the waist, she rested her hands on her knees and sucked in several deep breaths. "I was so worried."

"You should've been. Paul saved long and hard to purchase such a fine horse from Callen Lockhart's brood."

"Lockhart?" She popped back up and inhaled a lungful of air, tempting the strength of the pearl buttons trailing down her blue-green dress. "Is he any relation to Maclean?"

Aaron studied her face for a moment, looking for the hint of hopefulness at the mention of Maclean. "He's Maclean's brother and a well-known horse trainer in the region. His stock brings in some of the highest prices in all of Colorado."

"I'm so grateful that you found Edmund and that he's unhurt. Thank you so very much." When she pulled pins from her hair, the remainder of her silken strands fell down around her shoulders, distracting his thoughts all the more. "I tell you…I don't know how he escaped. I tuck him in every—"

"Tuck him in?" Aaron swallowed hard, grasping for patience and control over his rebellious thoughts.

She nodded, then held the pins between her teeth and threaded her fingers through her hair. "I check his gate every night before I go to bed. Just like you said," she said, enunciating around the pins. Twirling her hair around, she fastened it at the back of her head again in no time flat.

But it was not fast enough. With the way his chest was

pounding so hard watching her, a person would think that he was the one who'd just run two miles.

His heart was so traitorous. How could he be acting like an oat-sowing, whipped puppy schoolboy? He loved Ellie. He had vowed to take care of her, to love her and cherish her until—until death.

The reality stung hard and deep.

Too deep to know what hit him and deep enough to feel pain.

"I am positive that the gate was securely fastened." Hope's gentle voice was like some lifeline out of his realization and a reminder of why his loss had become so tangible.

"Well, apparently not." Desperate to ease his pain, he grasped for a reason—*any* reason—to dislike Hope. "Because the stallion made his way over here and had a grand ole time with my mare."

Hope winced at his gruff tone, sending shame barreling through him at breakneck speed.

She didn't deserve his anger; after all, she'd run all the way over here for help. "Look, I know you've been trying very hard to make a go of things, but doggone it all if you don't frustrate me with the headlong way you go about huge tasks."

And he was also frustrated with the way her very presence called up from within him age-old, innate emotions that rocked him deep.

"Would you rather I sit back and whine about my circumstance?" she challenged. Lifting her chin a notch, she glanced to where the mare nickered softly by the fence, dipping her head in an effort to get the stallion's attention. Understanding as to what had transpired between the two horses dawned in Hope's innocent expression. Her throat convulsed as she swallowed. Her eyes grew wide.

And her mouth, glistening with moisture, fell open ever so slightly.

She patted her sleeve across her perspiration-beaded brow, dodging his rapt focus. "I am terribly sorry, Aaron. I will not let this happen again."

"It's a little late."

"I don't know how he escaped," she said, meeting his intense gaze. "But I will do my best to ensure that it doesn't happen again."

Nodding, Aaron guided the horse away from the corral—away from all of the sensations this woman called from within him.

When she caught up to him as he trudged toward her house, he tried to stay focused. "Hope, this is the second time something like this has happened. First it was the goats, and then it was Paul's stallion." He tried to ignore the endearing image that flashed through his mind of her chasing the goats or the brave way she'd forged through the cattle or the stalwart way she'd stood behind the plow in the field. "And then there was the headstrong way you insisted on trying to plow."

Plowing should be easy enough for a child. Jane's words sprang to the forefront of Hope's mind. She grappled for composure in the face of Aaron's exasperation. "I was simply unaware of the correct method."

Tired from running all the way over to Aaron's place, she struggled to keep up with him as he headed back to her home through the meadow. His back muscles bunched beneath his shirt, his powerful legs ate up the ground with long, steady strides.

"That's for sure. Your rows couldn't have even qualified as rows the way they snaked all over the field."

"I tried," she defended quietly, his words stinging. She

pulled her mouth tight, remembering how she'd done her best. But her three meager rows had looked uncommitted and rambling, at best.

When Aaron brought the horse to a halt and pivoted to look at her, regret hung in his gaze. "I'm sorry I said that. I know that you tried. You've been trying very hard."

She swallowed a bit of her anger. "Thank you."

"But where would you get the idea that plowing is easy?" He furrowed his brow. "Unless they have some fancy, new contraption out East that does the work of a man, there's no substitute for good, old-fashioned hard work. At least not in these parts."

Hope worried the French linen fabric of her dress, its refined elegance in direct contrast to the raw, earthy nature of the West. For three weeks she'd lived in Boulder, and each moment that had ticked by and every task she'd put her hands to had taken her further from her roots, further from a true sense of who she really was.

She was so confused, because at times she wondered if she'd ever truly known who she was. Or maybe she was only now discovering the real Hope Gatlin.

Smoothing a hand down her skirt's tiny pleats, she was tempted to tell him exactly where she'd gotten her information. Instead, she stuffed any vindictive or blame-casting words back down her throat. For the most part, she could handle Jane's caustic barbs and hateful looks just fine. Besides, they'd lessened a great deal. But from here on out, she'd be a fool not to take what Jane said with a heavy grain of salt.

"Well, you're definitely not going to be plowing again." His words ruffled the hairs at the back of her neck yet gave her a warm and wonderful sense of comfort that she'd longed for. "I'm sure that *any* woman who's ever had to plow would tell you that it's backbreaking work—and that she'd rather not do it."

Hope wholeheartedly agreed, but that wasn't something she was about to admit. Even now her back still ached.

When he held out his hands, revealing the blisters that marred them from three days of plowing with gloves on, she felt an abrupt sense of guilt. "Hands down, there's no question as to whether it's hard labor."

Hope stared at the angry red blotches covering his palms remembering how her own hands had been unbearably sore. They were still rough and ridged with torn skin. "I'm sorry about your hands. If there was any way—"

"I didn't show you my hands for sympathy but to let you see how hard it is, even for a full-grown man." Sighing, he folded his arms at his chest. "I just have to wonder if you're trying to take on too much and that's why you're making mistakes. Like leaving this guy's gate open." He nodded over his shoulder toward the stallion.

"But I—" Hope severed her excuse, fuming inside as she reached out and trailed her fingertips over Edmund's downy-soft nose. The goats…she had to wonder if they'd somehow finagled a way to open the gate. And the plow… Jane had led her wrong there, although Hope would've attempted the feat even if Jane hadn't spurred her in that direction. But the stallion…she was sure that she'd secured the gate last night.

Aaron's questioning look of disappointment sent her frustration climbing even higher. This man could charm her and delight her and make her emotions swirl out of control in the span of a few moments. He was nothing like Jonas or other men she'd known back in Boston—refined, neatly manicured and cunning. He was without guile. He was genuine, loyal. He was every bit a gentleman yet without the pomp and circumstance.

And that was refreshing and completely unnerving.

Desperate to ease her pricked pride, and eager to find a shaded spot away from the warm sun, she beelined toward a gigantic pine tree, surrounded by smaller ones in the meadow. If the sense of guilt she carried didn't subside, she'd have to hire someone with or without Aaron's consent. No matter how much Aaron had said he was fine with helping out, there were moments like these when she saw something different, some distinct struggle in his eyes, his tone, his demeanor.

When she reached the tree, something caught her eye on the trunk. She peered closer at the bark, her stomach pulling taut. She traced a fingertip over the sentiment carved into the craggy bark. *Aaron loves Ellie, 8th of May, 1886,* and a heart-shaped etching surrounding the sweet declaration of love.

She'd always dreamed of some man making such a bold announcement, etched into nature, but had long ago given up such a fanciful dream. Once Jonas had turned his nose up at her, she didn't know if she'd ever be able to believe in true love. But Paul's sweet words had made her believe. He just hadn't lived long enough for her to find it in his arms.

"That's the day I asked Ellie to be my bride," Aaron uttered, his voice barely audible right behind her.

Compelled by his openness, she turned to look at him. He was so strong and mysterious at times that when he made himself vulnerable, like now, she felt privileged— privileged that he would share his private world with her.

The way he stared at the etching, as though remembering the day he'd conveyed his feelings there, made her chest squeeze tight. Anguish ran deep in his expression, cloaking the carefree glimpses she'd seen of him recently.

"How lovely to remember the moment in such a way,"

she whispered, trying to control her emotions as she took in the beautiful surroundings. "The way this tree sits out here like some steady beacon, it's perfect, really."

He shrugged. His mouth grew all tight. "It was our tree. We loved sitting out here at night and listening to the wind whisper through the branches." He stared up the enormous trunk then shot his gaze down to the ground. "I haven't visited here once since she died."

"It can't be easy facing familiar places for the first time. Alone." She remembered well the disorderly state of his home and how he'd appeared to have left things just as they were the day his life had changed so suddenly.

Aaron flipped Edmund's lead rope around a low-hanging branch and hunkered down to the right of the tree where the ground lumped in places. He parted the tall, dead weeds that had probably been last summer's splendor to reveal two grave markers.

Hope's breath caught. Her eyes stung with tears.

"These are Ellie and Jeremiah's graves." He gently touched the simple stones, his hands trembling.

Kneeling down beside him, she could almost feel the pain radiating from his soul. "What a perfect burial place, Aaron."

His throat visibly convulsed. "It's so overgrown."

"Winter is harsh," she whispered, grasping for some consolation.

Clutching a handful of dried grass, he dragged it out of the ground and flung it to the side, his motions stiff, almost mechanical. "I should be a lot better about keeping up on the weeds."

For several moments they knelt in silence, the seconds likely ticking away memories in his mind. When he finally levered himself to standing, his hands trembled as he covered his face.

Hope's throat had gone raw with emotion as she stood beside him, compassion for him drowning all frustrations she'd had only moments ago. When his shoulders shook on a silent sob, she thought her heart would break right in two. "Oh, Aaron. I'm so sorry."

Moved by his utter vulnerability, she stepped closer and wrapped her arms around his thick muscular chest. She was desperate to bring him some kind of comfort, but being around him made her feel so undone. And her faith, it felt so shaky.

Since Hope had committed her life to God six months ago, she'd assumed her burden would ease, but things had seemingly gotten worse—and the way Aaron's shoulders heaved on another silent cry, he could likely say the same. How could someone as kind and as good as Aaron go through something so harsh and cruel? Had God looked the other way when Aaron's wife and baby had died? She didn't understand enough of God to know the answers. Perhaps she'd never know. All she had to base her faith on were the remnants of Paul's beliefs that he'd sprinkled into his letters—the seedlings that had started her faith.

She silently prayed for Aaron as she had many, many times before. She tried to trust that God would hear her prayers, that He really was as close as her next breath. An ever-present help in times of trouble.

She wanted to believe so, because life without Him had seemed unbearably empty. But life with Him…

When Aaron drew in another heart-wrenching, shuddering breath, Hope struggled to shove aside her doubts to pray that Aaron would truly find God in the midst of his pain, because even though she had her own questions regarding her faith, she had a very tangible sense that God was Aaron's only hope.

She splayed her hands at his back where his heart

pounded wildly into her touch. She pressed her cheek to his chest where his masculine scent seeped into her senses. She held him for a long and lingering moment, was undone by the way he slowly, almost fearfully wrapped his arms around her in return. After a measurable pause, he seemed to relax into her embrace, but it was several moments before she felt his violent shaking subside, before she felt her own shaking subside.

Chapter Thirteen

It was nearly impossible for Aaron to focus on his lines as they stood on the town hall stage and rehearsed. His pulse pounded loud enough that he was sure Hope could hear it as she stood next to him. All of the sensations that had shaken him to his very core as they'd embraced this morning still made his heart thump wildly.

He'd grieved the loss of his wife and baby but always in private and never like he had this morning. So when he'd faced the graves, and sorrow had hit with such ferocity, all of the emotions he'd penned up came rushing out with mudslide force. Hope's arms had been a lifeline.

And it was also a captivating promise of what could be if he let his heart lead. When she'd chucked propriety aside and wrapped her arms around him, it had felt so right, so consoling. It was so much like healing that he hadn't wanted to let her go.

"Aaron. Your line," Callie prompted quietly from the front row of seats.

His face flushed hot as he flipped to the next page, searching for his line yet barely able to focus on the words. His anxiety only deepened knowing that the end of the play, just a page from now, concluded with sweet nothing words and an embrace.

He swallowed hard, straining to find his voice as he forced his line out of his mouth. "I've been a fool. I hope you can forgive me." The words tasted like dust in his mouth.

All day long he'd barely accomplished one doggone thing other than the chores at Hope's farm. Even Joseph had questioned him at work as to his preoccupation. And if matters hadn't been bad enough, when he'd returned home for supper, he'd found that Ellie and Jeremiah's graves had been cleared of all weeds. His chest had grown so tight that he'd struggled to breathe when he saw the small posies of wildflowers that had been laid there as a memoriam.

Hope.

Her thoughtfulness infused his heart with faith. Her sweet concern soothed his weary soul. And her spunk lit a fire in him that had been all but doused by death's dark and stormy cloud.

"Uncle Aaron," Libby whispered, tugging him to the here and now. "You need to say your line."

"Sorry, sweetie." He glanced up to see Ben and Callie staring at him with looks of bewilderment. "Which one was that?"

Libby leapfrogged the five feet over to him and pointed at his line. "See, it's right after mine. I say—" she scurried back to her position, her expression turning all serious "—I hope there will be a bride for the wedding," she recited. "And you say…"

He cleared his throat of all trepidation. "I'll have to remedy that," he recited, his words sounding as lackluster as his dirty windowpanes at home. "Because it wouldn't very well be a wedding without a bride, now would it?"

Clamping his jaw tight, he pinned his gaze to the page

as he scrambled to find his footing. But it seemed that everywhere he stepped there was a potential trap leading him to Hope.

Perspiration beaded his brow at the way she'd set her unwavering focus on him as she recited one of her lines, her voice washing over him like a cool breeze on a sultry day. Her faint touch on his arm was a tender connection, an irrevocable draw for his soul. She probably didn't have the foggiest idea what was wrong with him and deserved some kind of explanation, but how could he tell her what kind of battle raged in his soul? Sure, he'd been able to talk with her some about his loss, but if he gave her a true glimpse into his heart, he would risk hurting her. And he'd grown so fond of Hope that he couldn't imagine doing anything to cause her pain.

Jane's voice pierced the air with lightning-bolt force as she recited one of her lines and walked across the stage—stomped, actually—with the big black bow she wore in her hair flopping around like some big old coon dog's ears.

"Not so clompy, Jane." Callie winced, slicing a breath through her teeth. "You're supposed to be excited, not mad. Can you try it again, only walking a little softer this time?"

Can we just go home? Aaron silently pleaded.

But he wouldn't do that to Ben and Callie or the rest of the cast. He'd committed to being in the play, and that was what he was going to do. He could just go through the motions—that's all he needed to do. This was a play, for land's sake. He was playing a role. But hugging Hope again would be too tempting, too wonderful and too much like a gun aimed at his vows to Ellie.

With a disgruntled huff, Jane pursed her lips, pivoted and stalked to the other side of the stage.

"Now, this is where you're going to want to put your arm around her, Aaron," Callie directed.

He shot a distraught look her way.

"Just wrap your arm around her shoulders," Callie directed as he pried his arm from his side, feeling as stiff as a craggy old oak tree. "That's right. Now pull her close, like you really care."

Libby giggled then, and it was all he could do to keep his focus on what he was supposed to do. There was no *supposed to* about it, really. If he was to follow the errant beat of his heart, he'd wrap Hope in an embrace like he was doing at this very moment and never let her go.

"Perfect. That's just perfect," Callie praised, her voice a little too enthusiastic to suit him.

Jane marched across the front of the stage. "If there's going to be a wedding then I better—"

She stumbled and screeched. She threw her hands up, the script flying into the air as she tumbled slowly down the three shallow steps to the floor.

"Jane!" Callie screamed as she and Ben dashed to Jane's side.

"Ow!" Jane wailed.

Collective gasps filled the stage as several pages wafted down to the floor. The entire cast rushed to perch at the edge of the stage.

"Are you all right?" Ben grasped Jane's shoulder. "Where does it hurt?"

She braced her hands behind her and held her left leg out like a child sticking out a sore thumb. "My ankle. I twisted my ankle."

Aaron dropped the short distance to the floor and hunkered down at Jane's other side. Grappling to tamp down the overwhelming sense of relief he felt for the diversion, yet concerned for Jane, he fixed a worried expression on his face.

"Oh, there you are, Aaron." On a sniff, she lowered her leg, turned toward him and…and smiled.

Aaron gave Ben a what-in-the-world kind of glance then peered down at Jane, dragging out whatever amount of compassion he could find in his heart. "Are you all right, Jane? That was quite a spill you took."

He played the whole thing over in his mind. He'd purposely focused on her large clomping feet. He hadn't noticed where she'd tripped. It almost seemed like she'd made a run for the steps then did a weak kind of tumble down the three perches—on purpose.

"I don't know. I just don't know." She rubbed her *right* ankle, wincing. "But I don't think I can do any more tonight."

"That's all right, Jane. We were almost done, anyway," Callie assured her as Libby and Elsa came to stand next to her.

Callie wrapped an arm around each girl, giving them needed assurance—but especially Elsa, whose face drew so tight with concern that Aaron considered heading out to find Maclean for the girl.

Ben grasped Jane's right foot gently in his hands and peered with a keen kind of focus at his patient. "It's this one, right?"

Nodding, Jane added another set of sniffs as Hope made her way down the steps and knelt beside Aaron.

"Do you mind if I have a look?" Ben slipped a suspicious glance to Aaron then eyed his patient.

"Oh, I suppose," she mumbled as he unlaced her boot and eased it from her foot. She winced, her vigilant eyes darting to Aaron's.

"Can I get you something?" Hope's voice sounded more

like she was broaching a slumbering bear than a harmless woman. She folded her hand around Jane's. "Some water or perhaps a blanket?"

"No, thank you," Jane snapped then waved her hand in front of her face. "Goodness, why would you think I'd need a blanket? It's already blazing hot in this place."

When Hope gave a small sigh, Aaron had to wonder what would prompt such a brusque answer from Jane. He'd been concerned by Jane's peculiar behavior regarding Hope, but her tone, just moments ago, was uncalled for.

"Ya want me to go git yer bag for ya, Ben?" Luke asked, dropping to the floor, his half-tamed golden mop of hair drooping into his eyes as he hunkered down next to Ben. "Cuz I can. Wouldn't be no problem at all."

"Thanks, Luke, but I don't think I'll be needing it," Ben answered as he inspected Jane's ankle. "But if I do, I'll know who to send. You're my right-hand man."

"I could go with him, Papa," Libby offered, pulling Elsa with her to stand next to Luke. "I know where you keep your doctor bag."

"We'll see, sweetie." Ben gave Libby a wink as he continued inspecting Jane's ankle.

Aaron smiled at the innocent endearing way Luke shadowed Ben. The boy admired Ben in every way possible— and rightly so. Well over a year ago Ben had taken Luke under his wing when the boy's mother had been so deep in prostitution that she didn't seem to care for her own child. The boy would go on house calls with Ben and eat meals with him. Ben had made time for a young boy yearning for love and attention. To see Luke and his mother now, well on their way to healing and wholeness after all they'd gone through, was all Aaron needed to remind him of just how important the Seeds of Faith boarding house was to this community.

After several moments, Ben drew back on his haunches and peered at Jane. "Your ankle seems to be fine. I don't feel any broken bones, and so far I don't notice any kind of swelling."

"But sometimes that doesn't happen right away. It could be broken or sprained, right?" she inquired as though she was searching for a measure of hope following a grave report.

Disbelief flashed across Ben's face. "Sure, that *could* be the case, but I think that if you take it easy for a few days, you should be just fine. You'll probably feel as good as new tomorrow, in fact."

"That's wonderful," Callie exclaimed. "Isn't it, Jane?"

Hope laid a hand on Jane's arm. "If you need someone to stay with you tonight—"

"Absolutely not," Jane bit off, yet Hope didn't even flinch. Dousing her boorish expression some, Jane shoved her boot on with barely a wince and continued. "I mean, I wouldn't think to impose on you like that. You already have *more* than you can handle with the farm."

"That was nice of you to offer, Hope," Aaron breathed, relieved by the amusement he saw in her gaze. When other women might have marched out of the building, offended, Hope remained at Jane's side in spite of the woman's churlish behavior. It was all he could do to stuff down the appreciative grin that tugged at his mouth.

"Aaron, do you think that you could take me home?" Jane's whiney voice dripped into Aaron's thoughts like a leaky roof.

"Sure, I can." He glanced at Hope. "Could I give you a ride home, too?"

Jane's audible harrumph echoed in the quiet hall.

"If you wouldn't mind," Hope said.

After the play cast cleared, Aaron hauled Jane out to the wagon—at her insistence that she simply could not walk. With each laborious step—her arms looped around his neck so tight that he had to wrench his head free to breathe—his mind strayed to the time when he'd carried Hope from the field. She'd felt so perfect in his arms that he hadn't wanted to set her down. Aaron angled a forced smile down at Jane, trying not to grimace at the stale breath she fanned over him in a big sigh. Once he had her settled in the wagon, and Hope had taken the backseat, *again,* he drove the distance home, the setting sun glinting like an orange flame as it made its slow descent on the horizon.

"I don't know how I'll be able to manage at home," she whimpered, reaching down and rubbing her left ankle.

"Hope offered to stay with you." He cast a wink Hope's way. "Maybe you should take her up on that."

"Like I said, she can't even keep up with things." Jane wrenched around in her seat to peer at Hope. "I wonder if the play is too much for you on top of everything else you're doing, dear?"

"As far as I'm concerned, she seems to be handling it just fine. Aren't you, Hope?"

Hope smiled as sweet as the apple pie she'd brought out to him after chores the other day. "I tend to memorize things very quickly, so truly, it hasn't been a bit of a problem."

"But are you able to get your chores done?" Jane needled, hauling her loglike eyebrows over her eyes. "Are things at Paul's farm suffering on the evenings you have to come in town for practice? Perhaps you're making mistakes on the farm?"

"Hope would probably be the first one to recognize a mistake if she'd made one," Aaron quickly defended, knowing, firsthand how important it was to Hope to do things right.

But remembering the mishaps that had transpired…he had a moment of doubt.

"I appreciate your concern, Jane, but you mustn't worry. I'll be able to manage," Hope reiterated.

"I do worry, though." Jane gave an insignificant cough. "After all, I did hear that you left the gate open and that Paul's stallion got loose."

While Aaron turned into the short lane leading to Jane's home, he knew that Hope was probably fit to be tied about now.

"The horse did get out, yes." She shot Aaron a bewildered glance as though she'd just been struck across the face. "But how he managed, I have no idea. I didn't—nor would I ever—leave his gate unlatched."

"You see, *this* is why I worry," Jane announced, waving her index finger as she turned and pinned her incensed gaze on Aaron.

Aaron heaved a sigh. "She said that she didn't—"

"You could be so tired that you don't even realize what you're doing, Hope," Jane continued with forced concern. "And thereby, make a *very costly mistake*. And let me tell you…losing Paul's stallion would be a *very* costly mistake."

At that, Aaron reined in his team in front of Jane's house—about ten seconds past too late. He dismounted and stalked to the other side, loading Jane into his arms and hauling her into her home. After he made sure she was all settled in, he beelined outside to find Hope gone.

He peered into the gathering darkness, searching for her pale green dress or lily white skin, but he saw nothing.

"She couldn't have gone far," he muttered under his breath as he climbed into his seat.

Snapping the reins, he spurred his team to the road and didn't get more than a hundred yards before he caught up with her walking alongside the wagon path.

"What are you doing walking home when it's almost dark?"

"The opportunity to stretch my legs will do me a world of good," she called over the clattering wagon. She didn't even bother to spare him a glance.

"I don't mean to scare you, but wolves have been scouting the area lately. You need to be very careful."

She paused, her focus drawn across the field to the tree line, darkened by nightfall.

"That's not like you, Hope, to take off without a word." Her feistiness, the way she held her shoulders back and spine arrow-straight, confirmed her irritation. "Surely, there's more to this than stretching your legs?"

She flipped her attention to him then yanked her shawl tighter around her shoulders. "I should think that you would know *perfectly* well, Aaron Drake."

Reining in his team, he set the brake and vaulted to the ground. When he reached Hope, he caught her arm and brought her to a gentle stop. "Actually, I don't have the foggiest idea what's wrong other than Jane being insensitive and surly, that is."

Hope lifted her chin a notch, avoiding his gaze. "*That,* I can manage just fine."

He snatched his hat from his head. "So, tell me then, what's the problem?"

Smoothing a hand down his horse's neck, her gentle touch was wrought with that same wordless awe he'd seen in her the first few days here. "I know that it should not matter, but *someone* told Jane about Paul's stallion escaping. And, rest assured, it wasn't me."

"Is that why you took off? You think I said something to Jane?"

She nodded.

"Well, I had nothing to do with that." He jammed his hat back on his head.

"And I can assure you that the information didn't come from the stallion. Jane would never hold a conversation with a horse. Believe me." She eyed Aaron with clear speculation. "So, how, exactly, do you suppose she found out about the incident?"

"I don't know." He held up his hands. And he didn't, but he wasn't so sure that she believed him. "Listen, I didn't say a word to anyone—especially not Jane."

She studied him as though mining for a vein of dishonesty. When her gaze softened some, he breathed a sigh of relief because the idea that she might question his integrity rankled like nothing else.

"You're right." Her shoulders sagged a little. "I'm sorry that I even alluded to such a thing."

"Don't give it a second thought," he responded, concerned with the way distress wrinkled her faultless brow. "With the touchy way Jane has been since Paul's death, she's definitely not one I'd feed that kind of information to. Believe me."

She rubbed her hands up and down her arms as though chilled. "She's harmless. At least I think so, anyway."

"What do you mean, at least you think so?" Shrugging out of his coat, he draped it over her shoulders. And just like that, he envisioned his arms wrapped around her, holding her tight, keeping her warm.

"Thank you," she whispered.

He no sooner shoved the image aside than the alluring scent of roses wafted to his senses. "Has Jane done something that would make you question her?" he ground out, pulling the front of his coat together. He held it closed, peering deep into her eyes where he was almost sure that unshed tears shimmered.

She nestled her cheek against his butter-soft leather collar, hesitating as she swept her glistening gaze across the moonlit field. "No," she finally said, shuddering as she moved her focus to him. "Jane's grieving the loss of her only brother. I'm sure it can't be easy for her to have me taking over the place."

"Yeah, I have no doubt that it's been hard for her—*and* you." When her chin quivered faintly, he moved a little closer to offer comfort but not knowing how.

He wanted to bring her warmth. He wanted to speak words of hope and encouragement to lift her spirits. And he wanted to make sure that she was happy and safe and comforted. When she peered up at him, her gaze so honest and confused and hurt, it was all he could do not to draw her into his arms. He shoved his hands into his pockets, knowing that if he held her again, he might never be able to quell the growing desire in his heart for Hope.

For once, Hope disregarded her mother's strict proprietary guidelines as to comportment and hugged her arms to her chest beneath Aaron's warm coat, desperately clinging to the few strands of dignity she had left. She'd been on the verge of tears all day. First, she'd been profoundly moved by Aaron's grief this morning and had recognized that any feelings growing inside her heart for him would never blossom. He was far too in love with Ellie and her memory. And it was rightly so, which was why Hope had felt compelled to clear the tangle of weeds and dead grass from the graveside, leaving two posies of spring blossoms as a token of her heartfelt sympathy.

And then this evening at play rehearsal, Aaron had been

noticeably edgy, as though he was uncomfortable in his own skin. But tonight, when she'd assumed that he'd fed Jane the stallion story, Hope had ricocheted between tears and red-hot anger.

"I don't know why Paul didn't mention anything to you or anyone else about my arrival. I must believe that he was eager for our marriage. He'd said so many times in his letters." She quietly sniffed, struggling to swallow the thick emotion lodged in her throat.

"I'm sure he was looking forward to it. And he never made a flippant decision. Paul was a good and honest man."

"He was, wasn't he?" she sputtered as she peered at him, frantic to believe that with all of her being. Because ever since she'd discovered that Paul had kept her presence in his life a secret, she'd been plagued with shame and doubt. What if Paul wasn't really the man he'd presented himself to be? Just like Jonas?

"Are you all right?" Aaron settled his hands on her arms. The way his gaze seeped deep into her soul was a threat to her determination to stay strong. "I know this hasn't been easy on you. None of it has."

It had been absolutely terrible—and completely wonderful at the same time.

But she couldn't let him know just how often she questioned herself as to whether she could handle the gift Paul had deeded her. The end of summer was fast approaching, and she'd need to make a decision about the farm. She had to wonder if Paul questioned whether she would be able to handle things. Maybe that was why he'd put that stipulation in the deed.

"It hasn't been that bad. Although, were I deathly afraid of animals like my mother, matters could be far worse," she said on an weak chuckle.

He shook his head. "There's more to you than meets the eye, Hope. Maybe someday I'll find out what it is that drives you."

She couldn't let him know how she'd been hurt by Paul and also by Jonas or how often she'd found herself thinking of Aaron, longing for a good, trustworthy, loyal man like him to care for. But she refused to play on his sympathies or garner his comfort or kindness based on his fiercely noble sense of obligation or pity.

She took a step away from him yet pulled his coat in a warm embrace around her, the manly rugged scent permeating the fibers, wholly Aaron. "I should probably get home. Theodore will wonder where I am."

"We wouldn't want to worry Theodore, now, would we?" He gave her a pulse-pounding grin, then nodded toward the wagon. "Come on, I'll give you a ride the rest of the way."

When she approached the wagon and he eased his large hands around her middle to lift her to the seat, a fluttering stirred the base of her stomach. And when he took his place beside her, she had to resist the urge to nestle closer to his warmth, to his care, to the protective power of his strong arms.

Even though he possessed a deep, unending love for his late wife, Hope couldn't seem to stop caring for Aaron.

Chapter Fourteen

"So, tell me Aaron, how's Hope doing?" Zach folded his arms at his chest and gave Aaron a goading wink.

Wariness had crawled up Aaron's spine from the moment Ben and Zach had joined Joseph and him at the wood shop this afternoon. He could ward off Joseph's comments here and there about Hope, and he could fend off Ben's overt remarks, too, but the three of them together...

He braced himself. "What do you mean how's Hope doing?" Aaron pinned his focus to the long pine board he was measuring on the workbench. "She's getting along just fine, as far as I know."

"Well, I would hope that you'd know." Zach leaned against the workbench, hooking one foot over the other. "You're out there for several hours every day."

He eyed Zach. "I don't always see her when I'm there, you know?"

"Why? Are you avoiding her?" Zach prodded.

Ben approached and dipped his head toward Aaron's ear. "Just so you know, you've measured that five times already."

Aaron fisted his hands. "That's because you three are distracting me." He gave his oldest brother an impatient scowl. "You know I don't work as well when I'm distracted."

"Excuse me, but you never answered the question." Zach braced his hands on the workbench and jumped up to sit down right next to where Aaron was working. "Are you avoiding her?"

"No. I'm busy while I'm there, trying to make sure all of the chores get done."

"Well, you're certainly there enough to know," Joseph added with a half chuckle.

Making a dark mark where he needed to cut the wood, he stuffed the stubby piece of lead into his work apron. "Look, Joseph, I told you from the start that if it's too much for me to be gone from here—"

"I wasn't implying that." Joseph set his sandpaper on the sideboard he'd been sanding in the work area and approached the workbench, his steps in this familiar room as sure as if he could see. "Listen, you more than covered for me last summer after my accident. We've had a good system going, and it's been working just fine. You don't need to worry."

"I know you've said that numerous times, but I have to wonder if you've been feeling the pinch and you're just too prideful to say so."

"I'll admit that every once in a while I'd rather keep my mouth shut than to admit I need help." He raked a hand through his hair. "But this isn't one of those times."

Aaron studied him for a moment. "I could always work out something else to pick up the slack either here or on the farm."

"Like what?" Ben inquired, giving Aaron one of his big brother looks.

"I don't know. I suppose I'd finally have to give my consent to one of those green-around-the-edges farmhands

Hope would like to hire." Staring at the pine board in front of him, he drew his hands into fists. "But not one of them is acceptable."

"Not one?" Joseph questioned.

"If you could see the hungry look in their eyes when they see her, you'd know exactly what I mean." Aaron felt his blood churning and his hackles rise just thinking about it.

"So, who would you hire, then?" Joseph ran a hand over the workbench to make sure nothing was in his way then jumped up to sit next to Zach.

"I'm telling you, this is a classic damsel-in-distress scenario," Zach noted, elbowing Joseph in the ribs. "Any man would spring at the chance to clad himself in a suit of armor and ride in on a white horse to help the lovely Hope."

"Not just any man will do," Aaron ground out, feeling trapped by his own words. He would've wiped the grins from their faces had he been a lesser man. Instead he pulled in a steadying breath. "Zach, your head is in the clouds or the books or something." He unfurled his fists. "You need to get yourself a wife so that you can lavish all of that romantic whatnot on her."

Joseph knocked the Stetson off Zach's head and ruffled his hair. "I agree."

"Well, I'll just go to the mercantile today on my way home, then, and pick one up." Shoving Joseph's hand away, Zach leaned back for his hat and jammed it back on his head. "How does that sound, boys?"

"I'm sure Mrs. Duncan would be more than happy to help you out." Aaron grinned, remembering how many times the woman had tried to sell him on some young woman or another. "In fact, I think her niece is still here from Longmont."

"She's a looker, that one. Nice teeth. Hearty as an ox," Joseph teased, having been the recipient of Mrs. Duncan's good-hearted attempts more than a handful of times.

Zach catapulted off the bench, the heels of his boots hammering the hardwood floor. "Gentlemen, as you and I well know, a good woman is hard to find." He braced a hand on Aaron's shoulder. "That's why I think that Aaron, here, needs to stop long enough to look at what is right under his nose."

He'd looked, all right. And it had been all he could do to stop his thoughts from running straight to—

"Hope," Ben said. "She's a good woman."

Aaron stared at the pine board, scrambling to keep hold of the list of reasons why he couldn't love again. "But I love Ellie."

"And Ellie's gone." When Joseph reached out and found Aaron's arm, Aaron instantly recalled how much Joseph's presence and comforting touch had meant that morning when they'd discovered Ellie's body lying on Jeremiah's grave. "And your life has to move on."

"You were a great husband to Ellie." Ben's voice was low.

"The best," Zach added.

"But at some point you have to look to the future." Ben caught Aaron's gaze and held it firm.

Swallowing hard, he reminded himself that his brothers had only his best in mind. Even now, they probably thought that they'd put his well-being first. But their hearts were fully intact, not half torn by death's grip. "When I stood at the altar, I made a vow to love her and keep her—"

"Until death do you part," Ben uttered, his eyebrows raised. "I'm not saying that this should be easy for you. I would never say that. But I do think that you need to give this some thought, for yourself and for Ellie."

"And for Hope." Joseph gave his shoulder a brief squeeze. "Do you honestly think that Ellie would've wanted you grieving and alone for the rest of your life?"

"I don't know." Or did he? "We talked about this once, and we both agreed that if anything happened to the other, we'd move on. Marry."

"See?" Zach encouraged. "That's what I'm talking about."

"But we said that believing that nothing bad would happen," Aaron argued.

"What about you?" Zach probed, folding the fingers on one hand down and emitting loud popping sounds. "If you'd been the one to go, would you have wanted Ellie to be alone for the rest of her days?"

Grasping the edge of the workbench, Aaron resisted the urge to leave the building. He couldn't think. He couldn't speak. He could barely even force the next breath from his lungs as the seriousness of his brothers' words hung over him, like some force to be reckoned with.

"Just think about it," Ben half pleaded. "Please."

"Hope is an amazing woman, with more determination and strength than most women I've met." Zach folded his muscular arms at his chest.

"Whether you've accepted it or not, there's something between the two of you." Joseph set his unseeing gaze directly on Aaron. "The sparking tension is so real I can almost see it."

"Callie and I have noticed it, too," Ben agreed.

"What is up with you guys?" Prying himself from his brothers' intense attention, he stalked over to where Joseph kept a stash of jerky for his Newfoundland dog, Boone. "Here I am, just working away, happy as you please—"

he unscrewed the jar and popped a chunk into his mouth. "And then the three of you corner me like a pack of hungry wolves."

The air hung thick with the charged remnants of a rainstorm and even thicker with an eerie silence as Aaron tethered his horse near the barn. Most mornings Hope would poke her head out from the doorway to greet him in that hopelessly optimistic way of hers, but this morning she was nowhere in sight.

For four weeks she'd been doing chores and getting to know her way around the farm, but still he worried—a lot. And since he couldn't be there all day, every day, he found himself praying for her protection, that God would keep her safe. He'd probably gone overboard in his concern and worry, but having lost Ellie because he'd nodded off long enough that she'd made her way out to Jeremiah's grave, he couldn't seem to quell the incessant need to make sure that he had this situation well under control. Ben tried to comfort him with the fact that Ellie's profuse bleeding would have happened, regardless, but still Aaron felt responsible.

His heart stomped inside his chest as he peered in the corral, bracing himself for a horrific sight. The idea that Hope might've been trampled by the cattle she'd grown to love whipped through his mind with brutal force as he scanned the area where the herd huddled together as though a storm was brewing over the horizon. Seeing no sign of Hope there, he released the breath he'd been holding. He strode toward the barn entrance, trying to convince himself that Hope was just fine, yet uneasiness nipped at his heels.

"Hope," he called, wondering if maybe she hadn't heard him ride into the yard.

When a muffled groan from beyond the barn filtered to his hearing, chills snaked down his spine. He took off in that direction, the hair at the back of his neck standing on end as he rounded the barn. His stomach clenched with dread as he caught sight of Hope huddled against the henhouse, clothed in just her nightgown and a robe, her long hair a tousle of wayward strands, her bare toes peeking out from beneath her gown, a despondent expression blanketing her face as she hugged a chicken to her chest.

"Darlin', what happened?" Slowing to a stop, he hunkered down in front of her, holding her face in his hands. His throat knotted tight at the gruesome sight of chicken feathers and blood strewn from inside the henhouse to the outdoors.

When he spotted several large doglike, paw prints indented in the moist ground, he had his answer. Wolves. They'd feasted on Hope's beloved birds and left only one survivor.

"Are you all right?" he gently prodded, concerned with the cool, clammy feel of her face. Shrugging out of his coat, he wrapped it around her shoulders.

She hugged the quaking chestnut-colored hen to her chest. She inched her glassy-eyed, shock-filled gaze to his. "They were killed," she whispered, her voice raspy with emotion. "Killed, Aaron. It must have been just horrible for them."

"Aw...Hope. I'm so sorry. I know how attached you've become to them." Bracing a hand on her shoulder, he smoothed errant strands of hair from her face as he recalled the sweet and kindhearted way he'd seen her tend her little flock. "How long have you been out here like this?"

"I—I don't know. I heard them calling for me early—" her red-rimmed eyes filled with tears and pain "—and I heard some yelping. I just didn't get out here fast enough."

With the pad of his thumb, he brushed a glistening tear from her cold tear-dampened cheek. "Don't blame yourself, honey."

"But they're all dead." She slid a horrified gaze over what was left of her chickens. She had wrapped a side of her thick cream-colored robe around the lone survivor. "Everyone, except sweet little da Vinci." The way Hope dragged in a fractured breath just then, and the way her eyes spilled over with pooled tears as she gave a muffled sob, nearly broke Aaron's heart. "Do you know that they got my handsome rooster, Michelangelo, too?"

Out of the corner of his eye, Aaron caught a glimpse of what was left of the big chestnut-colored rooster, his stomach clenching with the distinct scent of slaughtered chickens. Compassion welled within his heart for Hope as he glanced at the coop, searching for signs of where they'd forced an entry. He'd never seen a woman become so fond of animals—let alone farm animals.

"I was afraid of that when I saw you holding just this one." He stroked the hen's head poking out from the robe then turned and eased down next to Hope. "I'm really sorry this happened. I know how much you enjoyed all of them." Wrapping an arm around her shoulders, he pulled her to his side, deeply moved by the way her whole body trembled with raw emotion. "Don't cry, darlin'," he soothed, desperate to ease her pain. "It's going to be all right."

"I sh-should've gotten out here s-sooner to protect them." She drew the chicken closer as a mooing sound came from the corral on the other side of the barn. "They count on me to be their g-guardian and their protector."

She was something...Hope. Here she was, the model of

elegance and propriety, her dark hair tousled in a tempting mess, and her feminine curves hurriedly clad in a night-gown and robe, half of which she'd pulled up to wrap around a chicken. His heart swelled with pride—pride and respect, and something else he wasn't sure he wanted to look at closely enough to identify.

Was it deep, growing affection?

Was it love?

His brothers' words, that he should take the time to notice what is under his nose, came rushing into his thoughts, begging for his attention. It was not that he hadn't paid their words any mind. For the past five days, he'd done nothing but consider their sentiments. All he'd been able to conclude is that Hope, though beautiful and spritely and witty and kind and determined, wasn't Ellie.

That obvious revelation had given him no peace or solace. In fact, it'd made his dilemma even more complicated.

Swallowing hard, he peered down at the heartbroken woman sheltered in his arm. He felt desperate to bring her some solace. "Wolves are cunning and very crafty, Hope. This sort of thing can happen so fast that most of the time you only get a shot at the bandits' backsides." He ran his forefinger over the hen's head, noticing the way it had stopped quaking in Hope's arms. "This one's a survivor, though, isn't she?"

Hope gave a solemn nod. She sniffled as the goats bleated from their pen. "I'm sure that da Vinci is traumatized after seeing the others." Her face instantly crumpled on another silent sob.

"Shh. It's all right, Hope." Aaron could barely swallow past the thick lump clogging his throat. He rested his cheek on her head, praying that she would find a thread of comfort in all of this. She'd been so stalwart these past four weeks. "Maybe we can purchase some more chickens so she won't be lonely. How's that sound?"

Dabbing at her tears with her nightgown's lace-edged sleeve, she peered up at him as though he'd just booked passage overseas on some fancy cruise liner. "That is so very kind of you, Aaron. I'm certain that she will be grateful." She trailed a fingertip over the hen's head. "Aaron."

"What is it?"

She sniffled. "What happened here is so very distressing. It's made me question whether I'm capable of doing this any longer."

He angled his focus down at her, touched by the thoughtful way she made sure the hen was covered, even at her own expense. Her bare feet and slender ankles stuck out from beneath her bed clothes. Swallowing hard, he shoved his focus to the hen. "Of doing what?"

"I've tried to do my best on this farm, but seeing all of this slaughter—" she leaned forward slightly and peered at the blatant evidence "—I wonder if I've taken on too much."

He eased her head to his shoulder, slipping his fingers over her silken strands of hair, trying not to notice how his heart felt so buoyant at being able to protect and care for a woman like this again. "That's nothing that can't be fixed, Hope. If you're feeling up to your ears in chores, well then, I'll just make a point to get over here more often." He angled his gaze down at her. "See? There's nothing that we can't deal with."

We?

That miniscule two-lettered word thundered through his mind and heart. When had he started thinking of Hope and him as *we?* True, he desired to see her every waking moment and would do whatever he could to help her and take care of her. But he'd also do whatever it took to avoid being near Hope because his growing feelings for her continued to chip away at his vows to Ellie.

His heart was torn, and at times the back and forth sway was almost dizzying.

She gave her head an adamant shake. "It's not that. As it is, you're already spending too much time away from your own responsibilities to assist me." She levered herself up to standing and turned to stare down at him. "It's just that there are lives depending on me on the farm. I've let them down, and I feel positively horrible about that."

He pushed himself up as she peered at the grisly carnage. "Don't make this harder on yourself," he implored, grasping her hand and coaxing her attention toward him. "You've done the best you can. No one can ask any more of you than what you're already doing."

"Well, apparently my best wasn't good enough." Pain darkened her normally bright and cheer-filled gaze. "Maybe Paul knew all along that this would never work."

"If that was true then I doubt he would've deeded the farm to you in the first place." He gave her a slow nod. "Farming and ranching are not easy ways of life, Hope. Ask anyone in these parts. Wolf and mountain lion attacks…these kinds of thing happen, especially living out here in the West." When a loud meow cut through the early morning, he glanced toward the house to see Hope's tabby kitten hanging by all fours on the black screen door, meowing with all its might. A half grin tipped his mouth. "Looks like someone's calling for you."

"He's probably afraid." She pivoted to face her kitten. "Don't be afraid, sweetie. I'll be there in a little bit," she called, waving to the kitten. Sighing, she adjusted her robe around the chicken.

Aaron had to bite his cheek to keep from chuckling at the completely innocent and kindhearted way Hope had with the animals—all of them—which is why he couldn't imagine her giving up now. "All farmers face risks, Hope, but they get through it. Take Zach, for instance. Just this past winter he lost a half dozen head of cattle to mountain lions and wolves."

She shuddered as she shifted her wary focus toward the rugged terrain to the west. The sense of confidence he'd seen in her these past weeks had seemed to dissipate in the past few minutes, and that near broke his heart. He'd do everything he could to see it return.

"Even with several ranch hands keeping an eye on things that kind of thing can happen. Livestock are easy prey for a hungry or lazy predator." He tenderly grasped her chin and nudged her gaze to meet his. "Just like your chickens were easy prey for a pack of wolves. That's why you can't blame yourself."

"That may be true, but look at all that has happened," she argued, adjusting her hold on the hen. "First the goats escaped and then Paul's horse and now this…"

"You can fence them in from the earth to the moon," he reasoned. "But when you figure wild animals into the mix, there's no guarantee."

She gave her head a defeated shake. "Maybe I'm making mistakes. Like Jane said."

"Don't listen to Jane." Seeing her desperation and misplaced guilt, he grasped her upper arms and pulled her to himself but not so far as to squash her one remaining chicken.

He could feel Hope tremble and wanted nothing more than to ease her mind and heart. He wanted to put that smile he found himself craving, back on her face. To see that stubborn tilt to her chin that tugged at his heart in a way he'd least expected.

In spite of the seemingly content hen sandwiched between them, she felt so right in his arms. To hold her and comfort her and support her when she needed it most felt so right.

"Aaron?"

"Yeah," he answered, drinking in the moment.

"The henhouse door..." She peeked around his arm at the door then nestled against his chest, filling him with a wonderful sense of purpose. "It was open when I got out here."

He swallowed hard. An open henhouse door was a careless way to lose livestock.

Closing his eyes briefly, he tried to remove any trace of disappointment from his face before Hope noticed. No doubt, the latch was sturdy. There was no way the thieving wolves could breach the entrance. He wanted to believe that she'd been thorough. He'd gained so much respect for Hope and her resolve to take on this mountainous task, but maybe she was missing a few things here and there.

He'd have to spend even more time over here, making sure that nothing slipped through the cracks, because the idea that she might give up and leave was almost more than he could bear.

When Aaron paused for a long moment, Hope pulled back to look at him, confused at his sudden silence. He'd expressed hints of misgivings after the goats and the stallion had escaped, but had his doubt grown to equal that of Jane's?

He slid his hands from her arms, and she felt an almost immediate sense of loss.

"The safety of my animals is first and foremost." She shielded da Vinci's eyes from the carnage as she faced the henhouse and mentally traipsed over the chores she'd done last night. "I distinctly remember latching the henhouse door—I've been especially mindful of doing so since you mentioned something the other day about wolves being in the area. I honestly don't know how that door was opened."

He crossed over to the door and examined it, opening and shutting it several times. "It hasn't been tampered with. And there's no other sign of forced entry. No claw marks. Nothing."

Self-doubt crept from her toes to her head like a wild and tangling vine. She couldn't return to Boston, but did she possess the skill needed to stay on here? Until Aaron would finally agree to an acceptable farmhand candidate, she would have to remain diligent. She had fortitude and determination, but when it came to experience, she was clearly lacking. The possibility of another life perishing under her care made her heart ache so much that it physically hurt.

It hurt almost as much as the way she ached for Aaron's caring and gentle touch again. For a brief and magnificent moment when he'd wrapped his strong arms around her, she'd felt that anything was possible and that she could endure any hardship as long as he was by her side.

But that was a fantasy, a flitting dream that passed by just out of her reach, like the downy chicken feather that wafted out and on, carried away on the morning breeze.

Chapter Fifteen

Hope felt alive with purpose as she exited the dress-maker's shop and breathed in the morning air, laden with the scents of summer. In spite of the hardships she'd faced, she loved it here.

There were few things in life she regretted.

Even fewer things she felt one-hundred percent, beyond a shadow-of-a-doubt, absolutely positive about—like moving to Boulder.

She'd had her reservations before she'd arrived here but hadn't allowed a few strands of uncertainty to keep her from moving forward. But last week, after those awful wolves had slaughtered all but one of her chickens, uncertainty had nearly shredded her assurance. Seeing beyond their gruesome death had brought her to her knees.

Situating her twine-tied package of floral cotton fabric she'd just purchased for a play costume, she recalled how her frantic prayers had not been so neatly packaged. On several occasions over the past few days, she'd pleaded for God's strength and help and for some kind of confirmation that staying on here would be the right decision. In a profoundly subtle yet impacting way, peace had filled her heart, and she just knew that she was right in the very center of her destiny.

Once she had her bearings about her and had dragged her good sense and expectant attitude into place again and after she'd walked about on the farm, taking in the tender shoots poking through her garden and field soil and after she'd visited all of the animals, marveling in God's beautiful handiwork, she'd felt even more fortified in her decision.

The warm reassurance she'd found in Aaron's arms after her chickens had been killed had stayed with her for several days. His strength had made up for her weakness. His protective ways had soothed her uncertainty. And his tenderness had settled into the deepest crevices of her heart, areas of hurt she hadn't been aware existed.

With a contented sigh, she smoothed a hand over her violet-colored dress and drew her French-made shawl up over her shoulders as she walked down the boardwalk back to the mercantile to meet up with Aaron. She'd joined him for a supply run this morning, grateful for the chance to spruce up for a trip to town. She'd caught Aaron's admiring gaze earlier, the way his eyes had grown deep and dark and fascinating, as though he was seeing her for the first time. And she'd been startled by his compliment, that she *took his breath away.* With the sweet memory of his words, and with the way the late June sun blazed in the cerulean sky, she couldn't help but smile.

"There you are." Katie's voice lilted into her musings. She and Joseph were standing outside the mercantile with Aaron, Sam Garnett, a native of Boulder and Julia, who Hope was convinced, was Sam's soon-to-be wife. Sam had arrived in Boulder just a week ago to set up a law office, and the townspeople were thrilled to have their very own Samuel Garnett back to practice law.

And Julia…she was just plain thrilled to have her very own Samuel Garnett.

"I wasn't expecting to see all of you here." She stepped up to the platform and exchanged hugs with Katie and Julia.

"I'm so glad we ran into you." Katie held Hope at arms' length then backed up to stand in front of Joseph. "We have something to tell you. All of you."

"So, it's something I can be privy to?" Sam asked, nudging Joseph's arm.

Joseph's smile deepened as he anchored his cane in the crook of his arm. "Of course you can hear this. You're like a brother."

"That's for sure." Removing his hat, Aaron winked Hope's way, his playful demeanor sending a tremor of delight from Hope's stomach all the way to her toes. "Growing up, I think he ate supper out at our place more often than not. Mama always made sure he got two pieces of dessert—said she wanted to keep him coming back."

"It worked, didn't it?" Sam smiled as he tucked Julia's arm in his in a beautiful and proper claim.

Hope might never know that kind of unabashed show of affection and desire, though she likely would never stop wanting as much. To have a man be so forthright in his intentions would go a long way to bolstering her wilting confidence in that area. Jonas's reserved and distant approach to their relationship—especially after her family's misfortune—had cut a wide rut in her heart she hadn't even realized was there until she'd witnessed such a beautiful contrast.

"So, what's the news?" Aaron puffed his chest out and braced his hands at his waist. "Are you expecting a big delivery at the shop that you haven't told me about? Building another addition?"

Joseph wrapped his arms around Katie and pressed a kiss to her head. "We're expecting a delivery all right."

Aaron glanced off toward the street, nodding to a passerby. "Well then, it's a good thing we have—"

"Katie and I...we're expecting a baby." Joseph rested his hands at Katie's waist.

Hope gasped. "That's wonderful."

"You're what?" Aaron's brow creased.

"It most certainly is wonderful," Julia exclaimed, peppering the moment with delicate applause.

"How soon?" Hope asked.

"Probably right before Thanksgiving." Katie smiled up at Joseph as he trailed the back of his hand over her cheek. "At least that's what we think."

"Katie, I'm so delighted for you." Tears stung Hope's eyes. "And you, too, Joseph. You're going to make wonderful parents."

"That's great news, Joe-boy." Sam clasped Joseph's shoulder. "I'm glad I'll be around to celebrate with you and to see your first little one grow up."

Joseph focused his unseeing gaze on Sam. "You can even be Uncle Sam if you'd like."

"I'd be honored," Sam replied in a low voice as he moved his attentive gaze to Julia. "And here I thought that, being an only child, I'd never get to be an uncle."

"Glad to oblige you, my friend." After a hearty handshake, Joseph grasped Katie's shoulders.

When Hope glanced at Aaron, his face ashen and his eyes filled with trepidation, her delight dissolved in an instant.

His throat visibly convulsed as he swallowed. His jaw tensed. When that tormented expression she'd observed twice before, clouded his brilliant blue eyes, she could only guess that visions of Ellie giving birth to a stillborn baby barraged his mind.

"Have you been to see Ben yet?" Aaron's voice had grown tense. "Does he think you should be out and about? I mean, shouldn't you be lying in bed and resting?"

Katie's elation had faded. "We visited with Ben just yesterday," she gently responded.

Joseph stepped over to stand beside Aaron, bracing a hand on his shoulder in a gesture of compassion that brought tears to Hope's eyes. "You don't need to worry. All right? He says that things are fine."

Aaron hauled in a long shaky breath. "Well, you need to make sure you take good care of yourself." When he glanced at Katie, moisture rimmed his eyes. "Do you hear me?"

Katie gave several quick nods, her brow pinched as she set quivering fingers to her lips.

"I'll make sure she's well rested," Joseph assured.

"I'll do everything I can at work so that you can be home with Katie as much as possible." Aaron shifted on the platform.

Guilt seeped into Hope's heart knowing just how busy Aaron had been between assisting her, his own job and then the play. As it was, he could hardly have a moment of time to himself.

"You're already busy enough." Joseph tapped the end of his cane against the wood planks. "Besides, I've been thinking about hiring on help."

Aaron flipped his concern-filled focus to Katie again. "Any sign of pain and you'll lie down. Promise me?"

"Of course." Her eyes welled with tears as she crossed to Aaron and wrapped her arms around his chest. "I'll be very careful. I promise."

"I've already lost Ellie and my baby boy. I don't want

to lose my sister-in-law, too." Bowing his head for a long and silent moment, he shrugged out of Katie's arms, then eased over to the parcel-stacked wagon parked alongside the loading dock. He pivoted to face them, his expression wrought with struggle. "Listen, I'm sorry that I dampened what should've been a joyful moment for you, Katie. Joseph."

Joseph shook his head. "Don't apologize."

"We understand," Katie added, glancing over her shoulder at Hope. "He needs you right now," she whispered. "He just doesn't know it."

Hope grappled for her meaning. How could Aaron need her when he mourned his wife? At times he almost seemed offended by Hope's company, as though her presence complicated his life.

"You care, Aaron. There's no shame in that. Do you hear?" Joseph held his cane out and moved toward Aaron as Julia and Sam stepped aside for him to pass.

Tears pooled in Hope's eyes, seeing the torment that Aaron faced and witnessing the very sensitive way his family dealt with his struggle. His loss had been great. His pain had been unfathomable. She could be a friend, but as much as she felt herself being drawn to him, and sometimes even by him, she doubted that there would ever be a place in his heart for another.

When he climbed into the wagon from the dock, Hope made her way over to him, took his outstretched hand and stepped into the sturdy wagon. She hugged her parcel to her chest as a flourish of emotions washed over his face—pain, fear, anger, frustration and something else she couldn't quite identify.

"Just don't be hard on yourself about what happened here." Joseph came to a stop at the edge of the platform.

"You've been through a lot. I'm sure it's natural to fear the same fate for those close to you."

"I'm thrilled for you both. Really. It's just that—" when a wagon clattered by, Aaron paused "—I'm sorry that I couldn't just ignore my fears and be happy for you." Releasing the brake, he gave the reins a gentle slap, guiding his team of horses through Boulder's busy street.

They'd almost reached her farm when he finally spoke again. "I owe you an apology. I don't know what came over me back there."

Her chest tightened at the way he worked so hard to be strong and unaffected. "Remembering...facing your fears...grieving...that's what came over you. And it's perfectly all right." She reached over and gave his hand a brief squeeze, feeling her heart slipping even closer to loving this man. "Really."

He pulled his team into her yard and set the brake, his hand tingling from her touch, his blood churning at her nearness. He'd been pummeled by fear and sorrow just minutes ago, but in an instant, he'd been wholly distracted by Hope, her sweet presence and the look of affection in her eyes. She was so caring and thoughtful and understanding in the face of his struggle that sometimes he didn't feel worthy of her warm companionship.

Swinging down to the ground, he crossed to Hope's side. His jaw tensed as he met the almost timid look in her eyes. "Again, I'm sorry. I didn't mean to make you uncomfortable back there."

"I didn't feel uncomfortable." She hugged her twine-bound package to her chest.

"I sure didn't expect news like that," he said, heaving a sigh.

"The baby?"

Nodding, he continued. "It near buried me six feet under. All I could do was clamor for something—*anything*—to set my world right again. I don't know if I could endure what happened to Ellie and Jeremiah, again. All I want is some kind of assurance that everything's going to be all right."

"I wish I could give that to you." Hope's voice was a mere whisper. Her soft gaze warmed his cold heart.

When he lifted her down, his pulse pounded at her nearness. He could've drawn her into an embrace right then and there, if he'd let himself. But what would that mean for him? For her? His arms ached for Hope. Was his heart just as eager?

Glancing toward the fence line, he nodded at where the cattle nudged their way to front and center to gawk at Hope. "Looks like you have a welcoming committee."

The way she smiled, first at him then over at the cattle in such an attentive considerate way coaxed a grin to his mouth. "They're such beautiful creatures."

"I suppose they're cute, at times. But beautiful? *You* are beautiful." The heartfelt compliment had slipped right out of his mouth.

Her face glistened with pure pleasure. That endearing look—that vulnerable, sweet, rewarding look—made him long to put that expression on her face again and again and again.

He grasped for solid ground, feeling himself losing his footing in good sense. "They must trust you. That's for sure," he said, struggling to shift his focus.

"I hope so. In fact, I'm sure that I could take most of the chores from you now." She fingered the twine. "That way you can be at the shop more often now that Katie's with child."

"I don't want you to feel any pressure or guilt for my time spent here, Hope. Do you hear?"

"But you want to ease Joseph's load now since—"

"I do. And I wish that I could be both places all of the time, but I can't," he admitted as a low moo wafted their way. He spanned the farmyard, noting again how the animals seemed as if drawn to Hope, just as he was drawn.

"You care, Aaron. Like Joseph said, there's no shame in that." Raising her hand, she added, "And before you go deflecting his praise, you must remember that he's honest. Just like you." Her voice, like the rest of her, was cloaked in quiet strength. Her eyelashes fluttered down over her eyes, beckoning him in a way she was unaware. Peering up at him, her gaze grew earnest and tender and vulnerable, and so compelling that he couldn't fight his attraction. "Your loss is very real, but I believe that if you'd ask God for peace, it would help. I know it did for me after the wolf attack."

"I'll try." He stared deep into her eyes and raised a hand to trace the gentle slope of her hairline. "You have a way of getting to my heart. Do you know that?"

She shook her head. Swallowed.

Trailing his fingertips to her cheek, it seemed that the closer he was to her, the further he was from grief's clutch. The seconds stretched before him, as if heralding a brand-new horizon.

"Honestly, Hope," he ground out, his pulse ripping through his veins. "If you asked me to scale every single mountain in the Rocky range right now, I would."

Whisper light, he slid his fingers to the base of her slender throat where her pulse raced beneath his fingertips, sending every one of his nerve endings humming to life.

He exhaled a breath he hadn't even realized he'd been holding. As much as he'd tried to ignore his attraction to her, he couldn't. Every waking and sleeping moment was filled with thoughts of Hope. Quaking in spite of himself, he took her package and laid it in the wagon. Grasped her slender hands in his. If he was ever going to move forward in his life, she was the one he wanted at his side, right?

Hope.

She was nothing like he'd expected and everything he never thought he'd wanted, yet he was undeniably moved and affected by her nearness and the steady, uncompromising sparkle of her charm and gentle ways. Even minutes ago, when he'd found himself deep in the face of his greatest fear, he'd longed for her touch, the caring way she'd look at him and the comfort he found in her sweet voice. Had God dropped her into his life? Was she his very own golden lifeline out of grief and pain? When he'd let his guard down and enjoy her for the compelling, caring, beautiful woman she was, he'd felt more alive and free than he had in many, many months.

"There's not a day that goes by where I don't worry about you out here by yourself." He smoothed his thumbs over the backs of her fingers, savoring the feel of her satiny skin and remembering how her hands had blistered raw in her resolute attempt to plow.

Her eyes glimmered in the late morning sun as she peered up at him, all innocent and genuine. "You don't need to worry. I'm fine. Like I said, I'm almost certain I can do most of the chores by myself now."

The very thought of not seeing her every day shadowed him like a menacing cloud. Besides, he'd made a promise to watch out for her, to hold on to Hope. "You're not taking into consideration the fact that I *want* to be here."

She studied him, her penetrating gaze seeping into his soul. "You don't trust me?"

"I don't trust God," he admitted, as he shoved his gaze

to the ground where her roly-poly kitten had appeared and was doing figure eights against the hem of her dress. "Another one of your admirers."

She smiled softly and shifted her focus down to her kitten. "Hello, sweetie."

"You do not lack for admirers, Hope." He drew a step closer, his pulse pounding at what the next few seconds held. And what it would mean for him. What it could mean to the vows he'd viciously clung to. "Somewhere along the line I'm going to have to find it in myself to trust God again with the lives of those I care about." He swallowed hard, sliding his hungry gaze from her brilliant eyes, to her perfect little nose, to her full lips. "At least if I ever hope to know what it's like to love again."

Her gaze grew wide then. Her lips parted on a quiet sigh. Her breathing grew as shallow as his, the sweet smell of her breath fanning over him, stoking the dim embers in the core of his being.

He worked his hands up to her arms, his chest pounding, his ears whooshing with every single beat of his heart. His hands trembled as he moved them to her shoulders, then to her neckline, where tendrils of her silky hair whispered over his knuckles sending radiating bolts straight through to his feet, fastening his boots in place. Cradling her head in his hands, his heart swelled at the slow and innate way she yielded to his touch.

He was close enough to hear the unbridled beat of her heart and near enough to feel the way her body quivered at his touch. He ached with the desire to cherish her and make her feel every bit as alive as she made him feel.

Closing his eyes, he lowered his head. When he brushed his lips over hers, a shudder of satisfaction ricocheted through his body, knocking his world off-kilter. He settled his mouth over her velvety lips in a tender and solid

Chapter Sixteen

For the past four hours since Hope had melted to Aaron's touch and had carelessly indulged herself in his tender kiss, she'd been grappling for any thread of control she could find. His restrained emotions, the way his heart had hammered inside his chest and the cherishing way he'd held her had impacted her far more than she wanted to admit.

Grasping the edge of the stage, she vaguely listened as Ben made some last-minute rehearsal notes, with the play performance being only three nights away. She chided herself for being so vulnerable, so helplessly malleable to Aaron's touch. She'd been hurt once by Jonas. How could she be so careless as to set herself up for the same with Aaron? He likely had no idea the strength of her attraction and affection. As much as she'd tried, she could not deny that she wanted to be cared for, nurtured, loved.

But finding those things with Aaron was impossible. If she had any hope of making a life for herself here in Boulder, she'd have to disregard her feelings for him. He had his vows to his wife to consider. And although nearly seven weeks had passed since he'd made his promise to Paul, he still felt compelled to watch out for Hope and take care of her based on that honor-bound obligatory vow.

Well, she couldn't bear the idea of being some man's obligation. No matter how noble he was, how upright, how well-intentioned.

She'd felt angry, hurt, guilty…and grateful.

Torn by so many emotions, she tucked her hands beneath her legs and stared down at her booted feet dangling from the edge of the stage. She was barely aware of the other cast members around her as images of Aaron plowing for many laborious hours slammed into her mind, bringing with it instant remorse. For seven weeks he'd arrived at the crack of dawn, working tirelessly and without complaint. She couldn't have managed those first weeks without him, but in light of the deep distress he'd expressed for Katie's condition, she wasn't about to let him continue.

He had his carpentry job to do, and he had a wife to grieve. Hope couldn't compete with that—nor did she want to.

The confusion that had crossed his expression when she'd backed out of his embrace had almost compelled her into his arms again. Instead, she'd turned and forced one foot in front of the other, into the house. She'd even refused his ride to play rehearsal and had driven herself this evening.

Lifting her gaze, she focused on the last-minute directions given by Callie and Ben, but it was nearly impossible with Aaron sitting less than ten feet from her. Despite her distress, the spine-tingling effects of his kiss still sizzled from her lips to the core of her stomach. She grazed her fingertips across her mouth, recalling the tender yet certain way he'd pressed his mouth to hers.

Never, in her two years of being engaged to Jonas, had she experienced that kind of earth-shaking feeling. Jonas had given her a chaste kiss on the top of her head every now and then—never when they were out in public. But her knees had certainly never threatened to buckle beneath her as they had under Aaron's touch, his kiss.

He'd made her heart beat wildly. Something had happened in that moment—something beyond a simple kiss. She'd stripped herself of all doubt to believe…and to feel. And what she felt for Aaron was far more than just congenial. It was real, it was big and it was love.

But his sense of duty and his deep devotion to his first love had shadowed over any other desire, no matter how strong. He'd had a weak moment. He had just dealt with some very real fear. His emotions had been like particles of dust blown about in a storm. And she'd been a safe haven, a voice of compassion, and a friend.

When Callie and Ben dismissed the cast members just then, she avoided the gazes of those in the room and made her way out the door and into the gathering darkness. Unbidden, images of Jane hovering near Aaron all evening long, like a spider hoping to catch some prey in her well-spun web, crawled into her thoughts.

Jealous or not, Hope had no claim on Aaron and never would, she conceded as she reached her wagon.

"You look beautiful tonight."

She came to an abrupt halt at the familiar voice. Her breath caught as she peered through the pine boughs next to where she'd parked. "Jonas?"

He stepped out from a long shadow into dusk's waning light, the usual picture of good taste in his fashionable jacket, cravat and winning smile. "Surprised to see me?"

"Shocked seems like a more appropriate term," she uttered.

She gulped. She hugged her script and handbag to her chest in an effort to settle her jarred nerves. She'd not spoken with Jonas since she'd called off the engagement well over a year ago. He'd crossed her mind countless times, but she'd never allowed herself to dwell on him.

"What are you doing here?" She fingered the ivory brooch at the front of her scoopneck bodice.

"I couldn't stay away." His intense gaze met hers in a way that sent a sudden wave of shyness lapping at her composure. "It's been so long. How are you, Hope?"

"H-how did you know I was here?" Glancing back to the town hall, she saw a few others filing out the door, but Aaron wasn't among them. "What brings you all the way out to Colorado?"

He arched his dark eyebrows in that charming way of his that he'd use like some well-tuned instrument. "Like I said, I couldn't stay away." Draping a hand on the rim of her conveyance, he inched his admiring gaze from her toes to her head. "I spoke with your mother a few weeks ago, and she told me where you'd gone off to."

She barely worked a swallow past the harsh lump in her throat. "She did?"

Her mother had all but disowned her when she'd broken off the engagement with Jonas. She'd wept repeatedly, begging for Hope to change her mind and crawl back to Jonas, asking his forgiveness for being so fickle. Hope was far from fickle. But with the financial stress her parents had been under, she'd refused to divulge the real reason she'd called off the engagement. It didn't come as any surprise that her mother would try to finagle some sort of reunion.

"She told me about your fiancé, too, Hope." He braced a hand on her shoulder and peered at her with a tangible amount of compassion and concern—something new for Jonas. "I'm terribly sorry you've had to go through so much. I wish I'd have known sooner."

He'd been every mother's dream for her daughter—dashing, intelligent, witty, chivalrous. But she'd never known him to be compassionate. Had he discovered a new and meaningful side of himself?

"Thank you, Jonas," she responded, oddly moved by his kindness. "I appreciate your concern, but really, I'm getting along fine."

"I'm relieved to hear that." He patted his chest.

She searched for any amount of insincerity in his gaze but came up surprisingly short.

"Well, like I said, you look beautiful. The fresh mountain air must agree with you, Hope, my dear." He draped his arms at his chest and peered off toward where the sun had dipped behind the mountains. "You know, I've never been west of the Mississippi. It's really something out here, isn't it?"

"I love it," she breathed, taking in the horizon's beauty burning all pink and orange and purple behind the mountains.

"You're a rare jewel," he said, his voice low. "You could find something good to say about the hottest, driest desert if you had to. That's one of the many things I love about you." Brief and whisper soft, he skimmed the back of a hand down her cheek. "Hope…the eternal optimist."

"How have you been?" she asked, inching away. She chided herself for the squeezed sound of her words, but she was still dumbstruck by his presence here. He was the last person she'd expected to see.

"Lost without you."

"Oh, come now, Jonas. Surely, it's not been that bad." Out of the corner of her eye she caught sight of Aaron, his intense gaze leveled this way. Even with the dimming light of day she could see the way his brow furrowed, the way he'd drawn his mouth into a grim line.

She appreciated his concern, but he had to stop taking *watching over her* so seriously. Jonas was just an old acquaintance.

"A friend of yours?" Jonas nodded to where Aaron stood, watching like some mountain lion on the prowl.

"Yes, his name is Aaron Drake. He's been assisting me on the farm," she said, wishing that he was so much more.

"I see." Jonas sidestepped, blocking Aaron from view. When his expensive cologne wafted to her senses, she was instantly transported back to her days in Boston, where she'd dine at one of the lovely little eateries with Jonas. "I've missed you, Hope. I've missed you a great deal."

She couldn't exactly say she'd missed him. That would be a lie. Yes, she'd thought about him, but her thoughts had usually been carried on a bed of hurt.

But seeing him now, the concern he showed, the compassion and his attentiveness, she had to wonder if he'd changed.

"After your mother told me what had happened to your fiancé, I couldn't get out here fast enough."

"What do you mean?" she asked, concerned that something awful had transpired and he'd been sent to let her know.

"Oh, it's nothing to worry your pretty little head about." The condescending way he touched his finger to the tip of her nose, irritated her, but she forced herself to appreciate the apparent changes he'd made. "I'll tell you all about it over a nice dinner. Or maybe breakfast?"

She tightened her grip on her handbag, worrying the

beaded tassels to the point that they might fall apart. "Why not now?"

Jonas heaved a sigh, removing his fashionable rounded hat from his head and working his hands around the brim. "Honestly, I'm exhausted from my journey, but I couldn't wait to see you, which is why I tracked you down here."

Jonas had never gone out of his way for anything, and the fact that he had on her account struck her as peculiar. Endearing. "You went to a tremendous effort."

"Not really. Although you, my darling Hope, would have been worth it." He gave her one of those dashingly handsome sideways grins of his that had stopped her in her tracks early on in their relationship. "Really, I just stopped into the mercantile, and Mrs.—"

"Duncan?" She smiled.

"Yes. Mrs. Duncan." He chuckled, settling his hat on his head again. "She offered quite a pallet of information. She told me more than I asked and surely more than I wanted to know. But it was worth my time," he said, grasping her hand. "*You* are worth my time."

"Jonas, I—"

"What do you say?" He twined his smooth, manicured fingers through hers.

Self-consciousness rained down on her—especially when he paused and slid his thumb across one of the work-induced calluses that had formed in the past few weeks.

When he moved his hand up to her elbow, she had to wonder if he was offended by her work-roughened hands. "Why don't you join me for breakfast in the morning? I'm staying at the Boulder Inn. We could eat there if you'd like."

With Jane doing all of the baking there in the mornings, Hope could only imagine what kind of gossip she'd concoct. "I don't think—"

"The accommodations seem nice enough." He dipped his head, catching her focus. "Hopefully the restaurant will be equally satisfactory."

Curious as to whether Aaron was still monitoring the situation, Hope craned her neck to see, unnerved at the sight of him standing just a few feet behind Jonas, his arms folded at his chest. An unattractive scowl was marring his good looks and an undeniable look of warning showed in his gaze.

Vexation pricked thorn-sharp. How could Aaron be so bold? So unfriendly? So possessive? He couldn't just kiss her whenever he pleased and then keep his heart far from reach. She refused to allow him to act as though he had some claim on her when he clearly didn't.

"It would have to wait until I get my morning chores completed."

"Chores?" Jonas was not a man to be put off, especially after he'd traveled so far. But this time he'd have to wait.

"Milking Gertrude, feeding the cattle, the goats and the horses. I'll need to get some weeding done in the garden, too. Before the sun gets too hot," she added, distractedly reviewing her mental checklist. "I can meet you just as soon as I'm finished."

"Hope Gatlin doing chores?" Jonas gave a wry chuckle. "You have fallen from grace, my dear. Though I must say, the idea of you filling the role as a domestic goddess is appealing."

She nervously clasped her hands at her waist. "I'm doing what's necessary."

"Had I known you'd needed a hand with all of those chores, why, I would've arrived far sooner."

"That's very thoughtful of you, Jonas, but—"

"She won't be needing your help." Aaron appeared from behind Jonas and planted himself at Hope's side. "She has me."

In an instant, her irritation increased tenfold. "But I—"

"You're Mr. Drake. Hope just told me about you." Jonas stuck out his hand, his squinty-eyed gaze nailed to Aaron. "I'm Jonas Hargrave. The Second."

He met Jonas's intense gaze and set his back teeth, tensed his jaw. Aaron seemed to take pleasure in swallowing Jonas's manicured hand in his, large and work-worn. The air around him seemed charged with maleness and challenge and strength as he finally released his hold.

Jonas moved a step closer to Hope. "Hope and I, we were engaged to marry at one time."

"Funny, she's never really talked about you." Aaron slid his gaze from Jonas to Hope then back again.

"That doesn't surprise me with what happened between us. I'm just grateful that she's not one to hold grudges. Although, when it comes to me, she has every reason to." Jonas's candid contriteness almost knocked her feet from beneath her.

She whipped her disbelieving focus to him. She'd never known him to willingly admit to any fault. The fact that he'd taken some kind of responsibility for the demise of their engagement—and in front of Aaron, no less—took her by complete surprise.

Jonas turned his undivided attention on Hope. "This town certainly seems nice enough. Pleasant folks—for the most part."

"Aaron. Oh, Aaron." Jane's grating voice shattered the evening air. The woman stood on the town hall steps, her hand flapping about madly from her wrist. "Are you ready to go?"

"Looks like you're needed over *there*," Jonas said, on a provoking wink.

Heaving a sigh, Aaron threw a frustrated glance over his shoulder then settled his focus on Hope. "I'll follow you home."

"There's no need. I'll be fine." From the corner of her eye, she noticed Jane slinking their way.

"It's getting dark, Hope. And I'm going to make sure that you get home safely." Aaron's I-will-not-argue-this tone brought any remaining protest up short, and when she remembered the marauding wolves, she felt a small sense of relief.

"He's quite a welcoming fellow," Jonas remarked under his breath as Aaron stalked to his rig and gave Jane a hand up.

Returning to Hope's side, he circled her waist and lifted her up, his touch searing straight through her dress, setting her skin afire. "I'll wait for you."

She struggled to hold in place her thin membrane of poise. But sorting through the past few hours, let alone the past few minutes, set her head to spinning. Here was Aaron, taking his promise to town and then acting like he had some claim on her when just a few hours ago he'd made it clear that he wasn't ready for any kind of relationship. And then there was Jonas, his humility and caring ways in direct contrast to what he'd ever shown of himself in the past. Just this afternoon, she'd prayed that God would bring some kind of clarity to her situation. Had He answered her prayers in a way she'd least expected, dropping Jonas into her life once again, even when her heart yearned for Aaron?

On the heels of a gallant bow, Jonas reached up for Hope's hand, the kiss he pressed to her fingers inciting none of the magnificent sensations invoked by Aaron's touch. "I will be expecting you tomorrow morning around eight-thirty. Will that be all right?"

"That will be fine," she muttered.

Jonas gave her hand a parting squeeze. "Until then, I bid you good night."

Good-night? There was nothing good that she could find about tonight.

Chapter Seventeen

The heifer heaved another anguished groan as Aaron rolled up his sleeves and entered the stall. In spite of Hope's determination that she'd take care of the chores, he couldn't stay away. And when he'd arrived less than twenty minutes ago to find Hope's face etched in concern and her eyes rimmed with tears, he knew he'd made the right decision. She'd been out here since before dawn had split the murky horizon, trying to comfort the laboring cow. The minute she'd caught sight of Aaron, her shoulders had wilted in obvious relief.

"What's going to happen to her baby?" Hope knelt in the corner of the stall, stroking the heifer's wide face.

"Hopefully, nothing." He hunkered down to check the heifer again. "Just pray, Hope."

"I will." She adjusted the small pink bow she'd tied around the cow's curly tuft of hair at the top of her head. "What else would you like for me to do? There must be something."

"You're going to miss your breakfast date if you stay any longer." He angled his focus her way to gauge her response. "Why don't you head into town? You can take my rig since it's already sitting out there ready to go."

When her jaw dropped, a small sense of satisfaction rose within him. "I wouldn't think of leaving Daisy in her condition."

"Suit yourself."

"Thank you, I will." Hope's feisty whisper tipped his mouth to a half grin. When the cow eased to its side, straining with another contraction, Hope hunkered down, almost nose to nose with the creature. "Aw…poor Daisy. It's all going to be over soon. And you shall have a new baby calf to show off."

Unbidden, a mesmerizing image of Hope tenderly cradling a baby flashed through his mind. His heart swelled as if he was witnessing the real thing. But an instant later, when he pictured himself standing with her as they peered down at the baby—*their* baby—he was rattled to the core.

He swiped a sleeve across his perspiration-beaded brow, sure that she could see straight through to his thoughts. "I'll need you to hold on to that rope around her neck," he ground out, grasping for control over his thoughts. "Just in case she decides to get up and move around. With her baby being breach, I'm going to have to get it turned around so she can push it out."

"You would do that for her?" When Hope's eyes misted with tears, he felt his control slip a little more.

He nodded then shoved his sleeve up as high as it would go, preparing to inch his arm inside the enormous animal. "You can be sure that she's not going to like it much, so be prepared for her to balk."

She nodded with a fair amount of confidence, and that tugged at his heart.

"You can do it, Daisy. Aaron's going to help you." She gave him the most endearing smile then. "You'll do just fine."

His heart surged at her vote of confidence. Especially when he wasn't feeling overly confident, himself. "Thanks. Something about bringing a baby—animal or human—into this world pretty much strips away my general confidence."

"You'll do very well. I know you will, Aaron."

He sighed, holding on to her words as though they proclaimed a new day. "Do you have a good hold on her?" He flipped his gaze up to Hope.

"Yes, as much as I can."

"Good. Now that this contraction has let loose, I'm going to inch my arm inside of her." He maneuvered through the tight opening, pushing all the way up to his shoulder. "I'm feeling for the front hooves. There's the calf's head," he grunted as another contraction bore down on the cow and the fleshy walls surrounding his arms constricted tight as a noose.

"Did you get him turned around?" Her voice was laden with sweet innocent hope.

He held still so as to not disturb the cow. "Kind of. But at the moment she has me wrapped tight. Until this contraction lets loose, I'm stuck."

"Oh, my. That sounds horrible."

After the walls had relaxed again, he found the front hooves and started inching the calf around. When he finally got the job done and was able to slide his arm out, he gave the mama a pat. "It's all right now, Daisy. Next contraction, you give it all you've got and push your little one out."

Glancing up, he saw Hope staring at him, her eyes pooled with tears. "You're so sweet," she whispered.

He held her gaze, loving every minute he'd spent with her this morning, loving that she was here with him and not in town having breakfast with her city-slicking former fiancé.

"I think she's starting to have another contraction, Aaron." The concern he saw in her expression near broke his heart.

"You're right," he agreed as the cow began straining. "Here we go, Daisy. You may be new to this, but be a good girl and push that baby of yours out."

After several more contractions, a black-and-white-spotted calf finally appeared. Aaron eased the good-sized male down into the fresh hay he'd spread for bedding. "There you go, little one."

"Oh, how precious." Hope heaved a relief-filled sigh. "The baby's all right?"

"Alive and well." Tears stung his eyes as he braced a hand on the heifer's rump. "You have a little—well, not so little—boy, Daisy. How do you feel about that?"

The cow's low moo tugged a smile across his face.

"Aww, a baby boy." Hope eased the lead rope from around the cow as the new mama heaved her tired body to standing and shifted around in the stall to inspect her newborn.

Dipping his arms into a pail of fresh water, Aaron scrubbed himself clean then dried himself off as he watched the heifer attending to her newborn, licking him off and giving him a tender nudge now and then.

"How does she know how to do that?" Hope's awestruck gaze remained fixed on the cow and her calf.

Aaron crossed to her and settled an arm around her shoulder, loving how the rawest, most innate things in life seemed to incite absolute awe from this city girl. "I suppose that, just like with other things, they follow their instinct. And their heart." Pulling her into his side, he rested his cheek on top of her head. If he were to follow his heart, would it lead straight to Hope? "You did good work, darlin'. I couldn't have done it without you."

"There you are." The unmistakable sound of Hargrave's smooth voice broke the mystical tender moment and set Aaron on edge. He stood at the doorway of the stall, clad in every kind of fashion contraption there probably was for a man. "I was worried."

"I'm sorry I didn't make it in for breakfast." Hope's moist gaze flitted over to Hargrave. "But Daisy was having a difficult time giving birth."

He barely looked at the mama and calf. "I see she managed all right."

"Oh, Jonas, you should've seen it." Hope eased over to the doorway. "Aaron had to reach inside and turn the calf around so that Daisy could push him out."

"Really?" Hargrave spared him a brief and bland glance.

If not for the fact that Hope just flashed Aaron one of her appreciative heart-stopping smiles, he'd have scowled all the way to tomorrow.

"Can you believe that someone would be so caring and tenderhearted as to do something like that?" That wonderful sense of awe filled her voice yet again and settled into his heart like warm honey.

"I can't," he remarked, giving Aaron a cursory nod. "That's really something."

Hope clasped her hands beneath her chin. "It was so—"

"Are you ready to go now?" Hargrave's congenial tone might have fooled some, but Aaron could tell the man's feathers had been ruffled, and for some reason that brightened Aaron's dour mood.

She peered up at Jonas. "I still have all of my chores to do."

"She's been up with Daisy since four o'clock this morning," Aaron explained, irritated that the man gave so little consideration to Hope's situation. "She's probably exhausted."

"I'm fine, Aaron." She half glared at him. "Really."

Bracing a hand on her arm, Jonas directed a triumphant smile Aaron's way. "That's my little farmer girl. You're really something, Hope."

"*Your* little farmer girl?" Instant disdain swirled in Aaron's stomach. Folding his arms at his chest, he sized up the man. "Did you grow up on a farm?"

Jonas held his hand up. "Ease up, Drake. It was just an endearing expression." The easy way he wrapped an arm around Hope's shoulders yanked at Aaron's control. "We used to do that all of the time, didn't we?"

An unconvincing half of a smile tipped Hope's mouth as she peered up at Jonas. "So, how did you find your way out here, anyway?"

"Mrs.—"

"Duncan?" She kept an eye on the new calf, wobbling in an attempt to stand.

Hargrave arched his dark eyebrows over his eyes. "So, Mrs. Duncan has a legendary reputation, eh?"

"She means well," Aaron put in, doing nothing to keep the irritation from his voice. He gave the heifer a pat then gathered the rope and bucket and squeezed around Hargrave to exit the stall.

"I'm sure she does," Jonas retorted with a superior chuckle.

That pricked Aaron's pride and also made him feel petty. He was a bigger man than to prove some point, prove himself. But jealousy's bitter sting pierced deep.

"She's a wealth of information, that woman," Hargrave continued trailing Hope as Aaron returned the items he'd used to their proper place. "I found out everything I needed to know, and I doubt our conversation was more than ten minutes."

"Jonas," Hope braved, her voice taking on an odd, almost insecure tone—nothing like the Hope he'd discovered over these past weeks. "Did you get a chance to look around the farmstead when you arrived? It's lovely, isn't it?"

"Perfect." Hargrave raised his too-perfect eyebrows over his too-small eyes. "It's probably worth a sizable amount of money."

Why that would be the first thing he thought of disturbed Aaron to no end.

"I'll have to introduce you to the animals and—"

"How long do you think it'll take you to get your chores finished? We could make it a noon meal if you like?"

Incensed by Jonas's complete disregard for Hope's enthusiasm, not to mention Hope's cowering behavior toward Jonas, Aaron stopped in his tracks at the wide-open barn doors and did a one eighty. "Tell you what, Hope, I'll do the rest of your chores for you so that you can go and have your breakfast with Hargrave."

He'd been as good natured as could be in making that offer, but he couldn't deny that a small part of him had laid it out before her just to see what she would choose.

Jealousy, dark and ugly, had fanned to life, burning hot and bright, and almost as threatening as the fierce protectiveness he felt for Hope. He didn't like feeling so spiteful, but there was something about Hargrave that didn't sit right with Aaron. He wasn't one to make rash judgments without good cause, but from the moment he'd met the man yesterday, he'd had a bad feeling. Hargrave's intentions were in serious question and would continue to be so until he'd proven different.

On a sigh, he realized that in the past few days things with Hope had been moving lightning fast. He felt himself slowly losing control over his heart. It was almost as if he was being pressed into making some kind of decision.

Maybe God was giving him every chance to man up, to accept his past, his present and his future—to move on, even when he didn't think he had it in him to do so. Grief and sorrow had been so near. As real and as heavy as those emotions were, he'd begun to wonder if moving on would take a conscious, determined decision and a final resolution with God.

"Thank you, but I won't be needing your help with the chores. This is my responsibility." Her unspoken words hung heavy in her gaze...now that Jonas was here, she didn't need Aaron any longer. "I'll finish the chores then join Jonas for a noon meal."

But she did need him. When he'd shown up this morning, she'd nearly cried, wrought with worry over one of her beloved cows.

And he needed her. He'd found more fulfillment over the past seven weeks than he had in months. Her sweet, loving ways had made him feel alive again.

If he could, he'd burrow his gaze deep inside her soul to discover the truth of how she really felt. He'd felt the rapid beat of her heart and had heard her sigh when he'd kissed her, but he'd tried to convince himself that she wasn't interested in him.

"All right then," he finally conceded.

"I'll be famished by the time I arrive, Jonas." She slid her focus to Hargrave. "Would you mind ordering for me?"

"I'd be glad to, my dear. It'll be just like old times." When Jonas gave her a wink, Aaron flexed his hands then curled them into rigid fists.

* * *

Hope peered over the table at Jonas, willing herself to focus on him even though all she could seem to think about was Aaron. She'd been flabbergasted by Aaron's behavior earlier when Jonas had paid a surprise visit at the farm. Aaron had been agitated last evening after play rehearsal, but this morning he'd been nothing if not rude.

She couldn't imagine why he was acting so out of sorts except for the fact that he was still traumatized by the kiss they'd shared. But was he always inclined to being so unwelcoming to strangers? He'd certainly exhibited a bias against her when she'd arrived in Boulder—he'd even admitted as much. If not for the promise he'd made to Paul, she doubted he'd have given her the barest compulsory nod.

When she'd arrived at the hotel restaurant, she'd recounted the excitement of her morning, and Jonas had listened—with far more attentiveness than she'd expected. He'd seemed so sincere in his interest. His words had been understanding, eloquent, caring—contrite.

But still, she couldn't seem to get Aaron out of her mind.

"Are you listening, my dear?" Jonas's refined voice seeped into her thoughts.

"I apologize." She willed him her undivided focus as she took another sip of coffee. "What were you saying?"

"I said that I would like to speak with you about something very important. If you'll be so kind as to permit me," he added with a coy grin that had the hair on the back of her neck standing soldier straight.

Just then Jane appeared at the table's edge—yet again startling Hope. She stuck the coffeepot in between them. "More coffee?"

"No, thank you." *For the third time,* Hope added silently

as she bit off a frustrated groan—one that her mother would've thoroughly chastised her for.

She tried to contain her irritation, but this was the tenth time Jane had shown up, bringing food, drinks and dessert and also checking to see if all was favorable. The woman had been as pleasant and amiable as Hope had ever seen.

That, alone, was enough to make Hope wary.

"I didn't know you were waiting on tables here, Jane. I thought you'd been hired to do the baking." She slid the last bite of her mouthwatering berry pie into her mouth.

"We…um…we've been exceptionally busy today so I offered my services." Jane fanned a hand down her flour-dusted apron. "I'm always willing to help out when there's a need."

Remembering how unaccommodating Jane had been over the past weeks, how seemingly determined she was to stand back and watch Hope flounder in the deep waters of inexperience and regret, Hope had to force down her blaring protest.

"Busy?" Hope glanced around the nearly empty restaurant. Two other waitresses stood behind the counter, boredom pulling at their young features as they gave a lackadaisical effort polishing silver stemware.

"Absolutely everything was delicious, ma'am." Jonas pressed the white linen napkin to his mouth. "The best I've have in a long time and certainly another reason to be partial to the West."

A ruddy blush blotched from Jane's neck to her cheeks. "I'm glad you enjoyed your meal, sir."

"I'll take that bill when you have the time." Jonas gave Hope a perceptive wink while Jane skittered off, moving with more stealth than a fox on the hunt. "She certainly is thoughtful."

"Jane puts a tremendous amount of thought into

everything she does," Hope diplomatically concurred, knowing, firsthand, how calculated the woman could be with her surprise visits, well-chosen words of discouragement and barbed looks.

"Hope, my dear," Jonas began as he laid his napkin on the table.

She squirmed beneath the liberal use of *my dear*.

"I know that this may seem a bit forward and abrupt—" he slid a finger down the crystal glass of water "—but I have something that I must say."

"Certainly." She folded her hands in her lap, dread hallowing out a pit in her stomach.

"I've been a fool for letting you go." His matter-of-fact, statement hit her between the eyes. It stung deep.

She stared in total disbelief. He hadn't let her go. She'd let him go, and she'd been disparaged for doing so. In fact, the steady stream of derision aimed her way had been one of the main reasons she'd answered the mail-order bride advertisement. As much as she was ashamed to admit it, Paul had offered her a way of escape when he'd proposed marriage.

"I've been lost without you all of these months. And I was wondering…" Reaching across the table, he laid his hand across hers, his fingers and palm lacking the telltale signs of hard work she'd found in Aaron's touch. His seemingly rehearsed manner and the damp feel of his palm only added to her growing irritation.

Jane skidded to a halt at their table and flattened a thick-fingered hand over the slip of paper as though it might blow away. "Here's your check, sir." She stared down at where Jonas clasped Hope's hand, her mouth tipping in the faintest of smiles. "Are you sure there's nothing else I can get for you?"

"No, I don't believe so." The patience Jonas exhibited

was a complete shock. In the past, he would've complained to the owner of the establishment by now. "Thank you, though. Your service has been very attentive."

Hope almost wished that Jane would sit down and join them, given the seriousness of Jonas's words and the bold way he held her hand.

"As I was saying," he began again, leaning her way, his hand feeling like a fish that had flopped over her fingers and died right there in the middle of the table, "I was wondering if there was any chance you could find room for me in your heart again?"

She tugged her hand from his. "Jonas, I—"

"Please, don't answer yet." Holding up one clammy finger to her mouth, he paused for a long moment. "Only promise me that you'll give it your utmost consideration."

She didn't owe him a thing.

But even so, she would commit to at least giving him that much. After all, she had to seriously look at what her future held. Although she could pine for Aaron, *if* she permitted such a thing of herself, she refused to be so weak. She'd come out to Boulder to start a new life, and although her path had taken an unforeseen turn at the outset, she had to make the best of it or decide to sell the place as Paul had made room for in his deed.

Could it be that her relationship with Jonas had come full circle? She'd heard it said that God's ways were higher than ours. Maybe Jonas arriving here was part of His ways.

She swallowed past the instant apprehension constricting her throat. Could it be?

"I will," she finally said, ill at ease with the instant and triumphant grin that stretched across his face.

"I'll wait as long as you need." He snaked a hand across

the table, his long thin fingers wrapping around her arm. "I love you, Hope. And I want to spend the rest of my days with you."

But did she want to spend the rest of her days with him? He was charming, to be sure. He'd surprised her with his concern and gentle nature, and he'd obviously discovered goodness within himself that before had been sorely missing.

But he'd not moved her to tears as Aaron had this morning when he'd helped Daisy. Nor had he made her laugh the way Aaron had when he'd allowed himself to relax around her. And he'd never caused her innermost parts to flail about with a single touch. In fact, she'd felt nothing with Jonas—not even the slightest tingle.

She wasn't so shallow to think that a relationship was based solely on physical sensations, but it was an integral part of attraction that she could no longer deny and one that she'd discovered had been missing with Jonas. There'd been no guarantee that she'd have found that in Paul's touch, but she'd been committed to him, to growing in her love for him.

Jonas hauled in an I'm-glad-that's-over kind of sigh that only furthered her irritation. "We can sell this place, take the money and go back to Boston," he remarked as he adjusted his cravat. "Where you belong."

Where she belonged?

How could Jonas think that he could waltz in here and presume to know *where she belonged*? The very idea had her blood boiling so hot she felt ready to explode.

Chapter Eighteen

Eager to breathe in the fresh air after being cooped up with Jonas for the last hour and a half, Hope guided the team home. He'd been generous with his compliments and wholly respectful, but still she'd been impatient to leave the hotel restaurant—especially after he'd asked her if there was room in her heart for him.

Bringing the wagon to a halt, she set the brake and climbed down from the seat. Spotting Aaron's wagon parked on the far side of the barn, she started off in that direction, recalling how painfully clear he'd made it that he was unable to move his heart forward. She'd been so caught up in the moment, in the way he'd cherished her with that kiss and the way she'd quivered at his touch, that when he'd slapped reality in her face with his words, she'd clambered to keep her foothold.

She'd considered Jonas's request because of Aaron's uncertainty—for a brief moment, anyway.

Staring down at the hard-packed earth, her stomach pulled taut as she recalled how when she'd looked at Jonas—*really* looked at him—her pondering had come to a screeching halt. His charm could win any heart—any heart but hers. And he was dashingly handsome with his dark hair, chiseled features and winning smile, but something deep and wise, something pure and wholly profound was missing. He'd gone to church on occasion, but the solid comfort of knowing that he had a personal relationship with God was sorely missing.

Despite the apparent changes he'd made, the stinging memory of his disdain after her family's highly publicized misfortune, flapped about in her mind's eye like a red flag of warning.

"How was your meal?" Aaron's voice broke into the discomforting thought.

She looked up to see him standing in the barn doorway, his arms folded at his chest, his face an unreadable mask. "It was pleasant."

"Pleasant?" he echoed, his tone harsh.

"Yes." Uneasy, she hugged her arms to her chest. "Jane makes the most delicious baked goods."

"I'm not talking about the meal." He leveled his gaze at her.

Vulnerability snagged at her composure. "But you said—"

"What happened with Hargrave?" he questioned, his tone charged with accusation. "Is he going to be sticking around?"

She avoided his discomforting gaze and slipped around him, making her way back to the stall where Daisy and her new calf were resting. "I don't know. Perhaps."

Aaron was close at her heels. "Jane said she saw Hargrave holding your hand."

She came to a sudden stop, her stomach growing tight at Aaron's interrogating attitude. Hope could've carefully chosen her every move at the hotel or made a scene when Jonas had reached for her hand, but she didn't have a thing to hide from Jane or anyone else. "She didn't waste her time, did she?"

"Well?" He came around to stand in front of her, jammed his fists on his trim waist. "Is she telling the truth?"

The reproach and hurt she found in Aaron's gaze tugged at her regret. "Yes, but why would this matter to you, Aaron?"

When she edged around him to enter the stall, he reached out and grabbed the door, barring her way. "I happen to think that I have a right to know. After all, I promised that I'd take care of you."

"Please. Will you let me pass?" She struggled to keep her voice even and worked a swallow past the thick lump in her throat. "And will you *finally* release yourself from that silly promise? Honestly, there is no need to—"

"Silly? It's serious. At least it is to me." He stepped aside and allowed her to enter. "When I give my word, it means something."

She gasped at the sight of the calf standing next to his mama, his knobby kneed legs holding up his sturdy body. "Aw...look at you standing, little one. Aren't you adorable," she whispered, amazed at the resilience of both mama and baby. "We'll have to come up with a name for your baby, Daisy. Maybe Libby can help me with that at play rehearsal today."

"Libby would probably love that," Aaron muttered, leaning against the doorframe, his gaze softening the slightest bit.

Hope's heart did a little flip flop at the way his utterly natural and masculine presence filled the room...and her heart.

But she couldn't keep subjecting herself to the heartache of yearning for something she couldn't have.

"Listen, Aaron," she began, moving to stand opposite him in the doorway. "I am officially releasing you from your promise. You do not need to burden yourself with it for another moment." She stacked her hands at her backside and leaned against the rough wood. "Paul was a dear to think enough of me to secure my future with a trusted friend, but I'm doing just fine."

"Fine?" he challenged, arching his eyebrows over his eyes. "Like this morning when you needed help with the calf?"

His jab stung, yet she maintained her poise. "I am ever so grateful. You saved their lives." Her heart swelled even now thinking about how Aaron's eyes had misted over when the calf had finally appeared alive and well. "It was a beautiful thing to see, a moment in time I shall never forget."

"But you couldn't have done it without me." The harsh gaze he narrowed on her sliced right through her composure. "And what about the crops? They wouldn't have been planted without my help. Or the other critters? They'd have flown the coop or barreled through their fenced enclosures without my help."

Pierced straight through by his callous words and the truth they carried, she edged into the corridor and took a few steps back. Why was he being so hurtful? He'd always been so encouraging, saying that she'd done far more than most women would have given the same circumstance.

"You're right," she conceded, hoping to waylay his obvious resentment. "Are you satisfied now?"

She couldn't help but wonder if he viewed Jonas as his ticket out of his vow to Paul. Maybe he was just grasping at the many strands of reasons why she was unfit to stay here in the hopes that she'd move on.

But she didn't want to move on. And if ever she did, it certainly wouldn't be with a man like Jonas.

Yanking his hat from his head, he slapped it against his leg. He raked a hand through his thick hair. "I'm just trying to point out that as much as you want to get rid of me, you still need me. Even if you had all of the chores down pat and could do them in your sleep, there are just some things that you'll need help with."

Noticing the way Daisy was shifting nervously in the stall, Hope strode down the corridor to the outdoors, Aaron eating up the distance behind her with his long strides.

He stepped up to meet her, that alluring masculine scent of his, all natural and woodsy and earthy, wafting to her senses. She felt her resolve slip. Reminded herself that she didn't want to need him. "I can find another way."

"*What* other way?" He jammed his hat back on his head as Theodore appeared, meowing sweetly at his booted feet.

"I—I can hire someone—whether or not you agree. There's got to be a good man or two out there." Hope slid her quivering fingers over each pearl button trailing down the front of her light blue-and-cream damask bodice, helpless to think of any other way.

"So far the rakes you've interviewed for a farmhand position would've presented a very real threat to you," he retorted, his voice laden with caution.

"Well, I won't have you helping out of obligation—not any longer." She tugged at her bodice. "I can find someone."

"This is the height of the busy season for farmhands, cowhands and the like. Anybody who isn't already employed isn't worth a look. So, what's your plan then?" When he stooped to pick up Theodore, her resolve slipped a little more at his show of tenderness. "Your garden is bursting with ripe produce. Do you even know what to do with all of it?"

"No, but I'm sure I can figure it out," she dismissed, bothered by the contented and unfaithful purr coming from her cat. Where were Theodore's loyalties? Didn't he know that Aaron was being insufferable?

"And what about your first hay crop? It's due to be cut any day now." With a deliberate measure of calm, Aaron stroked her fluffy kitten, as though to goad her. "How do you plan on harvesting that? Or the other things we planted?"

"I can hire someone." She leaned against the barn, the golden rays of sunshine seemingly blocked by the cloud of discord hovering over them.

"So, does that mean you're staying?" Setting Theodore on the ground, he pinned his defensive gaze on her, his throat visibly constricted. "I put my heart on the line when I kissed you, Hope Gatlin. I drug it out of hiding. I opened it up again. I took a gigantic painful risk."

Hope couldn't breathe for the way her heart thundered inside her rib cage. Had she really been so uncaring? So insensitive? She searched her heart for the hint of misconduct or thoughtlessness on her part but came up empty-handed. All along, she'd bowed to his lead, let him set the pace. Had he heard her thoughts or seen deep into her heart, he would've known how much she really cared. "Aaron, I didn't ask for you to kiss me." Her whispered words scraped across her throat.

"You didn't stop me, either." Squeezing his eyes shut, he paused.

"You said that you didn't know if you were ready," she whispered, moved by his struggle.

"I'm not."

"That has been made painfully clear."

"But I don't think I'll ever be ready. It's not been easy... letting go of Ellie." He pulled a hand over the back of his neck as he often did when he grew frustrated. "I've been fighting my attraction to you, Hope. And I can't seem to get rid of it."

She forced herself to look at him. "What a lovely thing to say."

Gazing skyward, he hauled in a deep breath. "What I meant to say was—"

"Aaron, I've fought the same thing." She grasped at what little pride she had left. "But I can't allow myself to care for you as more than just a friend. If ever I marry I'd like to believe that I'm not just some pale second."

His emotionless expression did nothing to ease her pain. "Hope, you're—"

"I can't live up to her—to Ellie's memory. Nor do I want to. She was special. She must have been to have acquired your lasting love and devotion." Plastering her arms to her side, she refused to reveal the fragility of her heart. "But more, I will not be some man's obligation."

"You're not an obligation, Hope. You've never been an obligation."

Her heart ached at the harsh reality she faced. "You're so very loyal and honorable, Aaron. But you hemmed yourself in so tight by the blind promise you made to Paul that you couldn't find your way out even if you wanted to."

"Who said I wanted to?" His demeanor was so rigid she thought that he might just snap in two. "I thought that he meant to stay strong in my faith, to hold tight to God. I had no idea that Paul meant I was supposed to marry you. But even so, I never said that I wanted out of the promise."

"Well, you can rest assured that, just like I stated from day one, I will *never* marry you. The past couple of days have confirmed that for me."

His defensive gaze bore straight through to her heart. The air between them grew stiflingly thick with tension and hurt as he stared at her. Slow and steady, he raked his gaze from her toes to her head. He gave his head a single measured shake. "I didn't see this coming," he uttered, his voice eerily hardened.

"What do you mean?" Chilled by the callous look flashing in his eyes, she hugged her arms to her chest.

"I didn't think you'd go off gallivanting with that fancy suit."

Aaron's heart ached as he watched Hope drive off toward town in his wagon since he hadn't finished reshoeing her horses. Even from this distance, he could see her chin angled slightly upward in that familiar, I'm-not-giving-in look of hers. But the way her brow had crimped in distress as she'd mounted his rig just moments ago had cut him deep.

Reaching down to where Theodore rubbed against his legs, he gave the kitten a scratch behind the ears. His gut pulled as taut as a readied bow just thinking about how harsh his words to Hope had been two hours earlier. He'd thought of nothing else as he'd busied himself mucking the stalls, reshoeing her horses and filing their hooves, all the while praying that God would make some sense of his turmoil so that he could have some kind of reasonable conversation with Hope—so that he could let her know exactly what was in his heart.

So that he could understand what, exactly, was in her heart.

He had his guesses, had been almost certain she was having similar feelings toward him—she'd even said as much. Her willing response when he'd kissed her had said as much, too. But as soon as Jonas had arrived, she'd changed, and he had to wonder if she viewed Hargrave as her way out of a very difficult circumstance.

Just a few minutes ago when she'd emerged from the house where she'd fled to stitch costumes for the play, he'd been prepared to apologize. Even if Hope was swayed by another man, he had no right to accuse her as he had—that much he knew to be true. He had no claim on her—none. And she was capable of making her own decisions.

But his apology would have to wait since she was already going to be late for costume fittings at the town hall. Offering for her to take his rig was the least he could do after he'd been downright rude to her and to Jonas Hargrave. He knew almost nothing of the man, other than the single, irritating fact that Hargrave had been engaged to Hope. That was enough to rake him the wrong way.

How could he blame the man, though, for caring for a woman like Hope? She was beautiful in every possible way.

And how could he expect Hope to wait in the wings while he stumbled toward some kind of acceptance of Ellie's death—at least enough to move on? Although he felt his grip on the past loosening more and more every day, he couldn't expect her to wait for him. He wanted her to be happy.

It just didn't sit right with him to think of her finding that happiness in another man's arms—especially Hargrave's.

The man was every bit as refined as Hope, his words rolling off his tongue like some well-rehearsed speech. His attire was impeccable and nothing like Aaron's simple way of dressing. His demeanor was commanding yet steeped in a certain air of self-importance that made Aaron want to haul back and hit him, hard enough that Hargrave's aristocratic nose would be permanently cocked off to one side.

Aaron released the chestnut mare's hoof, swiping a hand over his sweaty brow as he moved to the last and final hoof. Jealousy had never been so near as it had in the past few days. Nor had the absolute fear that if he let himself love Hope, he could well lose another gigantic chunk of his heart if something were to happen to her.

Most folks probably didn't think along those lines, but he did. He had to know if he could withstand that kind of heartbreak again. If there was some way he could ensure her well-being then maybe he could step ahead. But life offered no guarantees. Aaron had to know if he could trust himself and God with the life of someone he loved—at least enough to follow his heart.

Closing his eyes, he hauled in a breath as he recalled that morning, almost a year ago, when he'd found Ellie's body draped over the freshly turned grave of her baby boy. All night long she'd begged and pleaded to see where her newborn son had been laid to rest, but she'd been so weak. Aaron had promised to show her just as soon as she gained strength. He couldn't have fallen asleep for more than twenty or thirty minutes when she'd managed to crawl out of bed and make her way out to the place where Jeremiah's body had been laid to rest.

That's where he'd found her that gray and stormy morning—dead. Her nightgown was stained with blood, and the booties she'd knitted for little Jeremiah were dangling from her lifeless, dusky hand.

Aaron pried the last horseshoe off as he swallowed past the harsh lump clogging his throat. The horrifying image burned into his mind. There hadn't been a day or night that had slipped by without that memory playing over and over again, blasting away any and all peace. The memory had resounded in his soul like a clanging bell tolling the way he'd failed to protect the love of his life.

As much as he'd blamed God, he'd faulted himself equally so. He was the one who'd fallen asleep. By the time he'd found her, she was gone from his arms forever.

Filing the hoof, he lined up the new shoe and tapped it into place. Until he could line up the gross discrepancies in his heart and forgive God and himself, he would never be able to fully give his heart to another—at least not in the way Hope deserved.

She deserved his whole heart. She deserved to be cherished, not suffocated—loved for the treasure she was, not compared to another.

Laying his tools down, he scooped up a purring Theodore and peered out the double doors as he realized just how hard he'd tried not to compare Hope to Ellie. Some of the differences were just so glaringly apparent, though.

But maybe the stark distinctions were for the best.

Where Ellie had been as natural and carefree as a mountain wildflower, Hope was as manicured and rich as a rare and costly orchid from some faraway land. Where Ellie had enjoyed life around her, Hope was in a constant state of awe. He'd wanted to wrap her in his arms and kiss her soundly on more than one occasion because of that, too. Just being with her, looking at things through her eyes, renewed his awareness of creation. Where Ellie had been content to stay indoors, knitting or baking, Hope couldn't wait to greet the day, traipsing out to the barn at dawn's first light. She'd grown so attached to the farm animals, had named each one. And she'd marveled over every single inch the crops had grown. Ellie didn't know an enemy, but Hope had made friends with even those folks Ellie had sometimes avoided—like Pete O'Leary.

Aaron would never forget the day of Paul's funeral, when Hope had lingered at the grave after everyone else had trailed off to the wagons. He'd watched her from afar, marveling at the tender and patient way she'd dealt with the undertaker, Pete, and his sneaky little ferret, Conroy. She could've dismissed the rough weedy-looking man and his furry-faced counterpart, but instead she'd put aside her own distress to show kindness.

Just then he heard the distant jangle of a rig coming this way. He glanced up to see two horses, *his* two horses, ambling down the lane toward the house. When he noticed the hitch dragging in the dirt behind the team, his heart came to screeching halt.

"Hope." The strangled sound of his own voice called up his worst fears. It couldn't have been more than twenty minutes since she'd left.

He dumped Theodore on the ground and sprinted to meet the horses, struggling to keep his mind from descending to the worst situation. But his wagon was nowhere in sight—and neither was Hope. When he scanned the road and saw no sign of her, his stomach bottomed out. His lungs seized up.

He turned and ran back to the barn, forcing himself to breathe even as he prayed for her. Mounting the freshly shoed chestnut mare, he rode hard down the road, his mind racing with dread and fear. Guilt battered him with relentless force as he thought of Hope having some kind of accident in *his* wagon. Had he done something wrong in hooking up his rig?

She'd left the house angry. But he'd never known her to be reckless. She knew that the road to town was wrought with beauty and danger and had even commented on as much a time or two. There were two precarious areas where the road wound around a bend, leaving little to no room for driver error.

The thought of Hope careening down one of those slopes in an out-of-control wagon played on his every fear.

He rounded a precarious bend, searching wildly for any indication of her. When he spotted his wagon resting on its side a good hundred feet down a steep slope, horror gripped his heart. His pulse whooshed through his veins at breakneck speed. His vision briefly squeezed to a narrow tunnel as he searched for signs of Hope.

"Hope!" he called, reining in the horse to scan the slope. "Hope! Can you hear me? Hope!"

Guiding the horse down the screed, boulder-littered slope, he willed himself to stay focused. But every second that lapsed seemed to drag Hope further from him. And that cut as deep and wounding as any long-edged sword.

Did he love her? Did he care for her the way he'd cared for Ellie?

"Hope!" He sidestepped the chestnut mare down a steep area when a flash of color some fifty feet away caught his eye.

His heart surged to his throat as he peered in that direction, the hem of her blue dress coming into view. "God, no. Not Hope. Please, not Hope, too."

He catapulted off the horse and ran in that direction. The thought of losing Hope constricted his chest so tight that he could barely breathe. He silently barraged heaven on her behalf, each prayer set like a foundation stone on which to build love. Had he loved her for some time, but had just been too wrapped up in his grief to recognize it? Too focused on his loss to find the hope that God had dangled before him?

When he reached her battered and silent body, slumped like a rag doll on its side, he knelt beside her, pleading for God to spare her life.

"Hope, can you hear me? Come on, darlin'." He cleared the ground of debris and carefully rolled her to her back, being sure to keep her neck stable. "Please. Don't leave me." With trembling hands, he felt for her pulse. It was weak, but the sign of life was there, beating just beneath his fingertips.

He breathed a small sigh of relief. "Thank You, God."

Pulling his kerchief from his back pocket, he dabbed at the streams of blood coursing from an angry gash that angled from just above her ear to mid-forehead at her hairline. He unbuttoned his shirt placket and shrugged out of his shirtsleeves, then ripped several strips to use for bandaging.

"Hope, darlin'? Can you open your eyes?" Hunkering down, he tried to get a closer look at the gash, caked with sticky blood-soaked hair.

When she gave a small groan, his eyes burned with relief.

"Just hang on." He gently clasped her shoulder, longing to pull her into his arms and hold her tight, but until he was sure that her back or neck wasn't broken, he wasn't going to move her an inch. "I promise I'm going to get you out of here just as soon as I can."

Her delicate eyebrows drew together just then and her mouth opened ever so slightly. The fact that she was even a little responsive was enough to infuse him with some much-needed hope. But the idea that she was in pain pierced his heart straight through.

Was he willing to let her go if he had to? He loved her. He did. He loved Hope. The way his heart would surge at the thought of her, and the way his mind raced with frantic thoughts of keeping her near and close and safe was proof enough. He longed for her gentle touch, her sweet voice and that tender way she'd look at him—as though he was all she could seem to see.

Was he worthy of her glance?

Or had her glance strayed to another?

The thought engulfed him with mudslide force, thick and dank and confining. Having been unwilling to settle his heart with God, had he pushed her into Hargrave's arms?

She deserved the world and then some. If her happiness was made whole in Hargrave's arms, then Aaron had to find a way to release her from his. He could be man enough to do that....

Except that she'd captured his heart—completely.

"That's the way. Just stay with me," he urged, choking the words past his emotion-constricted throat. He worked his hands down her legs and then her arms. "I'm checking to make sure you don't have any broken bones, Hope. Do you understand?"

She hadn't opened her eyes, but the slightest crease in her brow gave him encouragement.

When she groaned as he got to just above her left wrist, he lightened his touch. The way a bone protruded slightly was not a good sign—not at all. "I'm going to have to secure your arm before I'm able to move you, darlin'."

He searched the ground and found two sturdy sticks, then hunkered down beside her again, tearing four more strips from his shirt. "I'll get you out of here as soon as possible, Hope. Just bear with me."

With a tenuous touch and quivering fingers, he splinted her arm. It was impossible to tell whether she was in pain at this point, though. In the ten minutes it'd taken to secure the bone, she hadn't once responded. Her expression had gone stone cold, her coloring growing paler as each precious minute ticked by.

His heart wavered as he watched her chest rise and fall on a shallow breath. She was clearly unconscious—and maybe that was for the best. Broken bones or other wounds she'd suffered in the accident would be aggravated by the jarring motion as he transported her home.

He had to figure out a way to get her home. He'd give anything to have a little help right now—at least someone to let him know that he was doing the right thing. He was as sure as the setting sun not going to leave her side while he rode for Ben. With the way the wolves had been so thick in the area, he might as well hand her over on a great big platter for them to feast on.

His thoughts immediately ricocheted to Jonas Hargrave, prickling the hair at the back of his neck. His pulse slammed red-hot through his veins.

If he let go of the tenuous hold he had on her and gave her over to Hargrave, what would that mean? Would he be relinquishing her to one of the most cunning manicured wolves that had skulked all the way here from Boston?

Chapter Nineteen

"Other than a broken arm, the gash on her forehead and plenty of scrapes and bruises, I think she's going to be all right, Aaron." Ben balanced the basin of blood-tinted water, then reached behind him and closed the bedroom door with a quiet click.

Relief flooded Aaron's heart as he ran a trembling hand through his hair. "Has she regained consciousness yet? Because until I hear that sweet voice of hers, I won't be able to rest."

"She stirred a little while I was checking her over and setting her arm. I'm guessing that she'll come around soon." Ben led the way to the kitchen. "I'll say this much. It's a good thing you found her when you did."

"I have Brodie and Zach to thank for that." He passed a grateful glance to his brother and his friend seated at the table. "I don't know what I would've done if you two hadn't come along."

"Not another word about it. Glad I could help." The hint of Brodie's Scottish brogue hung in his words.

"Me, too. Hope's a pretty special lady." Zach rested his elbows on the golden pine tabletop, one of Joseph's creations. "But then, that's nothing you don't already know."

He'd known it almost from the moment she'd shown up here. And each interaction he'd had with her had only re-affirmed the fact.

"Are you sure everything checked out?" Aaron paced the floor. "I mean, she won't take a turn for the worse or anything, will she?" He eyed his brother, searching for any sign of hesitation.

"I'm positive." The solid way Ben peered at him helped relieve his apprehension a little. "But Callie, Lib and I will be glad to stay out here tonight if it'll ease your mind at all."

Jamming his hands into his pockets, Aaron scuffed over to the hallway, staring at the door to Hope's room. He swung back around and eyed Ben. "I've already decided I'm sitting up with her tonight. I'm not leaving her alone."

"She won't be alone. Like I said, we'll be here." Ben dumped the water down the cast iron sink, then pumped fresh water to wash the basin out. "But if it suits you to stay, too, then go right ahead."

"I'm definitely staying." Aaron pulled a hand over his face, sick at the idea of her injury somehow being his fault. "I don't know what happened. I mean, every time I hitch up the wagon, I check things over just to make sure they're in good repair. When I drove over this morning I didn't notice anything." He braced his hands on the table and leaned over it, burdened by guilt's heavy weight. "I don't know how that wagon separated from the hitch the way it did."

"I'll look it over," Brodie put in as he pushed up from the table.

Zach stood and grasped Aaron's shoulder. "Don't let this get to you. It was an accident."

"That section of roadway is notorious for mishaps," Brodie added, sweeping a thick clutch of dark hair to the side. "It can challenge the sturdiest rig."

"You know as well as we do that this kind of thing happens." Ben crossed to the table and shoved his stethoscope into his bag.

Unconvinced, Aaron gave his head a slow shake. "Not on my watch, it doesn't."

Shrugging from his brother's touch, he walked over to the window where the afternoon sun soaked the fields in a brilliant sea of golden warmth. Hope had often marveled over the way the crops would seemingly grow right before her eyes on a clear, blue day like today. And she'd found it so amusing the way her kitten would seek out the brightest patch of sunshine in which to nap. There were so many little things about Hope, so many innocent trusting traits, that had warmed his cold and hurting heart. There were so many endearing qualities that had captured him so completely that he no longer dreaded the sun's rise.

"I promised to watch out for her, and I failed." Guilt's weight pressed harder. "Just like I did with Ellie."

"Don't be so hard on yourself," Ben cautioned as Aaron pivoted to face him.

He longed for freedom from the overbearing weight and pain of guilt, but it had roped his neck like a heavy millstone. "You're wasting your time trying to relieve me of blame. It's the way things are."

Even as he uttered the words, he felt a prickle of unease work up his spine, a warning whip around his soul. Had he grown so used to that deep sense of responsibility over these months that he'd forgotten what life was like without the tremendous heaviness?

Zach puffed out a breath of air. "Well, if you ask me, you don't have to claim a patch of land in the valley of guilt and set up residence there. That's not healthy." He shoved his chair back under the table. "Not for you. And especially not for Hope—that is, *if* you have any kind of a future with her."

He opened his mouth to throw back a resolute protest, but for some reason, words failed him. Did he have a future with Hope?

"What happened with Ellie wasn't your fault," Ben said, conviction clamped tight to each word. "Believe me, I've blamed myself enough for her death, but ultimately God is the One who holds life, not me and certainly *not* you. You've taken on more than enough guilt."

"It's high time you let it go," Zach added. "If you don't, you're going to be so gun-shy when it comes to relationships that you'll end up being some holed up hermit who pops out in society every once in a blue moon."

"I'm not going to be a hermit." Aaron gave a heavy sigh.

Ben nailed him with a challenging look. "Neither will you be a very pleasant person to be around. Grief is one thing, but carrying around undo guilt is another."

"You're going to suffocate the ones you love," Zach heaped on, as if the portion of reasoning they'd already dished out wasn't enough.

"You think I don't know that?" he spat back.

Brodie came to stand next to Aaron. "They're just trying to help—my brothers and sister would do the same."

"We know it's been hard," Zach urged. The way his voice broke the slightest bit pierced Aaron straight through. "We also know you've been fighting your feelings for Hope for a long time."

"Probably since she showed up here," Ben agreed, grasping his bag.

"There's a time and season for everything, Aaron," Brodie urged. "A time to mourn. A time to rejoice."

Zach gave an adamant nod. "He's got that right. We're not saying that you're supposed to just go on as if nothing ever happened. But you need closure. For you and for her." Zach peered off toward Hope's room. "At least if you're going to pursue that little lady all the way to the altar."

Aaron exhaled a long breath. Hope had become such a meaningful part of his days. She'd been so understanding, so compassionate and so very tender. And she'd never ever asked for one thing in return—as if she thought that she was a bother.

She was far from a bother.

He'd scale the tallest and most dangerous mountain for her and more. She'd breached a very thick wall around his heart from the moment she'd braved her way through a throng of two-thousand pound cattle, and all for a scrawny kitten that she'd turned into a plump house cat—a friend.

"I know I need closure. But who's to say she's even interested in me?" he quickly added as Hargrave, all six feet—dressed for success, refined to the core—of him stumbled into his mind's eye. "I mean with Hargrave in the mix."

"Watch out for him," Ben warned, holding up his index finger. "I don't know him from a stranger, but I can tell you this much, I don't trust him."

"You met the man?" Zach inquired.

"Outside of play rehearsal last night. I went up and introduced myself after Aaron followed Hope home." Ben shrugged into his coat sleeves. "He was polite as could be. He seemed nice enough, but something about that man just didn't sit right with me," he said as he adjusted his collar.

"Even Libby acted a little timid with him, and she'll make friends with anyone."

"I'll see what I can find out about him." Brodie fingered his U.S. marshal's badge pinned to his vest.

Just then the front door rattled with a knock. Weary, Aaron scuffed over to the door and opened it to find….

"Hargrave." He set his back teeth. "What are you doing here?"

The man pulled his rounded hat from his head, his hands trembling and his upper lip beaded with perspiration. "I heard about Hope. What happened? Is she all right?"

"She's resting." Aaron didn't feel inclined to go into any great detail.

"Is she all right?" Jonas's tone was cloaked with the kind of weak desperation that scratched at a man's soul.

"She should be," Ben clipped off as he approached the door. "But we won't know for sure until she comes to."

"Can I—can I see her?" He patted his face with a crisp white handkerchief.

Aaron pinned his gaze to Hargrave. If the man truly did have feelings for Hope, and she felt the same, then he wasn't about to finagle a situation just to appease himself. That would hardly be fair. But he could carefully monitor the man. Like an eagle scouting a newly harvested field for an unsuspecting rat.

Stepping aside to let Jonas enter, the pit in Aaron's stomach deepened. "You can look in on her but not for long. Since she hasn't regained consciousness yet, we don't want to disturb her."

Jonas pushed the rest of the way into the house. "I'll stay as long as I want, Drake. You may be her helping hand here on the farm, but other than that you've no claim on her."

Aaron eyed him, struggling to maintain his calm. The

way the man couldn't look him in the eye only furthered his already foul opinion.

"Five minutes. That's all." The muscle at Aaron's jaw ticked with anger. He scraped his gaze from Jonas's head to his toes, taking the man's full measure and pretty much disliking everything he saw.

"You heard him," Brodie said, stepping toward them.

"If she happens to ask for you later, we'll see what we can do about having someone fetch you at the hotel." Zach gave Hargrave a condescending wink.

Narrowing his gaze on Aaron, Jonas turned on his heels and walked back to the bedroom, his gait a little too smooth, a little too practiced to make him seem like much of a man. And that small observation pricked Aaron all the more.

"Please do not blame yourself, Aaron." Hope held her breath, trying not to wince as she shifted on the sofa. She'd insisted on getting up this morning even though she'd been down for less than a day and even now regretted her decision.

"You should be resting in bed." With great care he adjusted the pillow under her arm, his hands trembling.

She plastered the brightest smile she could on her face. "Had I languished in bed for even a moment longer, my patience would've been tried past the point of decency."

"I doubt it," he argued.

Mostly, though, she hadn't wished to further Aaron's sense of guilt. He'd been so attentive to her needs right along with Callie and Ben, Joseph and Katie. Even Jane had offered to get her a drink. Once.

"I should've checked things over just to make sure that the wagon was sound before you took off for town."

"Accidents happen." Hope grasped one of his hands and

looked him in the eye, desperate to ease his guilt. "It was a simple mishap, Aaron. An accident. In my frustration, I was probably going a bit faster than I should have."

His cheerless gaze was as vulnerable as she'd ever seen. "You've given me a few scares over the past two months, Hope, but this one—" a pained expression creased his brow "—I don't know what I would've done if something had happened to you. Especially after the things I said to you."

She could've cried right then. Just seeing his anguish gave her a deep and impacting glimpse into his heart.

"I want you to know that the things I said…I was frustrated. Nothing more."

"I responded in kind, Aaron. I'm every bit as guilty."

"I would never forgive myself if something had happened to you."

"But I'm fine. See, look." When she pushed herself out of the sofa to prove her point, her battered body silently screamed in protest.

"There you go again. Insisting on proving yourself," Aaron scolded as he shot off the sofa and eased her back to her seat. His strong hand at her back was like a warm, healing balm.

She forced a smile to her face in spite of her pain. How she wished that he could let go of the past and embrace the future. That he could finally move on instead of returning to that moment in time when his life had come to a screeching halt. "You can't blame yourself every single time something bad happens."

He peered at her, and for a moment she felt an overwhelming sense of responsibility for his pain.

She swallowed hard. "I'm so sorry I—"

"There's nothing for you to be sorry for." Gentle as could be, he touched a finger whisper-light to the gash

Ben had stitched on her forehead. "I'm just glad that you're going to be all right—at least once you heal up."

She scowled as she peered down at her left arm, trying to dismiss his overly attentive response as just an overreaction. But what if he felt even more obligated to her now? "This is a nuisance, to be sure. It will require me to have most of my dresses altered."

"That's a small thing, easily remedied. And it's a whole lot better than what could've happened." He fingered the delicate lace edging her sleeve, his soft touch sending tiny shivers of delight coursing up her arm and straight to her heart. "I want you to promise me something."

"Promise?" She couldn't help but grin at his peculiar choice of words. "From your experience, Aaron Drake, promises can be risky. You should know that."

The way he stared at her then, his gaze so earnest and honest and glazed with affection, gave her heart pause. "I have no regrets. Not one."

She wanted to look away, scared to death that she'd see guilt behind his words, or obligation, but she couldn't seem to pull her gaze from his. She longed for his gentle touch, for the sound of her name on his lips, for the feel of his breath whispering over her skin. One word from him and her knees would grow so weak that it would be hard to find her balance.

He was nothing she'd ever thought she'd want in a man, but everything she wanted. He was sincere, every inch masculine and yet so very gentle, compassionate, honest and loyal.

But as the coarse words he'd spoken yesterday inched into her thoughts, her rising emotions slipped from their heady height. Although he'd apologized for his sentiments, she couldn't bear the idea of following her heart only to find him facing another roadblock in his. Because love that wasn't pure and free of guilt or obligation wasn't love at all.

She just wanted to be loved. And she wanted to love.

She loved Aaron. She'd probably loved him from the moment she'd stumbled in Gertrude's stall and was caught up in his arms. But the more readily she set her mind on him being nothing more than a friend, the better off she'd be. And as quickly as she could give Jonas her answer, the better off she'd be, too. Because ever since he'd proposed that she sell the place and go back to Boston, *where she belonged,* she'd felt sick to her stomach—and absolutely sure about her decision a year ago to break her engagement. His words had shaken her from her minute, albeit odious, lapse of judgment.

What had she been thinking to believe that Jonas had actually changed? As distressing as it was to admit, it was becoming more and more apparent that his interest in her went as far as the depth of her bank account. When her family had lost their fortune, he'd lost interest but had been too prideful to make his shallow intentions quite so obvious. And when he'd learned from her mother that Paul had gifted her with a healthy sum of money, Jonas had come racing out here to cash in on her fortune.

Staring out the window at the summer landscape, she realized, yet again, that Jonas was nothing like Aaron. Nothing. Their similarities went as far as the fact that they both walked on two legs and breathed air.

"Did you hear me?" Aaron's voice was low and tight as he held her gaze. "I have no regrets."

Wishing to avoid his warm attention, she glanced over at where Theodore had curled up in a bright patch of sunshine. "So, what promise would you like for me to make?"

He set his hand beneath her chin, bringing her focus to

him. "Well, for one…for the next few weeks, you'll leave the chores to me. Deal?"

The very idea made her instantly sad. "But the cows will miss me. And the goats and poor da Vinci…she'll be lost without me."

"I didn't say you couldn't go out and visit with them." A smile strained at the sides of his mouth in a way that eased her some. "You can be out there with me or whenever else you like, but I don't want you causing more injury to your arm by doing chores. It'll be more than enough for you to take part in the play tomorrow night. That said, I want you to give yourself plenty of time to heal—just like Ben said."

"All right. I promise." She couldn't bear the idea of being separated from her animals. And quite honestly, she couldn't bear the idea of being away from Aaron.

"And another thing…" When he covered her hand with his, a trickle of fluttery sensations left her feeling heady with pleasure. "Promise me that you'll hold on to hope."

She eyed him for a long moment, the weight of his words blanketing her heart with expectation. Hope? For what?

The farm? The animals? Aaron?

She had to stop longing for anything more than a platonic friendship with Aaron. She'd just have to make it through the play tomorrow night, and the next few weeks of him huddling over her, then she would hire someone else to help out. She'd finally realized that if she waited until Aaron felt comfortable with a new hire, she'd be farmhand-short and experience-poor for the rest of her life.

"I promise," she finally uttered.

Unbidden, thoughts of Jonas suddenly dropped into her mind. Since Aaron was always close at hand, she'd not had an opportunity to speak with him alone when he'd visited.

But if she was to completely break free from the past and move on, then giving Jonas her answer was of the utmost importance. "Can you please promise *me* something?"

Aaron's gaze grew so sincere, her heart melted a little. "Anything."

"Promise me you'll locate Jonas. I know that you are not fond of him, but I need to speak with him. It is imperative."

Chapter Twenty

Agreeing to retrieve Jonas Hargrave was the hardest pledge Aaron had ever made. But if he loved Hope, then the only right thing to do was to let her go, to let her choose. If she wanted to be with Hargrave for the rest of her life, then he wouldn't stand in her way.

What he could do, however, is push himself closer to reaching a resolution with himself and with God. That way the playing field would be leveled, because ever since Ellie and Jeremiah died, he'd been mired in grief so thick he couldn't even see things straight.

Since Hope had seemed so weary, he'd left her with Jane and insisted she go back to bed and rest while he went after Jonas. After he'd dropped Hargrave off, he'd gone home, and for the past two hours he'd been packing away some of the things he'd clung to, gathering all of the items that he'd left untouched after the deaths—the cradle he'd crafted, the baby blanket Ellie had knit along with the hand-sewn baby items…he'd packed all of it up to be donated to the Seeds of Faith. The thought of some mother in need, using these things, made his heart swell with pride.

Ellie would've been proud of him. She'd have been proud, too, for the way he'd gone a step further and had begun to wipe the slate clean in his home. He'd left one picture of her on the chest of drawers in his bedroom. Everything else he'd packed away in her hope chest.

He'd felt a tangible sense of peace—that is, until he'd returned to Hope's farm just a few minutes ago and found Brodie and Sheriff Goodwin on the porch with Jane.

Dread crept up his spine as he dismounted and jogged over to them. "What is it? What's wrong?"

"It was no accident," Brodie announced, his words measured and firm as Aaron leaped up the three steps.

Sheriff Goodwin hooked his thumbs into his vest pockets. "No sirree. No accident at all. Someone meant you harm, Aaron."

The sound of the goats bleating and cows mooing echoed in the farmyard. Chore time was past due, and by the way they were carrying on, they were determined to get someone out there to feed them.

"What a huge relief you weren't hurt," Jane gushed, perching a hand on his arm.

"I wasn't but Hope was," he ground out, caring little that his curt response made her flinch. He shrugged from Jane's touch and leveled a disbelieving gaze on the woman, wondering how he'd been so blind to Jane's spiteful ways.

Aaron gathered a lungful of air to keep his calm. "What in the world are you talking about, Brodie? I mean, I can't imagine why someone would want to do something like this."

"It was a spot of misfortune that Hope happened to be driving the rig." Brodie gave his head a slow, serious shake. "That's for sure."

"So, you're saying that someone tampered with my wagon?"

Brodie removed his black Stetson. "I investigated the

rig and the hitch, thoroughly. And there's no doubt in my mind it'd been compromised. I've seen it before."

Pulling a hand over the back of his neck, he let the information settle in. "Are you sure?"

"Absolutely."

"Sure fire shootin', we are." Goodwin hacked, the echo reverberating across the peaceful farmyard. "That's why Brodie here got me all involved in this thing." Wrenching his mouth off to one side, the sheriff focused his beady eyes on Aaron in that self-important way of his. "We got ourselves a rogue out there who's lookin' to cause a body harm. Namely you, Aaron Drake. And we're gonna catch 'im if it's the last thing we do."

Jane made an all-out show of clearing her throat. She raised her loglike eyebrows over her eyes. "Maybe it wasn't the work of someone else. Maybe—"

"What?" Aaron prodded, impatiently. "Maybe what?"

She clasped her hands in front of her, her gaze flitting from one thing to the next. "Well, maybe Hope did this to herself. Maybe she was desperate for a way out of the farm, seeing as how it's been so hard. Honestly, I wouldn't put it past her to cause her own accident just so that she could shirk her responsibilities here."

Incredulous, his jaw muscles tensed harder with every moment that ticked by. "How could you possibly think that Hope would deliberately try to hurt herself just to get out of a few chores?"

"Well, it's obviously been hard for her," she argued, threading her fingers together so tight that they blanched white. "Anyone can see that."

Aaron jammed his hands at his waist, grappling for calm. He felt far too close to losing his temper with this woman than he wanted to admit. "Have you *ever* seen her complain? Even once?"

She slid back a step, bracing her hands against the house. With a shake of her head, she blurted out, "She doesn't belong here, Aaron. Can't you see that? Paul had to have known this seeing as how he didn't even tell me about her."

"Sure was a surprise," Goodwin added on an irritating chuckle.

Out of the corner of his eye, Aaron could see Brodie nudge the sheriff's arm as though to shut the man up.

"Paul didn't tell me about her either, Jane, and I was one of his best friends." He grappled for a thread of manners, his pulse pounding as he glanced down to find Theodore rubbing against Jane's skirt. "He was sometimes a very private man. Maybe he was worried that the whole thing would fall apart before she got here. I don't know. But for some reason he wanted to keep this to himself until she arrived."

"Get away, you nasty cat," Jane growled, swatting then rustling her skirt as though the kitten had spread some dread disease over the garment. She set her focus on Aaron again. "I'm just surprised she didn't bow out at the last minute."

"Why would you think she'd do something like that?" he probed, her accusation pricking his ire as he reached down and scooped up the yellow tabby.

"She had to have known what she was getting herself into—that alone should've scared her away. And if she didn't know, then you can be sure that just as soon as she got off the train, she'd wished she'd never set foot here."

"You're wrong on that account, too. Hope understands what commitment is all about. She wouldn't have done that to Paul." He narrowed his gaze on her, downright angered by her blatant vindictiveness. "You just need to accept that fact."

Jane hugged her arms to her chest. "She should've gone back home after she found out that Paul had died."

"If you remember, she'd been given a responsibility." Pulling in a steadying breath, he grasped for some thread of calm as he pet the purring tabby. "One that she's been good natured and determined about, too. And she's loved it."

The way Jane's chin quivered just then tugged at his compassion. "She's ruined everything. Absolutely everything."

"*What* are you talking about?" he prodded, confused as all get-out, now. "Is it that you wanted the lead role in the play?"

She gave her head a decisive shake.

"Well then, was it that you wanted to live in Paul's house? Or were you put out about the bank account?"

"No," she spat. "But as soon as she showed up, all of your attention was spent on *her*." Tears formed at the corners of her eyes as Goodwin gave her back an awkward pat. "I thought that you and I were becoming—"

"You and I, Jane, we're friends." He willed his anger to subside as he dipped his head to grab her attention. "Do you understand?"

On a sniff, she pulled her chin up a notch. "Friends?"

"Yes, *friends*," he stressed, trying to ward off her fantasy for something more. The idea of Jane Thompson being anything more than a friend nearly turned his stomach inside out. She'd likely make a good wife for someone, someday, but it as sure as shootin' wouldn't be Aaron Drake.

"If you took the time to get to know Hope a little," Aaron continued, wanting to completely douse Jane's aversion to Hope. "Perhaps you'd realize how much she's loved it here—in spite of the blisters she suffered from plowing, the goats escaping and the stallion getting out. *Even* after she'd lost all but one of her chickens to wolves, she could see the good here. She doesn't want to leave."

He was sure of that just a few days ago, but Hargrave showing up had dealt his confidence a big blow. Still, he knew that she loved it here on the farm. "When I told her that I didn't want her doing chores, her first thought had been of the animals and how much she would miss them. Does that sound like someone who's looking to get out of a responsibility?"

Jane plucked a handkerchief from her sleeve and blew her nose, emitting a honklike noise that startled Theodore. "Oh, my…"

"What's the matter?" he prompted as he smoothed a hand down the kitten's fluffy fur.

"I've really done it now. Paul would be very unhappy with me if he were alive to see this."

Hope appeared at the door then, her silken hair perfectly mussed up, her eyes droopy from sleep. She cradled her arm against her chest.

Aaron set Theodore down on the porch as he held the door open for Hope, wishing that he could scoop her up in his arms and comfort her for the rest of her days.

"Hope?" Jane howled, a deep crimson blotching her neck and cheeks. "Can you forgive me?"

"Forgive you?" Confusion creased Hope's brow.

"For what, Jane?" Aaron dared, a deep pit hollowing his stomach. "What did you do?"

"I'm the one who let the goats out. And the stallion, too. And I'm the one who came over and unlatched the chicken coop that night." Jane twisted her handkerchief in her hands, shifting her timid focus to Hope. "I didn't dream there'd be wolves. I was only hoping to scare you off."

Aaron's blood swished red-hot through his veins. He'd figured that Jane had been upset by Hope's presence, but to go so far as to try to scare her off...

"I even lied to you about plowing being easy work," she confessed, her eyes pooling with tears. "When I've never, ever even touched the thing. Paul would've never allowed it."

Hope touched the hair at the nape of her neck then drew her hands to her sides. Although she was the picture of poise and calm, she had every right to be angry.

"Forgive me. Please say you will," Jane pleaded, her voice tinged with that familiar whiney tone that grated Aaron's nerves.

"I think I've known all along." Hope glanced at where her kitten rubbed against her dress.

"Jane, you better have a good explanation," Aaron ground out, moving a step closer to Hope. She may have let Jane off the hook, but Aaron wasn't feeling so generous.

How could he have been so blind as to miss what had been occurring right under his nose? He'd even gone so far as to almost agree with some of Jane's *observations* about Hope a few weeks back.

Hope had never said one word about Jane's behavior—not one. Alone, she'd endured Jane's vengeance. After the wolf attack, she'd even started doubting herself.

And Aaron had so much as accused her for making mistakes when the truth was she'd done nothing wrong.

Like a worm struggling to escape the baking sun, Jane slid her gaze to Aaron as though looking to him for help.

He wasn't about to come to her rescue. If she'd been so sneaky and downright mean as to sabotage Hope, then it was only right for her to make amends.

She heaved a sigh, her hands trembling as she pinned

her gaze to the porch floor. "I'm so sorry. I've been horrible to you, and you haven't deserved it. First I was mad at Paul for bringing you here and not even telling me."

Hope rested a hand on Jane's arm, causing the woman to startle.

Huge tears sprang from Jane's eyes as though on command. "But then I thought that maybe," she sputtered, glancing at Aaron, her thin mouth pulled tight, "well, that maybe Aaron had set his heart on you." A loud sob escaped her lips, followed by a wail that nearly broke the glass paned windows behind her.

Theodore suddenly turned into one gigantic fur ball as he scraped and scurried off the porch so fast that he nearly tumbled head over heels. Even the songbirds in a nearby tree grew quiet, as though anticipating another outburst.

Aaron dragged in a steadying breath as the woman's cries pierced the late afternoon summer air. Visions of her peculiar behavior over the past two months flashed through his mind with lightning speed—the way she'd *supposedly* injured her ankle at play practice and then insisted on being carried and the way she'd always make sure to sit in front with him, leaving Hope to ride in the wagon bed. He also thought about the little seeds of misgivings she'd try to plant in his head regarding Hope. He should've paid more attention to his suspicions.

Hope encircled Jane in a hug. "I understand, but I can assure you that as far as Aaron and I are concerned, you have nothing to worry about." Her words nearly deflated his hope.

Jonas had been here earlier, and from what she'd just uttered and from the way she'd moved from his side just moments ago, she'd obviously made her decision. She must've affirmed her affection for Jonas, though, Aaron couldn't figure what she saw in the man. He was white as a blizzard, stiff as a train rail and far too buttoned up and smoothed down to constitute a man. Aaron nearly choked on the image of her walking out of his life on that man's arm.

He loved her. And if he had any hope of winning her heart then he'd have to make his intentions known—as boldly and as clearly as the beautiful July day.

Chapter Twenty-One

With the afternoon chores past due, Aaron had torn himself away from the house and headed out to the barn. He'd been eager for an opportunity to talk with Hope, but Brodie and the sheriff had wanted to ask her some questions. And Jane had hovered over her, seeing to every need as though paying penance for her spiteful deeds. Hope had been unbelievably kind and gracious in the face of Jane's confessions, comforting the woman who'd sobbed so loud that Theodore had scrambled for cover.

"God, what am I going to do? I think I've lost her." Returning the pitchfork to the barn entrance, he made his way over to the closed gate leading to the corral. He draped his arms over the top wood slat and peered at Daisy's newborn, strong and sure on his feet as the little guy stood close to his mama.

Closing his eyes, he breathed in the scent of fresh hay he'd spread out for the horses. He'd done a one-eighty in the past weeks—from blaming God and himself, to beginning to realize that life's seasons can't necessarily be dictated. And he'd gone from believing that he could never love again to his heart being tugged by love's unseen force.

There'd always be a place in his heart for Ellie. She'd been his first true love, but the painful yearning and aching void he'd lived with this past year had waned. Sometimes when he was with Hope, he couldn't even conjure up those feelings. She'd captivated his attention, his affection and his emotions. She'd made him believe in hope and love again.

And his brothers and Brodie, they'd tugged him through some tight spots when he would've otherwise gotten stuck if left to his own strength.

And God…Aaron had to believe that He'd been there all along, walking him through his valley of grief, even when he'd railed against Him.

"Forgive me," he said, his throat constricting tight just knowing that God's forgiveness was there as the sentiment crossed his lips.

Paul's last words threaded through Aaron's mind again. *Promise me you'll hold on to Hope.* He'd been all but void of hope, and then Hope had come into his life. She'd turned it upside down without doing a thing.

Just then a shuffling sound came from behind him. Turning, he expected to see the sheriff or Brodie coming down the barn aisle.

The peaceful feeling that had engulfed him just moments ago scattered at the sight of Jonas Hargrave.

"What are you doing here?" Aaron ground out, half-heartedly groping for congeniality and finding none. "I thought you walked back to town."

"That's not much of a greeting, now, is it?" Hargrave's gait was clumsy as he sidestepped, his foot knocking into an empty pail.

"You've been drinking, Hargrave." Even from a good ten feet away, Aaron could smell the scent of liquor tainting the earthy barn smells.

A smile curled Jonas's thin lips as the bellow of hungry cattle filled the air. "What would make you say that?"

Aaron nailed the man with a disgust-filled gaze. "You need to get yourself back to the hotel. And the sooner the better. When I get done feeding the goats and cattle, I'll take you back to town."

"That won't be necessary. And I do believe I'll leave when I'm good and ready." Jonas tugged at the sleeves of his fancy dove-gray jacket. Reaching inside his coat, he pulled a shiny flask from a pocket, uncorked the thing and emptied the last drops into his mouth. An insincere smile twisted his lips. "I'd offer you some, but as you can see, it's gone."

Aaron stalked past Jonas to retrieve the pail the man had kicked. "You'll either leave this property on your own accord now or you can wait right there and go with me when I'm done. Take your pick, or I'll make the decision for you."

"I didn't think you owned this piece of land," Hargrave spat as he followed, his steps heavy as he stayed close on Aaron's heels. "That being the case, and since Hope didn't ask me to leave, I believe I have every right to be here."

Aaron's jaw tensed as he dove the bucket into the grain bin for Penelope and Patience. Images of that day he'd shown up here to find Hope chasing the goats around to retrieve her fancy female garments flashed through his mind. He'd laughed that day. For the first time in months, laughter had erupted from deep within.

"I'm here to watch out for Hope, and that's what I'm going to do," he warned, as the bleat of two hungry goats filtered into the barn. He turned and eyed Hargrave. "And frankly, I'd feel a whole lot better knowing you weren't skulking around here—especially in the condition you're in. Hope doesn't need this extra stress right now."

"Just a few hours ago you came in town for me—at Hope's request, if I remember right." Hargrave attempted to straighten his cravat, but finally gave up and gave the fluff of fabric a halfhearted pat. "I'm worried about her. I want to make sure she's going to be all right."

"She's going to be fine," Aaron assured him, wondering if maybe he was judging the man too harshly. Jonas had been out here four times in the past day, though all but once Hope had been resting and Aaron had sent him away.

"We had quite a conversation earlier." Jonas stretched out his hands as though inspecting them for signs of dirt, then brushed them together in such a pristine way that Aaron disliked him all the more. "You see, Hope and I... we always could talk for hours."

Conniving and very astute, Hargrave knew just what to say to pierce Aaron's pride.

"Well, there won't be any talking now. Hope is likely worn out from a long day." Willing himself to calm down, he loosened his grip on the pail and walked out of the barn to the goats' pen. He unlatched the gate, moved around the goats and spread the grain in the trough. Pivoting, he peered at where Jonas stood just inside the barn. "You're riding with me in a few minutes—whether you like it or not."

Hargrave fixed his gaze on something off to the side. "I want to see her for myself."

"You saw her earlier. You should know that apart from a broken arm and that bad cut on her forehead, she seems to be faring better than any of us expected after such a horrible accident."

He'd wracked his brain trying to come up with someone who might want him injured or dead, but not one face flashed in his mind.

Except Hargrave's.

Exiting the pen, he grabbed a pad of hay from a square bail. He separated two equal chunks from the pad, fluffing them out and setting them on the ground so that each goat would have their own pile—a request Hope had made early on.

"You know," Hargrave began, "she wouldn't have been injured if she hadn't been on your rig."

He froze on the spot. He slammed his gaze to the man's pasty white, perspiration-beaded face. The hair at the back of his neck prickled to attention. "How would you know she had my rig?"

"She shouldn't have been driving, Drake," Jonas warned, his words sounding as sober and steady.

Aaron was as sure as Hope was beautiful that Hargrave was no saint. In fact, he'd be willing to bet that the man had no character or integrity, at all—that his smooth, gentlemanly demeanor was nothing more than a facade.

"How would you know she was driving my rig?" he questioned, his suspicions growing thicker by the second.

"Word gets around."

Alarm prickled every nerve. "I heard some news, Hargrave. Some very disturbing news."

"What's that?"

"I heard that someone sabotaged my wagon," he measured out. "Do you happen to know anything about that?"

Jonas planted his hands at his waist. "Now, why would I know about that?"

"You tell me."

"I'm just a newcomer here in Boulder, a lonely visitor who's been enjoying the lovely sights." Malevolence flashed in Jonas's eyes, belying his congenial tone.

Aaron clenched his jaw. The idea of this man ogling

Hope grated like harsh sandpaper over soft wood. He moved a step closer, his attention riveted to Jonas. He flexed his hands. He drew them into tight fists. What he wouldn't give to shove them right through Hargrave's face, but what would Hope say once she found out? How would she feel, knowing how unwelcoming Aaron was being to her beau?

At this point, Aaron didn't care. He had to consider Hope's safety, first and foremost. And the way the man was acting all shifty, he didn't trust him one bit with Hope's heart let alone her life. He'd rather follow his instinct and err on the side of caution.

And his gut feeling screamed that Jonas Hargrave was directly responsible for Hope's accident.

"I have to get the chores done. So if you'll excuse me…" Edging past the man, he walked to the gate where just moments ago he'd been watching Daisy and her new calf. If Jonas had sabotaged the wagon then Aaron had to make quick work of the chores so he could take him back to town—and deliver him to the jail.

With a large bucket of grain in his hands, he unlatched the gate and made his way inside the corral where a dozen cattle and three new calves were loping this direction, their bellows of delight echoing in the farmyard. "You all act like you're starving. You've spent enough time grazing in the pasture over the past few days that you should be full."

Over the past two months under Hope's care, these cattle had gone from being skittish to nearly tame, a feat that had surprised him. He spread out the grain in the large trough then returned to the barn for two more bucketfuls. After he fed them, he turned to see Caesar staring sadly over the slatted fence of his bull bachelor quarters.

"You're next, buddy." Grabbing the bucket from the

hard-packed ground, he retrieved a healthy dose of grain for the bull then walked out into the corral again and opened Caesar's gate. He kept his eye on the enormous beast as he made his way to the small feeding trough where Caesar stood ready to eat. For some reason, he trusted this bull more than he trusted Hargrave—and that wasn't saying much.

Never trust a bull. That very first day, he'd said those words to Hope after she'd swatted Caesar's nose, accusing him of picking on Theodore. In spite of his growing unease with Hargrave, a half grin tipped his lips at the endearing memory.

Hope. She was a wonderful and innocent breath of fresh air. She'd brightened his days in more ways than he could count. And she'd landed in his life at a time when he'd least expected it, when he was sure he'd never love again.

God had given him a gift. Hope.

His heart swelled with that knowledge as he emptied the bucket and watched Caesar dip his nose into the grain. While the bull munched away, Aaron crossed to the water pump by the barn, grabbed the handle and began furiously pumping, coaxing water to stream and splatter into the water trough.

"Jonas, no!" Hope's scream shattered the late afternoon calm, jerking every nerve ending to high alert.

Aaron pivoted just in time to see Jonas bringing the pitchfork down right on Aaron's head.

He fell hard. He hit the ground, his head spinning. His ears were ringing. Groaning, he squeezed his eyes against the bright flashes of light pulsing in his vision.

"No. Don't do this, Jonas." Hope's cry filtered to his senses.

He forced his eyes to open, labored to drag his senses

into place as he pushed himself up to his knees. He willed his eyes to focus.

"You were the one who should've been driving the wagon. Not her," Jonas snarled as Aaron caught him throwing a glance over at where Hope was trying to climb over the fence from the farmyard.

"Hope, no! Stay out!" Aaron's blood rushed through his veins like a raging river. He struggled to stand, his head pounding with obscene force.

"You should've been the one," the man accused again. He brought the pitchfork around, catching Aaron's arm.

Aaron stumbled to the ground once more, his arm searing with white-hot pain. His head was spinning out of control.

"She's mine. And the money would've been mine if you hadn't been so ready to lend a hand," Jonas accused.

"What in the world are you talking about?" Aaron forced through clenched teeth. He reached behind him and groped for the watering trough, his head whirling. His vision pulsing in and out of darkness. He drew in a deep breath as Jonas stood over him, the pitchfork poised to spear.

"No, Jonas. Leave him alone," Hope pleaded from the fence line.

Aaron angled his pulsing gaze to see her laboring to climb the fence, her tangling skirts and one able arm making it nearly impossible.

"Stay back, Hope. Don't come in here," he implored as she beelined toward the main gate.

Hargrave's expression contorted to feral desperation as he gave the pitchfork a quick thrust, the tines piercing Aaron's flesh.

Slicing a breath through his teeth, he struggled to get up. It was all he could do to stand, but he had to make sure that Hope was safe. Glancing around for something…anything to use as a weapon, he spotted the bull rope hanging over the fencepost. He'd kept in there just in case but had never needed to use the thing with Caesar.

Hargrave thrust the pitchfork at him, piercing his chest and knocking him down again. "I would've sauntered in here pretty as you please and won her over. She would've come crawling back to me, too, if it hadn't been for you."

Over the man's hissing breath, Aaron could hear the corral gate opening. Images of Hope entering Caesar's pen and falling at Jonas's rage flashed through his mind. "God, help," he breathed as he did a fast roll to the right and levered himself to standing. "Please, Hope. Stay away. Don't come any closer."

"Drake isn't worth your time," Jonas growled over the herd's agitated moos. He honed in on Aaron, the pitchfork poised for another strike. "He's just some dim-witted westerner who's deemed you, a helpless eastern beauty who just happened to land in a nice little sum of cash, an easy mark."

"Aaron would never be so vulgar!" she defended, her words bolstering his sinking heart. His sinking hope.

Jonas cast an enraged gaze Hope's way, pinning her with it long enough for Aaron to reach out and snatch the bull rope from the fencepost.

"Fella, if you think she's helpless," Aaron ground out, hiding the rope behind his back, "then you *don't know Hope*." He blinked hard, laboring to bring his world into focus as Hope unlatched Caesar's gate and rushed toward them.

"I know her a whole lot better than you do, Drake." Hargrave closed in on Aaron.

"Stay back, Hope. Please." Each time he moved or even dragged in a breath, his world spun out of control.

"Don't do this, Jonas," she pleaded, her eyes brimming with tears. She grasped Hargrave's arm and struggled to yank him away. "Please. Aaron has done nothing wrong."

"Get out of here, Hope." Jonas gave her a quick shove, sending her stumbling backward. Then he thrust the tines at Aaron, piercing his stomach.

Aaron teetered off balance as Hargrave's thin lips curled into a menacing smile.

"Are you all right, darlin'?" he ground out, barely taking notice of the stabbing piercing pain in his stomach or the warm trickle of blood oozing from the puncture wounds. Aaron fumed. In his book, any man who intentionally harmed a woman wasn't fit to breathe the air God gave him.

With a snarl, Jonas closed in on Aaron.

"No!" Hope's face crumpled in fear. She shoved herself to standing and honed in on Jonas again.

She swiped at a tear trailing down her cheek. Hugged her wounded arm to her chest. "Drop the pitchfork, Jonas, please. I'm begging you to come to your senses. Aaron has done nothing wrong."

His strong sense of protection hummed to high alert as he tightened his grip on the rope and whipped it around, hard and fast. The rope whipped around Hargrave's throat, the tail end snapping his cheek with a loud crack.

Jonas yowled and grabbed at the rope, desperately trying to free himself.

Aaron yanked hard. Out of the corner of his eye, he caught sight of Caesar staring intently this way, his nostrils flared. His enormous neck muscles, bunching. The bull lowered his head in a clear threat, snorted, pawed the ground once and then charged—straight into Jonas's side.

Hargrave flew ten feet into the barn. His wail pierced the air as he crumpled to the ground. He writhed in pain.

"Aaron, are you all right?" Hope's hand trembled as she held his arm.

"I'll be fine." Dragging in a deep breath, he clenched his jaw to keep from wincing as he stalked over and snagged the pitchfork from where it lay beside Jonas. He heaved it over the fence then gently wrapped an arm around Hope's shoulders, moved that she would risk her life for him. "How about you? Are you hurt?"

"I'm fine." The vulnerability and strength and deep affection he saw in her gaze as she peered up at him was enough to make a man realize his own heart.

Was there still a place for him in her life? Because he loved her. He loved Hope Gatlin.

"Get him away!" Jonas screeched as the bull stood over him, snorting and stomping as though preparing to finish the job. "He's going to kill me."

Aaron gave her shoulder a tender squeeze. He ignored the searing pain radiating across his stomach and chest, head and arm, and peered down at to where the man was whimpering, scrambling to sitting.

Hargrave inched back against the barn. Curled into a ball, hiding his face in his hands as Caesar closed in on him, his shoulder muscles bunching and quivering with untapped power. "Get this murderous beast away from me!"

The bull drove his front hooves into the ground inches from Hargrave, dusting the man in a plume of filth. He snorted and threw his massive head from one side to the other.

"He's killing me. He's killing me." Jonas peeked through his hands, his gaze wild and terrorized. "Somebody do something! Get this crazed animal away from me."

A strong sense of satisfaction rose in Aaron, seeing just what kind of man Jonas really was as he whimpered and whined—vengeful, weak, cowardly.

He was not much of a man.

Chapter Twenty-Two

"**W**ell done, Caesar," Hope whispered, sniffing quietly. Her stomach convulsed at the very idea that Jonas had tried to kill Aaron. She smoothed a hand down the bull's neck, alarm shooting through her as she spotted crimson stains seeping through the ragged remains of Aaron's ecru shirt. "Aaron, your stomach. You're bleeding terribly."

"It's nothing," he dismissed with a strained half smile. "Probably nothing more than flesh wounds."

Hope lifted her apron and secured a side in her teeth then tore a thick strip with her good hand. "These look just terrible." She struggled to keep from crying as she imagined just how empty life would've been had Aaron been killed. She pressed the cloth to each of the wounds, trying to determine just how deep they were.

"You could've been killed, Aaron. This never would have happened to you if not for me." She peered up at him, her eyes burning with the threat of tears. Her heart swelled at Aaron's steadying glance.

He grasped her shoulders, settling her with a look of assurance. "I'll be fine, darlin'. Trust me."

The reality of what Jonas had done over the past day hit her with full force then. When a quiet sob escaped her lips, she pressed her fingers to her mouth, struggling to hold herself together. "Are you sure?"

Aaron reached for her hand and pressed a kiss to her fingers, his hand trembling in a sure sign that he wasn't as unaffected as he'd like her to believe.

"I promise." He nuzzled her fingers to his rough cheek, sending quivers down her spine then back again. "I promise."

A gentle wave of peace lapped at her soul as she touched his lips. She could count on him. And she absolutely knew that she could count on God. Just minutes ago, when she'd stepped outside and had seen Jonas standing behind Aaron, a pitchfork in his hands, poised and ready to kill, she'd run as fast as her legs could carry her, all the way pleading with God to spare Aaron's life.

Even in that dire moment, when her world was seemingly spiraling out of control, she'd felt a tangible assurance that God was there—and more than worthy of her trust.

When the bull snorted again, Jonas whimpered, then squeaked out a pitiful cry as though he was no older than a toddler in nappies.

Aaron exhaled and raked a hand through his hair. "I'll have Ben tend to my wounds later, but right now I need to deal with him." He glanced down at where Jonas was huddled in a tight ball. "At least until Brodie and the sheriff get back from Jane's."

Hope shoved her gaze to her former fiancé. His words had been so smooth and polished over the past couple of days. She should've known better than to believe—if even for a weak second—that he'd actually changed.

"He loves you, you know?" He peered down at the huddled mass of quaking man.

"Jonas?" she choked out, horrified that Aaron would

think such a thing after what had just transpired. "How could you think—"

"I was actually referring to this big guy, Caesar," he said, nodding to the bull. Grimacing, he turned and grabbed a handful of Jonas's collar, then dragged him over to the fence as the bull stayed right with him, every step of the way. "For the most part, Caesar has always been cooperative with me. But from day one, he's been like a puppy with you."

A smile cracked the sadness on her face. "He's just a big old baby," she sputtered, feeling like she could laugh just as easily as cry. She remembered how adamant Aaron had been that she be very wary of the bull. The concern he showed time and again had given her a wonderful sense of security and protection she'd yearned for.

"I'm not so sure that Hargrave, here, would agree with you." Aaron unwound the bull rope from Hargrave's thin neck and wrenched the man's arms behind his back.

In a matter of moments, he had Jonas bound and secured to a sturdy fence post. "He won't be going anywhere now—at least not until Brodie and the sheriff get back." Standing, he swiped an arm over his brow as he gently nudged the bull aside. "Come on, buddy, you've scared him enough."

Hope crossed to Caesar's feeding trough and grabbed a handful of grain. "Come here, boy," she encouraged as the bull trotted over—just like a playful pup.

With a sigh, Aaron leaned against the trough. "Good thing that that bull was intent on protecting you." The steady, peace-filled expression she witnessed on his face just then filled her with an unexplainable joy. "The three of us and God...we make a pretty good team."

The packed crowd roared with applause in the town hall as the play came to a close. It'd gone off without a hitch.

Hope smiled as each of the cast members took their bows. Libby, Elsa and Luke held hands as they rushed to the front of the stage and gave a dramatic, unison bow, evoking a loud round of applause along with a smattering of chuckles in the room—and a heartening smile from Elsa.

When it was Jane's turn to bow with several other cast members, a twinge of compassion swelled inside Hope for the woman. Jane had been so wracked with guilt after her confession yesterday that she'd gone overboard to redeem herself, fluffing and fussing and fluttering about in an effort to tend to Hope's every need. With extreme gentleness and carefully considered words, Hope had eased the woman from her toil and guilt.

When it came time for Hope to take her bow with Aaron, her stomach grew oddly fluttery. She'd felt just fine all evening and had remained surprisingly calm throughout the performance, so why, now, would she be feeling as though she was on tenterhooks?

Aaron grasped her hand and stared down at her, sending her stomach into a series of flip-flops. Her knees grew weak. The smile he wore and the deep look of pleasure permeating his expression made her heart skip more than one beat.

"Are you ready?" he whispered in her ear.

She drew in a sharp breath as a tremor shimmied all the way down her spine to her toes. She chided herself for being so nervous and flustered, after all this was Aaron. Her good friend. "As ready as I'll ever be."

He paused for a moment, gave her hand a brief squeeze then led her to center-stage, his fervent gaze never leaving hers. Not even for a moment. His grin faded to a captivating look of intensity and…and something else that brought every wandering thought she might have to a staggering halt.

Aaron held her hand, her gaze, her heart—even when he was completely unaware of that fact.

The applause thundered louder, as whoops and hollers from Aaron's brothers rumbled to her hearing. When she took her bow beside Aaron, her eyes welled with ready tears, as though something big, something profound was stretching before them like some grand design.

She was blessed and honored to be a part of such a worthy cause, but her tears and the overwhelming sense of destiny and hope and expectation that hummed around and through her seemed to stretch beyond just this moment in time.

When the applause died down, Aaron dragged his focus from her and faced the audience—friends, family and neighbors. He held up his hand, the town hall growing so still and quiet that the sound of nighttime crickets chirping outdoors echoed in the large room.

When Hope took a step back in order to give him the limelight, he wrapped his arm around her and tenderly pulled her to his side. "Oh, no. You're not going anywhere."

Muffled giggles flitted, featherlight across the room as her heart surged all the way up to her throat.

"As probably all of you know," he began, his rich voice filling the room and her heart, "this past year has been a difficult one. Like many of you, I've been through loss. I've been angry with people, God, myself…. It's been hard, and most of the time I've bowed out of social events just because I didn't want to hurt any more than I already did. If not for my delightful little niece, Libby," he said, his voice breaking as he glanced over his shoulder at where

Libby stood waving at him, "I never would've been in this play."

Aaron drew in a long, slow breath, giving her shoulder a tender squeeze. "You folks...you've been so supportive." He gestured to the crowd. "And my close friends—" he nodded at where Brodie sat in the front row and very possibly where Paul might have sat had he lived "—you've been long-suffering. And my brothers and family...you've been more than a man could ask for in a family."

Pulling his fingers over his eyes, he cleared his throat. "The one thing I know that I lacked over these months was faith and hope. But mostly hope. Well, I want you all to know that I've found it. And I'm not letting it go."

Quiet awe-filled gasps and a sniffle or two wafted through the town hall.

When he pivoted to face Hope, her pulse swished and swirled, the noise almost deafening. "I'm never letting her go." His eyes misted over. "I'm not going to let you go, Hope," he whispered, his mouth tipping in one of those half grins of his that made her head swim. Her stomach all aflutter.

She couldn't take her eyes off of him. With each passing moment, she could almost feel her love for him grow. She loved the way he'd protected her, encouraged her and had been her strength when she was weak. And she loved the way he unabashedly cherished her at this moment. Suddenly everything around them, all of the people, the props, the chairs...all of it seemed as if to fade away.

"To find true love once is a blessing. To find true love a second time is an unexpected and beautiful gift," he proclaimed, his voice sure and steady and wholly unashamed. "You prayed for me when you didn't even know me. And you prayed for me when you knew me."

She remembered praying, even when her faith was so

new, for Aaron, that God would bring healing to his broken heart.

"I may have said what I'm about to before, but this time you have to know that it's not from my pride or obligation. It's from my heart."

Tears sprang to her eyes as he held her hand and dropped to one knee in front of her. "Hope Gatlin, I love you more than I ever thought I could love a woman. Will you marry me?"

A collective sigh filled the room as she held his adoring gaze. For as long as she could remember, she'd dreamed of something so beautiful, so loving and so very romantic. After what had happened with Jonas and then Paul, she'd concluded that love had passed her by.

But God…

God had redeemed over a year of heartache. He'd led her down a trail she would've otherwise never traveled— and all to find a man like Aaron Drake. He was honorable, loyal and loving. He was a man who'd not only divested himself of the past but had boldly stepped into the future. When he usually sought to avoid public attention, he'd been intent on capturing the limelight just moments ago—and all for Hope.

Through her tears she peered at him and nodded, knowing that he had her heart and that she had captured his whole heart. "Yes." She gave a silent little sob and then hiccuped. "Yes. Yes. Yes."

Epilogue

The viola's rich song infused the late afternoon with magnificent anticipation as Callen Lockhart played near the makeshift wedding altar. The small table had been placed smack-dab in the middle of Hope's field, bordered on two sides by mature trees. The pastor stood there, too, as well as da Vinci, who claimed a place right beside Callen, and could be heard making that chirping cluck kind of noise that hens use when they're content.

An amused grin tipped Aaron's mouth as he turned from the whimsical wedding ensemble. When he glimpsed Hope, some forty yards away, walking down the aisle, his breath caught in his chest. His heart skipped several beats. His arms ached to hold her…to hold Hope.

She looked as lovely as the day was perfect. The warm smile she gave him seemed to cast a glow over the field—the very same field she'd labored so hard to plow—as Ben walked her down the aisle, an unsophisticated path hemmed in by colorful scrap quilts and people. Lots of people. Aaron barely even noticed the throng of guests who'd stood from their quilts. It seemed as if the whole of Boulder had come out for the occasion, but Aaron had eyes only for Hope.

His Hope.

He gave a long and satisfied sigh, relishing every last detail as she moved closer. Each step ushered in by the viola's harmonious melody. And by nature's melody, too. The birds, the beasts of the field, the gentle wind's whispering song…

It'd been a sorrowful moment for Hope this morning, knowing that her animals would be watching from a distance. The fact that their furry feelings had even crossed Hope's sweet mind had only made Aaron love her more.

"Thank You, God," he whispered as his bride approached.

He'd once vowed that he'd never again marry.

That was before Hope. Before he'd voiced a promise to his friend that had at one time tasted like a bitter draught on his tongue, but had become his wonderful saving grace. A lifeline out of his agonizing grief. God had placed Hope, a beautiful city flower, right here in the rough-and-tumble West, and Aaron couldn't feel more blessed.

Two months ago Aaron never would've dreamed Hope would be walking through a mature hayfield, in kind and golden light, with the cattle calling from their pens and the goats bleating from theirs, and her rambunctious orange tabby chasing a butterfly down the pathway before her, to take his hand in marriage.

His heart squeezed inside his chest at the sight of her. She didn't look much different than when he'd picked her up from the train station several weeks ago. She wore the same lovely brocade wedding dress. The same hat. The same shiny brown lace-up boots. She looked as stunning and beautiful as she had then.

And yet Hope had changed.

And he'd changed.

As she drew nearer, a peace and calm washed over him.

A deep sense of destiny obliterated any last whisper of a hesitation—especially as Ben eased Hope to a stop and placed her hand in Aaron's.

"I love you, darlin'," Aaron breathed, fixing his gaze on hers and drawing her to his side.

The most satisfying, the most adorable, the most meaningful sigh he'd ever heard fell from her lips then as she peered up at him, her emerald gaze glistening. "I love you, too."

Aaron had changed, all right. He'd found God to be true, trustworthy and loving in the midst of uncommon and uncomfortable circumstances. And he'd found honest beauty in Hope's utter loveliness. Overwhelming joy in her innocent delight. And healing in her arms.

He'd found Hope.

"So I guess this settles it, doesn't it?" he whispered in her ear, remembering how lifeless and void of conviction those words had sounded many weeks ago. "We're getting married."

"You guess?" She peered up at him, her brilliant gaze taking in every inch of his face as though she couldn't quite get enough of him.

He placed a kiss on the angry scar blazing across her hairline, his heart clenching just thinking about how he'd almost lost her in the accident.

But he hadn't. She was here. And she was his.

"Oh, we're definitely getting married, darlin'." He pressed his face to her head and breathed in Hope. He held out his hand and stepped up to the altar. "I'm one blessed man to have you, Hope."

* * * * *

Dear Reader,

I hope you enjoyed reading Aaron and Hope's story as much as I enjoyed telling it. My characters are so very much a part of me—their likes and dislikes, dreams, struggles, fears, sorrows.… Writing them compels me to dig deep for honesty and openness.

Grief, along with other profound emotions born of circumstance, can carve ruts into our souls, grooves that can be difficult to overcome, as with Aaron and Hope. I very distinctly remember the sadness I felt when I left Aaron widowed so early in his life. As I stared at my computer screen and broke the news to him, it seemed cruel and unfair. Yet, being his creator, I was confident that he'd eventually discover realms of trust and faith and love he might not have known otherwise. Similarly, I believe that God knows our limits far better than we do, and the utter goodness of His heart for us overwhelms our limitations, our fears and our brokenness.

It is my hope that you will feel God's absolute love and enduring presence with you each step of your journey. And that, like Aaron and Hope, you will make amazing discoveries about yourself and God along the way.

Thank you so much for taking the time to read *Rocky Mountain Proposal*. Please check out the first and second books in the Drake brothers series, *Rocky Mountain Match* and *Rocky Mountain Redemption*, and watch for the fourth book, *Rocky Mountain Homecoming*, due out in September. I'd love to hear from you. Visit my website at pamelanissen.com.

With love,
Pamela Nissen

QUESTIONS FOR DISCUSSION

1. Desperate to comfort his dying friend, Aaron makes a promise, unaware of the full impact of his words. Have you ever faced a similar situation?

2. Imminent death has incited many promises and vows through the ages. What do you feel is the best way to honor such a promise?

3. Hope faces a very difficult situation when she arrives in Boulder. How would you have reacted, given the same scenario?

4. Aaron feels he will dishonor his marriage vows if he bends to the call of his heart. Do you feel his struggle is warranted? Have you ever walked through a similar situation?

5. Hope's stubbornness and pride are both her virtue and her vice. Have you ever dealt with a monumental task in the same way? If so, did you find your breaking point?

6. Jane's outright antagonism is a constant source of frustration for Hope. Have you ever dealt with someone like Jane? If so, did you find your breaking point?

7. Aaron's refusal to deal with the things that remind him of Ellie is a natural response. Have you had to walk through the pain of such loss, and if so, how did you respond?

8. As Aaron succumbs to the desire of his heart and experiences the full measure of his attraction to Hope, he experiences guilt's heavy weight. Do you believe his guilt is warranted?

9. Aaron's faith is shaken by the loss of his wife. How would you help him? What would you say? Do?

10. Hope's desire to feel "chosen" seems to be a recurring theme in her life. Do you remember a time when you struggled through something similar? How did you overcome?

INSPIRATIONAL

Inspirational romances to warm your heart & soul.

Love Inspired

HISTORICAL

TITLES AVAILABLE NEXT MONTH

Available June 14, 2011

GOLD RUSH BABY
Alaskan Brides
Dorothy Clark

MARRYING THE PREACHER'S DAUGHTER
Cheryl St.John

THE WEDDING SEASON
Deborah Hale & Louise M. Gouge

THE IRRESISTIBLE EARL
Regina Scott

REQUEST YOUR FREE BOOKS!

2 FREE INSPIRATIONAL NOVELS
PLUS 2
FREE
MYSTERY GIFTS

Love Inspired
HISTORICAL
INSPIRATIONAL HISTORICAL ROMANCE

YES! Please send me 2 FREE Love Inspired® Historical novels and my 2 FREE mystery gifts (gifts are worth about $10). After receiving them, if I don't wish to receive any more books, I can return the shipping statement marked "cancel". If I don't cancel, I will receive 4 brand-new novels every month and be billed just $4.24 per book in the U.S. or $4.74 per book in Canada. That's a saving of at least 23% off the cover price. It's quite a bargain! Shipping and handling is just 50¢ per book in the U.S. and 75¢ per book in Canada.* I understand that accepting the 2 free books and gifts places me under no obligation to buy anything. I can always return a shipment and cancel at any time. Even if I never buy another book, the two free books and gifts are mine to keep forever.

102/302 IDN FDCH

Name	(PLEASE PRINT)
Address	Apt. #
City	State/Prov.	Zip/Postal Code

Signature (if under 18, a parent or guardian must sign)

Mail to the **Reader Service:**
IN U.S.A.: P.O. Box 1867, Buffalo, NY 14240-1867
IN CANADA: P.O. Box 609, Fort Erie, Ontario L2A 5X3

Not valid for current subscribers to Love Inspired Historical books.

Want to try two free books from another series?
Call 1-800-873-8635 or visit www.ReaderService.com.

* Terms and prices subject to change without notice. Prices do not include applicable taxes. Sales tax applicable in N.Y. Canadian residents will be charged applicable taxes. Offer not valid in Quebec. This offer is limited to one order per household. All orders subject to credit approval. Credit or debit balances in a customer's account(s) may be offset by any other outstanding balance owed by or to the customer. Please allow 4 to 6 weeks for delivery. Offer available while quantities last.

Your Privacy—The Reader Service is committed to protecting your privacy. Our Privacy Policy is available online at www.ReaderService.com or upon request from the Reader Service.

We make a portion of our mailing list available to reputable third parties that offer products we believe may interest you. If you prefer that we not exchange your name with third parties, or if you wish to clarify or modify your communication preferences, please visit us at www.ReaderService.com/consumerschoice or write to us at Reader Service Preference Service, P.O. Box 9062, Buffalo, NY 14269. Include your complete name and address.

LIH11

*With time running out to stop the Lions of Texas
from orchestrating their evil plan, Texas Ranger
Levi McDonall must work with his childhood friend
to solve his captain's murder and thwart the group's
disastrous plot. Read on for a preview of OUT OF TIME
by Shirlee McCoy, the exciting conclusion to the*
TEXAS RANGER JUSTICE *series.*

Silence told its own story, and Susannah Jorgenson listened as she hurried across the bridge that led to the Alamo Chapel. Darkness had fallen hours ago and the air held a hint of rain. The shadows seemed deeper than usual, the darkness just a little blacker. Or maybe it was simply her imagination that made the Alamo complex seem so forbidding.

She shivered. Not from the cold. Not from the chilly breeze. From the darkness, the silence, the endless echo of her fear as she made her final rounds. She jogged to the chapel and flashed the beam of her light along the corners of the building.

Nothing.

No movement, no sounds, no reason to think she wasn't alone, but she couldn't shake the feeling that she was being watched. That somewhere beyond the beam of her light, danger waited. She did a full sweep of the chapel and of the office area beyond. Nothing, of course.

She opened the chapel door, stepping straight into a broad, muscular chest. Someone grabbed her upper arms, holding her in place.

She shoved forward into her attacker, pushing her weight into a solid wall of strength as she tried to unbalance him.

"Calm down. I was just trying to keep you from falling." The man released his hold.

"Sorry about that. I wasn't expecting anyone to be stand
ing near the door. We're closed for the day, but we'll be
open again at seven tomorrow morning." She cleared her
throat.

"No need to apologize. I'm Ranger Levi McDonall. My
captain said he was going to call and let you know I was on
the way."

"Levi McDonall?" Her childhood idol? Her best guy
friend? Her first teenage crush?

No way could they be the same.

"Come on in." She hurried into the chapel, trying to pull
herself together. This was the Texas Ranger she'd be work
ing with for the next eight days?

She flipped on a light, turned to face McDonall.

Levi McDonall.

Her Levi McDonall.

*Can Levi and Susannah put the past behind them
to save San Antonio's future? Find out in OUT OF TIME
by Shirlee McCoy from Love Inspired Suspense,
available in June wherever books are sold.*

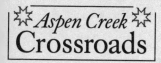

Love Inspired
HISTORICAL

INSPIRATIONAL HISTORICAL ROMANCE

Wedding bells will ring in these two romantic
Regency stories from two favorite
Love Inspired Historical authors.
'Tis the season for falling in love!

The Wedding Season

by DEBORAH HALE *and* LOUISE M. GOUGE

Available June wherever books are sold.